LOVEMe
TONIGHT

LOVEMe TONIGHT

GWYNNE FORSTER

The Harringtons

ARABESQUE®

LOVE ME TONIGHT

ISBN-13: 978-0-373-83187-6

Printed in U.S.A.

Dear Reader,

Since so many of you have written to me over the past several years asking if I would write another book about the Harrington brothers, my editor agreed that it was time to revisit that charming family. As you may know, there were only three Harrington brothers—Telford, Russ and Drake—and each had his own story. However, in my treasure trove of ideas, I discovered that the Harrington family is larger than I initially thought. As such, it gives me great pleasure to bring you this story of the sometimes sizzling, sometimes rocky relationship between another Harrington man and the woman he loves.

If you enjoy this story—and I sincerely hope that you do—you will be happy to learn that a character introduced in this novel, *Love Me Tonight,* continues the Harrington family series in his own story, *A Compromising Affair,* which will be published by Arabesque in 2011.

In case you missed the previous award-winning Harrington novels, *Once in a Lifetime, After the Loving* and *Love Me or Leave Me,* Arabesque is reissuing them, beginning with *Once in a Lifetime* in November 2010. I hope you have an opportunity to read them.

I enjoy receiving mail, so please e-mail me at GwynneF@aol.com. If you write by postal mail, reach me at P.O. Box 45, New York, NY 10044, and if you would like a reply, please enclose a self-addressed, stamped envelope. For more information, please contact my agent, Pattie Steel-Perkins, Steel-Perkins Literary Agency, e-mail MYAGENTSPLA@aol.com.

Warmest regards,

Gwynne Forster

Acknowledgments

To my husband and my stepson, whose love, affection and unfailing support are always with me and for which I thank God every day of my life.

Chapter 1

Judson Philips sat on his back porch looking at the sunset. He appreciated the longer days and shorter nights of mid-March, for time seemed to pass more swiftly than during the dreariness of winter. He needed the healing that the passage of time would bring.

Rick, his big German shepherd, sat beside him, occasionally rubbing against his leg. "Come on, boy, no use procrastinating. It has to be done, so let's do it." He patted Rick on the head, got up and went inside. He'd never realized how big that house was or how lonely he could be in it. With Rick beside him, he ran up the stairs and opened the door to his parents' bedroom.

For the first time in his life, he was alone in every sense of the word. Being adopted and an only child, he'd been the apple of his parents' eyes. They doted on him so much that, until he finished high school, achieving his independence had been one long struggle. When he was seven or eight years old, he had often fantasized about leaving Baltimore and becoming a saxophone player with a jazz band and traveling around the world.

He opened several chests of drawers in his parents' bedroom and found nothing of particular interest. He wasn't sure what to look for but decided to search in the bottom of his mother's closet. He found a two-foot square cardboard box with four drawers tucked away. He sat with it on his parents' bed and opened a drawer.

The sight of his father's passport gave him cause for hope. The phone rang, breaking the silence and startling him, much like a child caught in mischief.

"Hello," he said, expecting to hear the voice of one of his mother's friends calling to console him.

"How's it going, man?"

"Scott! Not so good," he began to unburden himself. "You know I loved my parents, and they certainly loved me. But I never got the courage to ask them about my birth parents, because I didn't want them to think I was unhappy or that they didn't do enough for me even though I never stopped wanting to know where I came from. Now they're both gone, and I'll probably never know. I feel…I don't know…but it's as if I have no ties. I don't belong with…hell! You know what I mean. I've just begun looking through my folks' papers."

"You gonna try and find your birth parents?"

Judson squeezed his eyes shut. "I have to," he said.

"I understand. I'm with you, man. You know that."

"Yeah. Thanks."

"I almost forgot why I called you. I know it's early after what you've just been through with Aunt Bev, Judson, but I thought it would do you good to get out. Tomorrow's my birthday. And my folks are giving me a party at the Hilton. Remember? What do you say?"

"Uh…all right. I'll…I'll be there." He'd forgotten about Scott's birthday. "Thanks for reminding me. I've…had a lot on my mind."

"I know that, buddy. I'm glad you'll come."

Judson hung up. Scott Galloway had been his close friend since kindergarten, and he couldn't think of anyone more reliable as a friend. He opened a second drawer and discovered a stack of papers, brown and dry with age. His heartbeat accelerated when he found an old newspaper clipping of a birth announcement. He discovered whoever it was about was born in Hagerstown, Maryland.

"Hmm." Why would his parents keep the newspaper clipping?

The next morning, Friday, Judson bought Scott a digital camera to replace one he'd lost, had it wrapped and delivered by messenger. He arrived at the party a few minutes after nine that evening, and Scott met him at the entrance to the ballroom.

"Judson," Scott greeted him. "Thanks for that terrific camera." He took it from his pocket. "Just what I needed. Uh…I have someone I want you to meet. Marks has been stalking her for the last hour."

Judson seemed indifferent. He tried not to let his frustration show, but he certainly felt like it. "Happy birthday, Scott. Sorry, but I do not want to meet another one of your cute buddies."

"This one isn't a buddy and you'd better not call her cute. She's a coworker and a friend, and you definitely want to meet her." He tapped Judson's shoulder. "Trust me."

Scott took Judson's arm and pushed him through the throng of birthday well-wishers, but suddenly stopped. "Judson Philips, this is Curtis Heywood."

"Judson Philips? Well, how do you do? You're precisely the man I need to see."

"How's that?" Judson asked.

"I've got a malpractice suit, and I had planned to call you, but meeting you through a mutual friend suits me better."

Judson handed Curtis Heywood his card. "Thank you. I'll be in my law office Monday morning." He couldn't spend more time with the man because Scott nudged him on.

He saw her from a distance. If she wasn't the woman Scott intended to introduce him to, too bad. The closer he got to her, the more certain he was that he wanted to meet her. But with her looks, he couldn't see how she would be unattached.

When he and Scott were about ten feet from the woman, Judson drew in a deep breath. For the first time since his college days at Harvard, he felt himself vulnerable to a woman. She turned in his direction and glanced directly at him. Her large brown eyes, shaded by long, silky lashes that fanned against her cheeks, seemed to calculate everything about him in that brief look. She focused quickly on the two men who had been standing in front of her.

Scott tapped his hand on the woman's shoulder and said to the two men with whom she'd been talking, "Excuse me, Pat, Orson," and stood between them and the woman. "Heather, I want you to meet my very best and oldest friend, Judson Philips. Judson, this is Heather Tatum, one of my colleagues. Heather is a lawyer, the same as you, Judson, except that she's also a special envoy with the State Department."

"I'm delighted to meet you, Ms. Tatum," he said, letting charm supersede his nervousness. "Scott hasn't told me any more about you than what he just said, and I suspect there's much more. Would you explain for me what a roving ambassador does?"

"I'm glad to make your acquaintance, Mr. Philips. Scott hasn't told me anything about you either, but I read the papers. I've also seen you on television." A smile softened her dazzling features and seemed to make her flawless dark brown skin glow. "As for being a roving diplomat, that only means that I do odd jobs in foreign countries at the behest of the president and the secretary of state. My father calls me a diplomatic gofer." The latter brought laughter from the three of them.

"I had to drag Judson out here," Scott said. "He lost his mother very recently, and he isn't crazy about big social gatherings anyway, so I'm flattered that he's here."

"I'm sorry about your mother, Mr. Philips. How recently did she pass?"

"Eleven days ago. Thanks for your kindness." He

didn't want to stand there staring at her like a love-struck school boy. He looked at Scott, who seemed overly satisfied with himself. "What time is your dad supposed to make that champagne toast?"

"Probably as soon as Mom is sure everybody has seen her dress."

Heather looked at Judson. "Do you think he's serious?"

"I certainly hope not. Aunt Ada is what you'd call a woman of substance. She is by no means frivolous."

"Excuse me a minute," Scott said and disappeared.

"Scott got me by the arm and told me he wanted me to meet a colleague," Judson said to Heather. "I saw you before we got to the middle of the room, and I decided that if he wasn't going to introduce me to you, I didn't want to meet whoever else he had in mind."

"Thank you. Where did you go to law school?" she asked him, changing the subject.

"Harvard."

Her grin and the wicked glint in her eyes gave him cause to exercise self-control. "What's amusing?" he asked her.

"We could never enjoy a Harvard-Yale game together."

"Say no more."

"You bet," she said, still grinning. "We lead 62–58. The eight ties don't count. I assume you played quarterback."

His eyebrows shot up. "Why do you assume that?"

"Because you look like one. Quarterbacks lead the team, and most of them are type-A personalities."

"I'm not sure I should thank you," he teased.

Their repartee ended when Scott's father stood and gave the toast. After the toast Scott rejoined them. "Being the oldest of three and the only boy carries much responsibility," Scott explained sarcastically. "At least that's what my parents have been trying to make me believe for thirty years. You're lucky that you were an only child," Scott said to Judson.

"I was lucky to be anybody's child," he said, but Heather's puzzled expression made him wish he hadn't uttered the thought aloud.

As the evening wound down, Heather seemed ready to leave.

"May I take you home?" Judson asked, anticipating her mood.

"Thank you," she said, "but I'm leaving tomorrow for Egypt, and I don't have much time. I've enjoyed meeting you. Good night."

Judson was admittedly a bit stunned. Wealthy, successful, handsome and a heart-stopper at thirty-four years of age, he was unaccustomed to rejection by anyone.

He stared at Heather's departing back. "Well, I'll be damned."

Scott rushed up to Judson. "What happened? Aren't you taking her home?"

"It appears she's very busy."

Scott's face contorted into a frown. "Didn't you two get along?"

"I thought we did, but she blew me off." He lifted

first one shoulder and then the other in a shrug. "Looks like I'm losing my edge."

Judson allowed himself a rueful smile. "Not to worry, buddy. She made a dent, not a chasm."

Scott looked into the distance. He'd known Judson since they were five years old. "Yeah," he said, mostly to himself. "If you say so."

Heather Tatum forced herself to walk out of the Americana Ballroom without looking back. She was not immune to Judson Philips's charm. Quite the contrary. But she had her own agenda, and he was not part of it. After years of study and long hours of work at the State Department, she had just begun to reach her goal of rising in the foreign service to become an ambassador, and she did not intend to be sidetracked by a charismatic, handsome, perfect specimen of a man.

Lord, but he's gorgeous, she thought to herself as she got into the waiting limousine, one of the few perks that came with her job. The evening had been fun. Indeed, Scott Galloway knew how to give a party. She'd liked his friend. Judson Philips had a masculine aura that set him apart. He knew who he was and exuded confidence.

"I'm going home, Garth," she said to the driver, leaned back in the soft leather seat and told herself to get her mind on something other than Philips.

She took out her cell phone and telephoned the woman who cared for her father at the family home in Hagerstown, Maryland. "How's he doing, Annie?" she asked the housekeeper who doubled as her father's caretaker. "He didn't seem to be in a good mood when I talked to him this afternoon."

"He's in a better mood. He even watched the baseball game until the Red Sox started knocking home runs. Don't you worry, Heather. You know I take good care of your father."

Heather smiled to herself. Annie had worked for the Tatum family since Heather was ten years old and had remained with them after Heather's mother had run off. She'd often wished her father would have married Annie, who clearly adored him.

"I know you do," she said. "I have a morning flight to Cairo, but I'll see you when I get back."

"I'll be here."

She hung up and began mentally sorting out last-minute details for her trip. She didn't believe in leaving anything to chance.

Heather walked into her room at the Ramses Hilton Hotel in Cairo shortly after noon that Sunday and looked around. As she always did, she tested the hotel bed for firmness. Satisfied, she went to the window and looked out. In the distance, she could see the great Giza pyramids west of the Nile and what looked like miles of sand. What a different world from Baltimore.

As she began to unpack, she glimpsed a large bouquet of calla lilies in a vase painted with the likeness of Queen Nefertiti. She adored calla lilies and had decided that if she married, she would carry them as her wedding bouquet. She made a note to thank the hotel management. She used the phone in her room to check in with the U.S. embassy in Cairo. Then she hung up her clothes and took a shower. From the time she departed from the Baltimore-Washington Thurgood Marshall International Airport until she walked into her room at the Hilton, eighteen tiring hours had elapsed. She ordered a sandwich and a pot of tea from room service and turned on the television.

When her sandwich arrived, she tipped the waiter, then got in bed and watched the news while she ate and drank her tea. Weariness caught up with her. She turned off the television, and when she put her head on the pillow, she noticed a note against the side of the vase and jumped out of bed to open it.

She read:

Dear Heather,
I wish you a safe, pleasant and fruitful mission.
Judson Philips

How on earth? What a resourceful man. And what a thoughtful one. She must have made an impact on him, as well. She smiled as she happily fell asleep.

She arose early the next morning, refreshed and ready for work. As she always did when in an Islamic country, she wore a white pantsuit—white was inoffensive and was appropriate for every occasion—with a pale yellow, sleeveless blouse and white shoes. She deferred to local customs to the extent that she could without compromising her values, but she refused to cover her hair or give up her three-inch heels. If anybody objected to her height, it was their problem. She loved her five-foot-eight-and-a-half-inch height, and she loved high heels.

Having made certain that she got to the conference room in time to check out the seating arrangements and have them changed if they didn't follow protocol, she sat in the place assigned to her and took out her notes and tape recorder. She wondered how many of those present truly cared about the suffering of children in Sudan, which was the subject of the conference.

The discussions got off to a slow start, and shortly after the coffee break, she felt a hand on her thigh. Shocked, she turned around to look at the man.

"Your husband is a fool to let you out of his sight," he said with a practiced smile, looking certain that he'd complimented her.

She stared at him. "How do you think these delegates will react when I slap your face?"

"Surely, you don't mean that," he said, his smile still in place. "Your country and mine are on good terms."

Her expression didn't waver. "Remove your hand. One...two..."

He removed his hand. "I don't know how the American men call themselves men."

Heather ignored the taunt, for she was accustomed to the attitudes of men from certain developing countries. At five minutes past twelve, she got her chance to address the group, and at the end of her prepared statement, she added her views on the way in which some delegates wasted opportunities to make a difference in the lives of disadvantaged children.

Later, after congratulations on her talk, Mr. Taliah, one of the delegates, asked, "Would you join my wife and me for dinner in our suite this evening? My wife doesn't go out because she isn't in purdah. She's a modern woman and she hates the snide remarks that she gets." Heather agreed; she knew Mr. Taliah and knew he was married.

However, the minute Heather walked into the room that night, she knew the man had lied. It wasn't a suite, but a room like her own. She realized the delegate intended a seduction. Without a word, she whirled around and walked out.

Back in her room, she had to admit that the calla lilies lifted her spirits, reminding her Judson Philips admired her as a person.

I must remember to send him a note of thanks, she thought to herself. *He went to a lot of trouble and great expense to send me these flowers. They're still so beautiful.* She threw her briefcase on the bed and heaved a long and heavy sigh. She lived a life that most people would not consider normal. At times, neither did she. In her mind she saw Judson Philips's handsome face, remembered his gracious manner and wondered if he could fill the awful void in her life. But after what she'd seen of her parents' bitter and loveless marriage, she doubted the wisdom of letting herself care for any man.

"Would you like me to request an apology from Mr. Taliah?" the chief of protocol asked her the next morning when she related the incident from the previous night as she was required to do.

"Of course not," she said. "It goes with the job."

She'd made light of it, but she would be glad to set foot in Baltimore that Tuesday afternoon. She liked Egypt, especially the Egyptians—who welcomed her as a sister—but she had little use for pompous diplomats who went to these conferences merely to exploit their status.

Her mission finished, she took one last whiff of the calla lilies in her room and—a smile on her face—made her way to the airport, home and dreams of Judson Philips.

She walked into her office Wednesday morning, locked her briefcase in her desk drawer and went to Scott's office. "Hi," he said when she walked in after one knock. "How'd it go?"

"Same old, same old. Great ideas, an excellent report that will be widely circulated and nothing substantial will change," she complained.

"Good grief, Heather. You're becoming so cynical."

"Not really. But I see the same guys at every one of these meetings, and it seems they get less courteous every time. Now, *you!* How did Judson Philips know I was at the Hilton in Cairo?"

"I know both of you, and I wouldn't introduce either of you to just anybody. What happened? Didn't you like him? He needs some cheering up, and so do you."

"He sent me two dozen of the most beautiful calla

lilies I ever saw. How would he know that calla lilies are my favorite flower? *You* don't even know that."

Scott leaned back in his swivel desk chair and rocked. "I said, didn't you like him?"

"Don't ask stupid questions. Why wouldn't I?"

"That is not the answer to my question," he continued.

"I liked him, Scott," Heather admitted. "But don't try to start anything between us. My life isn't an easy one. My dad isn't getting any better, and I want to spend all the free time I can muster with him. And you know I'm being considered for an ambassador post. I have to focus on that as much as I can."

"The two of you have so much in common, Heather. Why don't you give it a chance? You owe it to yourself."

"I'm sorry. It's the wrong time, Scott. He's…well, he's nice. I'll let it go at that. How can I get in touch with him? I want to thank him for those flowers."

He wrote a number on a notepad and handed it to her. "You can phone him."

"Thanks, but I want to write him a note."

"Yeah. You want to be formal. After the trouble he went to, he deserves better." Scott wrote the address of Judson's law firm and handed it to Heather. "Too bad. He liked you a lot."

Judson looked at the letter and wondered at the precise, forward-slanting handwriting. It had no return address. The sender had marked it personal, and he expected it was probably one more invitation to another stuffy affair. He opened it and sat up when he saw the handwritten note.

Dear Judson,
Thank you for the most beautiful calla lilies I ever saw. Two dozen in about five different colors. Calla lilies are my favorite flower, and you couldn't have known that. They were still in bloom when I left, and I hated that. But as you know, I wouldn't have been allowed to bring them into the country. Thank you so much for your thoughtfulness.
Yours truly,
Heather

"That's something," he said. He folded the note and put it in his pocket. She was an intriguing woman. Several different scenarios flitted through his mind. Did he really want a serious involvement with a roving ambassador? Maybe something casual was what he needed. He leaned back in the chair and made a pyramid of his fingers.

He phoned Scott. "Want to meet for lunch? I have to check on a few things not far from your office."

"Sure you wouldn't rather be lunching with Heather?"

"If that were the case, friend, I would have called her."

"Meet you at The Crab Shack."

They reached The Crab Shack at almost the same

time, and sat at their favorite table. "Your usual, gentlemen?" the waiter asked.

"Right," they said in unison.

"We have a president who's pushing education," Judson said to Scott. "I'm planning to start a boys' study group. And instead of sports, the focus will be academics. Why don't you start a girls' group, and we can have competitions that will keep them focused and interested?"

"Me start a girls' group? Why don't you rope Heather into it?"

"I don't want to involve her in this. You get a boys' group, then. It won't work unless they have competition."

"Okay. You do South Baltimore, and I'll form one in the Reisterstown area," Scott decided. "Have you made any further progress on your mother's estate?"

Judson shook his head. "I've had too many distractions. I'm going to look into it again tonight, see what I can find. You'd think my parents would have told me or at least left me some explanation. Suppose I need a bone-marrow transplant. Where would I turn?"

"You won't, and don't worry. You'll find what you're looking for. They didn't destroy papers that they could some day need."

"I sure hope you're right."

"This isn't good," Heather said to herself when she awakened that morning. *It isn't cold, so why do I feel chilly?* She got out of bed and padded to the bathroom. Maybe if she drank some coffee, she could pull herself together. She managed to make the coffee, but took a cupful back to her bedroom, put the cup on her nightstand and crawled back into bed. She didn't get sick. Never. So what was wrong with her?

She couldn't afford to get sick. She had to take care of her father and be ready for a permanent diplomatic post. If she wasn't up to it, someone else might get the assignment.

She fell asleep lying across the bed and awakened at a quarter of ten with a full-blown cold. After admitting to herself that she really was sick she phoned Scott. "Hi, this is Heather. I'm home, and I'm feeling rotten."

"You've got a cold. I can hear it in your voice."

"Looks like it. Could you please ask my secretary to print out that report I was working on and leave it with my doorman when you leave work this afternoon?"

"Sure. But why would you try to work? You're sick."

"I know, but it's due the day after tomorrow, and this is not a good time to start coming up short."

"All right. I'll deliver it. Do you have any food—juice, soup or something—for your cold in the house?"

"Scott, you're such a darling. Why didn't you and I fall in love? I need some milk, grapefruit juice and eggs. I have coffee and tea."

"You got it. You and I would never fall in love because both of us need the same thing—someone who's laid-back. Two type-A personalities would kill each other. Now, take Judson—"

"All right. I got the message," she said sleepily.

"Go to sleep. See you later." He hung up, and she

managed to do the same. She knew she should eat, but she didn't have the strength to cook.

The intercom buzzed, awakening her. "Hello."

"Ms. Tatum. A man is here with some things for you. Shall I send him up?'

"Thanks," she said and dosed off again.

"Philips speaking."

"This is Curtis Heywood."

"Yes. I've been expecting your call."

"I believe I have a good lawsuit against a medical diagnostic group, and I'd like you to take the case."

Judson listened while Curtis described the complaint. "Have you omitted anything that you might have done that could weaken your case? I need to know that up front."

"I'm certain that I'm not at fault in any way."

It sounded like a good case, but he wouldn't be certain until he dug into it himself. "Can you be here tomorrow morning at nine and bring your papers and any evidence?"

"I'll be there. Thanks for your time."

"You're welcome. See you tomorrow."

Judson hung up, saw the caller ID on his private line and lifted the receiver, smiling at the sound of his friend's voice. "What's up, Scott?"

"I need you to do me a favor—and hear me out before you get your back up. I promised Heather that I'd bring a report and some groceries to her today after work because she's sick at home. The thing is I can't, because I have to stay in D.C. and deal with an issue that just came in. Working in D.C. and living in Baltimore has advantages, but right now, friend, it's a disadvantage. As a favor would you please take the report and the care package to her on your way home? You can leave it with her doorman, if you don't want to see her."

"What's wrong with her?"

"Maybe a cold. She sounded really sick."

Judson wondered if it was one of Scott's tricks to try to get him to see Heather. "If she's sick, and you can't go, of course I'll do it. But if I find out that you're up to your old shenanigans—"

"Judson, if you'd rather not, I'll see if I can get somebody else to do it."

"I'll be at your office for that report around four o'clock. Did she say what she needs?"

"She said bread, milk, grapefruit juice and maybe some eggs. I guess she hasn't had time to do any shopping since she got back."

"Maybe. See you at four." There was something special about Heather Tatum, and he wanted to know what it was.

Later, he stopped by Scott's office at the State Department in D.C., collected the report and headed up I-95. Once in Baltimore, he went to a supermarket, where he bought bread, milk, eggs, grapefruit juice and butter. On an whim, he parked at a specialty restaurant on Calvert Street and bought a large container of chicken soup. *If she's got a cold, maybe I ought to get something for that,* he thought to himself. He stopped at a drugstore and bought some over-the-counter cold medicine.

* * *

"I have some things to deliver to Ms. Tatum," Judson announced to the doorman, careful not to identify himself. The doorman rang Heather's apartment.

"There's a man here to deliver some things to you. Shall I send him up?" He looked at Judson. "She said you can go up. Apartment 34–F."

Relief spread over his face when she hadn't asked who it was. He got off the elevator at the thirty-fourth floor, turned in the direction of apartment F, rang the doorbell and waited.

The door opened, and she stared up at him, blinking so that she could be certain to trust her eyes. "Judson? What—"

From her appearance, she'd just crawled out of bed, wrapped herself in a robe and made it to the door.

"Hi. Scott couldn't make it, so I brought your report and some groceries," Judson said, in a chirpy voice.

She stood facing him and staring at him. He grinned, hoping to put her off balance, and it must have worked since she smiled. "Why don't I put this stuff in the refrigerator for you?" he said, suddenly feeling less vulnerable. "And maybe you ought to go back to bed."

"If I'm taking orders, I must be sick for sure," she mumbled. Judson overheard her but decided to ignore the retort. "To your left," she said, and went back to bed.

"Are you in bed?" he called to her after putting away the groceries.

"I am, and I'm sorry, Judson. It's really nice of you

to do this, but I'm feeling too sick to be civil, much less good company."

At least she didn't apologize for the way she looked, and she needn't have. The woman looked great even with a runny nose, watery eyes. He walked into her room where she was clutching the covers tight around her neck. Why didn't that surprise him? He didn't laugh, but it took a lot to keep a straight face. "Have you had lunch?"

"I don't think I ate today, but if you brought me eggs, I'll scramble them and eat a bit later."

He removed his jacket and hung it on the back of a chair. "I can do that, Heather. Don't get up. I'll find what I need."

He awakened her sometime later to the aroma of chicken. He had placed a tray on a chair beside her bed. "Think you could eat a little something?" he asked her in a tender voice.

When she tried to sit up, Judson reached over, and propped some pillows behind her back. "If you'll give me a second, I'll get you a damp towel and you can wash you face." He came back with the towel and handed it to her. "You'll feel better."

She did as he suggested. "You're right. I do." She looked at the tray beside the bed. "You fixed all that?"

"It isn't much. If you eat a little of everything, you'll feel better. And take this Ester-C vitamin." He put the tray in her lap and sat on the chair.

"Chicken soup." She tasted it. "Judson, this is delicious. Why'd you go to all this trouble?"

"I wanted to make you feel badly for blowing me off," he said with a smile.

With the spoon halfway between the soup bowl and her mouth, she paused and looked at him with a curious expression. Suddenly she laughed. "You're sarcastic, and I wouldn't have thought so." She tasted the soup. "This is so good."

"Eat some of the eggs. You need the protein."

She ate the two scrambled eggs. "Hmm. You weren't kidding." She frowned slightly and seemed to be making up her mind about something. She finished chewing the toast and put her fork on the tray.

"I want to ask you about something you said the night we met, and if you think I'm out of line, just say so. I can handle it."

"Fine. As long as you don't ask me why I'm here."

"I wasn't going to ask that. The night we met, you said 'I was lucky I was anybody's child.' Scott didn't say anything, but it got me thinking. May I ask what you meant?"

He never had liked answering personal questions. He had nothing to hide, but he liked his privacy and guarded it tenaciously. Considering where the conversation seemed headed, it was better that she know now rather than later. "I was adopted, Heather, and now that both of my parents have died, I'm at a loss about my birth parents. I never asked my mother and father, because they loved me so much, and I was a happy child. But I always wanted to know about my background, especially who I looked like. I didn't ask them because I was afraid they'd think I was unhappy or that I was lacking something that I thought my birth parents could have given me."

"I'm sorry, Judson. Your parents seem to have done exceedingly well by you."

"Absolutely. They couldn't have done a better job, and especially since I was at times very wayward."

"You!" she exclaimed, in a teasing voice.

"I had a mind of my own, and if I didn't see the logic in something, I wouldn't do it. That caused friction between me and my parents until they understood and took the time to explain things to me. By the time I was twelve, we didn't have those problems."

"I can't imagine how important it is to you to know who your biological parents are, but will you be terribly unhappy if you don't find them?"

"I don't have to meet them, Heather. I just want to know who they are or were. Then I'll have a better sense of who I am. My adoption probably improved my chances for a good life, so I don't think I missed out on anything material."

She resumed eating her soup. "This is so good." She put down her spoon. "Judson, if your adoptive parents loved each other and treated you well, you are fortunate. My parents constantly fought. Dad claims that they were madly in love when they first got married, though I never believed it—they acted as if they hated each other. When I was nine, my mother had had it. She left, and I have no idea where she is. When I asked my father about her, he said marriage was very difficult for her, that the day-to-day discipline of marriage didn't suit everyone. I believe that."

He could see that it still pained her. "I'm sorry that your childhood was unpleasant. What does your father do?"

Her pride was obvious when she smiled and said, "He taught history at the university until he retired six years ago. They've named a distinguished chair for him in the department. Now, unfortunately, he's confined to the house and sometimes to bed. He hasn't been well for a couple of years."

"At least you still have him with you," Judson said. "Do everything you can for him, so when he's gone, you won't have any regrets."

She closed her eyes briefly, and he imagined that the thought of losing her father hurt her. He covered her hand with his because he couldn't help it. "Is there anyone close to you?" She let her hand remain covered by his.

"Thanks. There's Annie. She keeps house for my father and takes care of him. She's like a mother to me. Father hired her after my mother left, and…I used to wish he'd marry her."

"So you'd have a mother?"

She looked at him almost as if seeing him for the first time. "I don't know. I hadn't figured that out. Maybe. You are very perceptive."

He could see that she was beginning to tire. "Let me take that tray back to the kitchen. I've stayed too long, and you're getting tired." While he cleaned the kitchen, his mind traveled back to their conversation.

He hoped they would get to know each other, and after today he liked her even more than before. She was compassionate and caring, and those traits in a woman meant everything to him.

"I'd better go, Heather. Do you mind if I look in on you or call to see how you are?"

"I don't mind at all. I don't think I'll go in to work tomorrow, but I may. Mind can control matter."

"I don't doubt that one bit," he said.

"Thank you for the visit, for the company and for my wonderful supper."

"The pleasure was mine." He put a bottle of Ester-C vitamins in her hand. "Take two before you sleep." Then, he leaned down and kissed her cheek. He hadn't planned to do it, and he surprised himself. "Don't go to sleep without locking that door."

"It will lock automatically when you leave, but I'll double check." She seemed suddenly pensive. "Judson, I don't lead a normal life. If you invest your time in me, it may prove futile."

"Don't be so sure. Good night, Heather."

"Good night, Judson."

He got on the elevator and, after standing there for a while, realized that he forgot to push the button. As he descended, he felt a growing confidence. He took a chance, and it paid off. Heather Tatum wouldn't be easy. She had to be tended like a seedling in a garden. Fine with him. He had the time and the patience.

When he got home, he greeted his dog, Rick, checked his answering machine and saw that he had five calls from Scott.

He dialed Scott's home number. "What's eating you? I didn't get five calls from you all last month," Judson said.

"Where the heck were you? How's Heather? Is she mad at me?"

He sat down, rested his left ankle on his right knee and prepared to enjoy himself. "How would I know? To the best of my knowledge, she didn't mention your name."

"Come on, man. How is she?"

"Well, when I give a woman TLC, she becomes as soft as a pillow. You should try it."

"Judson," Scott said firmly. "Heather's my friend. Is she all right?"

"She has a bad cold, and she hadn't eaten all day. So I gave her soup, scrambled eggs and toast."

"Good. Are the two of you going to be friends? I mean…you know what I mean."

"We talked and got to know each other a little better. She's interesting and extremely likeable. We'll see how it goes. I'd better get something to eat and start going through my mother's effects. I don't know why, but I dread it."

"I'll get some pizza and a salad. You got any beer?"

"Always."

"I'll be over there in an hour."

He changed into blue jeans and a T-shirt and went into his mother's bedroom. Rick trailed behind him as usual. He got the cardboard box from the closet, put it on the bed and sat down. After removing the rubber band holding the bundle of papers, he carefully opened each sheet. Some sheets of paper had already begun to crumble with age.

"What's this?" he said as he stared at the death certificate of an infant who had died. He wondered if that was why he'd been adopted. He put the death certificate aside along with the newspaper clipping of the birth announcement. They could prove useful.

Before long, Scott arrived with a pepperoni-and-mushroom pizza, a Greek salad and a cheesecake. "You planning to feed a football team?" Judson chided him. While they ate, he told Scott what he'd found so far.

"You mean you've never seen your birth certificate?" Scott asked him. "How'd you get into school?"

"I've had a passport since I was three, and my parents renewed it every year. When I became an adult, I did the same."

"You have to find your birth certificate."

"I found a newspaper clipping about a child who was born in Hagerstown. I'm going to see if I can find anyone who knows why my parents would save that birth notice."

"Well, do it without making a fuss. Don't forget that you're pretty well-known in this area."

"Yeah. I hadn't thought of that.

"I don't see anything else in these papers, except property deeds, an infant death certificate, their marriage certificate and that sort of thing. I'll go through this stuff again after time puts some distance between me and all this."

Chapter 2

Heather got up, put the chain latch on the door and went to the kitchen for some water. She wanted to take the vitamin that Judson had brought her. She had expected to see dirty dinner dishes, pots and pans and cooking utensils piled up in the sink. Instead, the kitchen looked immaculate. She looked into the refrigerator and saw that Judson had put away the eggs and butter precisely as she would have.

"Hmm." She wouldn't have suspected that he was a neat freak. She got a glass of water and went back to bed. She owned several sexy negligees, yet Judson Philips had caught her looking frumpy. But so what? He had shown her that he could be sweet as well as charming, that he was thoughtful and kind. She couldn't say that she was sorry about Judson's visit, but she had a little pang in the region of her heart. Maybe the day would come when she could let herself freely go with a man she cared about and who cared for her, but she couldn't for now. She had too far to go and a rough road ahead. But somehow…

Judson had grown up in a loving family. She needed to talk to her father. The explanation that "marriage didn't suit everybody" suddenly did not suffice. There was always a reason why a marriage was in turmoil.

She reached for the phone and dialed Annie. "Hi. How's Daddy?"

"I was reading the paper to him and he dosed off to sleep. He does that a lot lately."

"I've got a cold, but if I can get better soon, I'll be over there Friday and spend the weekend."

"It'll be good. He always cheers up when you're here."

Heather drove her own car to Hagerstown. She always felt guilty whenever her chauffeur spent a weekend sitting in the limousine with nothing to do, because she didn't want to go anyplace. She parked in front of the family home, a white-brick Georgian, and went inside.

She hugged Annie, who met her at the door. "Hi. Is Daddy awake?"

"Yes, indeed. And he was so excited when I told him you'd be here. He's in his room."

She dashed up the stairs to her father's room and knocked on the door. "Come in." His once-deep baritone had become the voice of a weaker, older man.

"Hi, Daddy," she said as she walked in his bedroom and saw him sitting in his big chair looking out the window. She leaned down, kissed his cheek and hugged him.

"Heather! How good to see you. Talking to you on the phone is one thing, but it's always so good when you're here. How was Cairo?"

"I always enjoy Egypt, Daddy. But progress is slow, and those conferences often seem more of a diplomatic liability than an asset."

"You're impatient. Until people begin to share information about their problems and look for solutions together, no progress will be made at all. Scott called me yesterday. I always wished you two would get together, but once you started that brother-sister thing, it didn't stand a chance," he teased.

She couldn't help smiling. After three years, her father still hoped for the impossible between Scott and her. "He's my best friend, Daddy."

She didn't think it time to bring up what she came there to discuss with him. Her father wouldn't jump right into a conversation about his personal life, so she'd have to ease into it.

On Sunday morning after breakfast when the time approached to leave, she figured that she had no choice but to bring it up. But, he surprised her by saying that he had something to tell her.

"Let's sit out on the back terrace where it's sunny and warm," she said, walking with him, matching his slow, unsteady pace.

"I guess you know I'm not getting better, Heather." She leaned forward, knowing her father would say it, yet not wanting to hear it. "Nothing's imminent, but we both have to prepare for it. I am not going to get better. I know it, and my doctor knows it."

"But, Daddy, how can you say that? You're much better today than when I was last here."

"And I may be much worse tomorrow. That's the way it goes, dear," he said kindly. "But I don't want you to worry. I've had a very good life, and you've been the best part of it."

She patted his hand and counseled herself not to shed a single tear. "You know, Daddy, a couple of weeks ago Scott introduced me to his closest friend, Judson Philips. We're attracted to each other, and he's kind and—"

"The lawyer?"

She nodded.

"I've heard a lot about him."

She had told him about Judson's visit when she was sick earlier that week.

"He's obviously interested in seeing whether the two of you can make it," her father stated. "What's holding you back?"

"Dad, you said some people aren't suited to marriage. Maybe I'm one of them. After all, my mother wasn't."

"I see." He looked into the distance, took a deep breath and shook his head.

"You were twelve or so when I told you that. It was an explanation that a child could understand, but I see that it gave you the wrong impression. You see, I was crazy in love with your mother, but Linda was in love with someone else, and I knew it. I thought I could teach her to love me. For a while, she tried to make a go of it, but she never stopped loving him. The relationship between us got worse, much worse. She knew how much I loved her and, because she was miserable, she baited me and every conversation led to an argument. One day, she called me at work and said she wouldn't be there when I got home and that I should tell you whatever I thought would make it easier for you."

"And you never heard from her again?"

"Not once. I have a strong feeling that she went to the other man, Lyle Carter. I didn't blame her for that. I knew she was in love with him, but I always worried about her because he could be cruel." At her silence, he continued. "I know this is a lot for you to take in. Don't hate her. She thought I would be her salvation, but as hard as I tried, I couldn't make her forget him."

"Do you still care about her after all these years?"

He leaned back in the chair and closed his eyes. "I won't say I'm still in love with her. That ended long ago. But the pain's still there. After all, she gave me you, and for that, I'll always have feelings for her."

"You're right. I wasn't expecting this."

He sat forward and braced his hands on his knees. "I want you to listen to me because what I'm telling you is important. Go ahead and pursue your goal of becoming a diplomat, but if that's all you accomplish in life, you won't have a sense of fulfillment. You need friends, spiritual fulfillment and the love of a man who loves you. If you're fortunate, you'll have children. Give Judson Philips a chance."

She thought about what her father had said for a minute and then spoke before thinking. "Why didn't you give Annie a chance? She's devoted her life to you."

A smile played around his lips. "You're a smart one. We settled that years ago. She was afraid people would think she was living in sin and refused to be seen with me outside of this house. I told her that I wouldn't settle for a woman who was ashamed of me. No woman was going to hide me in her closet."

Driving home that afternoon, Heather carried a weight on her mind that she hadn't before. Her father was terminally ill. What she'd believed about her parents' marriage was suddenly called into question. Her father and Annie cared for each other but were too stubborn to do anything about it. And the person she loved and respected most had challenged her to find out what kind of man Judson Philips might be. She could take his advice, or she could be stubborn. Stubbornness had always been a part of her makeup. She didn't know what to do. Maybe she wouldn't do anything.

By the time Heather arrived home, she admitted grudgingly that Judson was as likeable as he was attractive. She was accustomed to trusting her mind, but it wasn't working properly because her father had unsettled her in a way that would have put Einstein in a quandary. "What the hell!" she said to herself as she unlocked the door of her apartment. "I'll deal with it."

More that ever, Judson felt an urge to know who he was. He was thirty-four years old, and the time would soon come when he would want to marry and raise a family. He figured he ought to know more about his background, if only for his children's sake.

"I suspect I'm going to need all the financial resources I can muster," he said to Scott when they spoke by phone Sunday evening.

"So you're going to really pursue it, huh? A lot of adoption papers are sealed. It won't be easy."

He tapped the nightstand with his rubber eraser. "I'm going a different route. I believe I know where I was born, and I'll take it from there. If I hit a blank wall, I'll figure out something else. Right now, my gut instinct is to begin with the bits of information I have. I'll be busy. I've taken on a new case and it's going to be tough."

"What's the topic?"

"A radiology report that led to a misdiagnosis."

"Did the patient die as a result?"

"No. The patient's and the doctor's reputations were injured. I'll file suit in about six weeks."

"You sound pretty confident."

"There's no guesswork." He paused. "Have you seen Heather this week?"

"She was at work Friday. She told me she was worried about her dad."

"I gathered as much the day I visited her. Gotta go."

He hung up and dialed Heather's number. "This is Judson," he said when she answered. "How are you feeling?"

"Not much of my cold left, Judson. How are you?"

"I'm fine. How's your dad?"

"I just left him. We had a good visit, but he told me that neither he nor his doctor expects his condition to improve. I had to keep a straight face. I didn't want him to start worrying about me. But th-this is awful, Judson."

"Believe me, I know. If you don't have any plans, would you have dinner with me? I know it's a last-minute invitation, but I want to see you. Maybe you'd feel better with some company."

She didn't hesitate. "I may not be good company, but if you think I won't ruin your Sunday evening, okay. Give me about forty-five minutes."

Just the kind of woman he liked. Not a hint of coyness. "I'll be there at seven o'clock." He hung up. Whether she agreed because of her mood, or because she liked his company was immaterial. She'd agreed to see him; he could handle the rest.

At least he'll see me without a runny nose, Heather thought, rationalizing why she'd agreed to have dinner with Judson. She rarely got depressed, but her father and Annie were all she had, and the thought of losing her father was more than she was able to contemplate right now. She went to her closet and scanned it for anything that was attractive and red, a color that always made her feel outgoing and confident.

Her V-neck, sleeveless dress had a wide, multitiered skirt, and when she looked at herself in the full-length mirror, she thought of her college graduation.

"You've come a long way in a short time," she said aloud. The doorbell rang. She looked down at her red toenails peeping through the straps of her three-inch heel, black patent-leather sandals and wondered what Judson would think of them. She was who she was. Tossing her head, she strolled to the door and opened it.

"Hi. You're right on time. Come in."

He handed her three calla lilies—red, purple and yellow—wrapped in cellophane and tied with a red ribbon. "Hi. How are you feeling?"

"I'm making it. These flowers are lovely. I think they're precisely what I need. Just the right touch."

"Thank you. I've chosen an Italian restaurant that specializes in seafood, but if you'd prefer something else, I have a couple of alternatives."

"Excuse me a minute." She went into the kitchen, put the flowers in a vase with water and returned with them. "I think I'll put them in the living room on the coffee table. When I get back I'll put them on my nightstand. And by the way, I love Italian food. Italian is always your best bet with me."

"I'm glad to know that," he said.

Heather grabbed a white cashmere sweater and joined him.

"Ready?" he asked.

She locked the door to her house and followed Judson to his car. "How did I know you'd drive a Buick?" She said aloud and immediately wished she could have kicked herself.

"Now, you are definitely going to have to explain that," he said.

"You are not ostentatious, but you like quality. My

second guess would be a Mercedes, but that's got status written all over it, so you'd choose something else."

He glanced at her as he pulled away from the curb. "And to think I've had the impression that I'm complicated. I'm not a show-off. You're right about that. I love the Mercedes coupe, but this car uses less gas and is kinder to the environment. How did you get to Hagerstown?"

"I drove. State Department gives me a chauffeured car, but I'd rather not use it for personal business, unless I have to. I do use it at night. My car's a Lexus." She held up her hand. "I know. I should be helping our environment, but at least I'm helping our employment rate, since that car's made here."

"How long does it take you to drive to Hagers-town?"

"An hour and a half or so, but one day I'll get caught."

"I won't go there," he kidded. "I'm planning on visiting Hagerstown soon to begin looking for my birth parents. I found a birth announcement for a boy who'd be about my age. Coincidently, my adoptive mother was born there."

Heather didn't want to discourage Judson, so she said, "You have to look everywhere until you're successful, so starting with the birth announcement newspaper clipping is as good a place as any. Will you be looking for any relatives?"

"That's the idea. Some of them may know some-thing."

"If I can help you in any way, you know I will."

"I appreciate that. First, I'll find the names and contact information of African-American newspapers."

"Judson, you don't have to research that. Most of that information is available in the local library or the Internet."

"Thanks. This is very helpful."

"I think you have an angel on your shoulder. It's probably not an accident that Scott finally decided to introduce us. He's told me before that he had a friend he wanted me to meet, but I wasn't interested."

He parked in a lot a few doors from the restaurant and walked around to open the door for her. "Thanks for letting me be a gentleman," he said. "I know you can open the door, get out, close it and also fasten your seat belt by yourself. But it will give me great pleasure to do those things for you. I may be old-fashioned. Is that going to cause a problem for you?"

She thought for a minute. "I don't think so. It's when a guy gets too possessive that it becomes a problem."

"I can well imagine."

"Let's just say that he is no longer relevant."

After entering the restaurant, the maitre d' seated them, and when Heather looked at the menu, her eyes widened. "This menu is full of things that I love," she said brightly. In the end, she settled for Parma ham with figs in Marsala wine for a starter and a soup of scallops, lobster, cuttle fish, shrimp, clams and spicy tomato sauce for the main dish. He ordered the same.

Judson strummed his left fingers on the white tablecloth, then leaned back in his chair and looked at her. "You said the guy who got out of line with you is no longer relevant. Was that your choice or his?"

"I told him how I felt, and we agreed that we had no future. If he hadn't agreed, it still would have been over for me."

"Is there a man in your life right now?"

"You cut right to the chase. No, there isn't. My father lectured to me about that today. He's probably right, but when I focus on something, it takes priority."

"You mean your career in the State Department?" She nodded. "Don't you want a family?"

"Of course I do, but I think I can have both."

"I agree. You can. But not unless you make the effort." Suddenly, he leaned forward. "The more I see of you and the better I know you, the more I want to know. And there is definitely more than a spark between us."

"I'm honest, Judson. Yes, there is. But I've worked hard to get where I am, and I want a diplomatic post."

"If I can balance a medical malpractice suit, a family fight over a rich man's will, a case involving banks in different countries and a lawsuit against an accountant and deal with all of them, I'm sure we can manage a get-together from time to time. You're as smart as I am, maybe smarter. You can handle it. So how about it?"

"I see you've figured out how to respond to certain kinds of challenges."

He lifted her hand, and she noticed not for the first time his long, tapered fingers. They were the beautiful hands of a capable man, and she wondered how they would feel on her naked body. She looked up, and shivers shot through her at the longing in his eyes.

"I know myself, Heather. I know what I want."

The waiter then brought their first course. She looked at the food covering the dinner plate. "If I eat all this, I won't want my seafood course."

"The owners are generous by nature. They're also forgiving, so leave what you can't eat." He called the waiter. "I'd like a bottle of pinot grigio Santa Margherita." He turned back to Heather. "So, do you know what you want from us?"

She savored the ripe fig. "My, you're tenacious. No wonder you're successful. It's a trait that I admire."

He stopped eating and looked at her. "You haven't answered my question."

She laughed with joy. "Oh, Judson. I'm so glad you called me today. I needed this."

"Did you need me?"

She gave him a brilliant smile. "Possibly. I'm not sure."

Outside the restaurant, the warm spring wind brushed his face as he gazed down at the woman beside him. Six weeks earlier, he'd stood in a cool, caressing wind watching as his mother's friends threw roses at her grave site, thinking that he never again wanted the wind to touch his face. He had loved the woman who took him in and mothered him when someone else hadn't wanted him, and losing her left an awful hole.

He needed a family of his own making. As he looked at Heather, a smile lit her face, and he took her hand

and began walking to his car. Maybe she could fill the void in his life. He wasn't sure, but he did know that that feeling of loneliness had disappeared.

"It's early," he said. "If your day hasn't tired you out, we could stop by the Eubie Blake National Jazz Institute and Cultural Center for a short while, or—"

"I'd like that. I'm not bubbling with energy, but I won't turn down an opportunity to hear live jazz."

"I'm glad you like jazz. I could listen to the great jazz players of the past forever. I have a good collection of their records."

"Interesting. Of course, I have quite a few Duke Ellington, Louis Armstrong, Fats Waller and Billie Holiday, but the collections are not nearly complete."

He squeezed her fingers. "What else do you like?"

"Everything that isn't ultramodern—classical, opera, blues and country. If I can't remember it, I don't want to hear it."

"If you had asked me that question, my answer would have been just about the same as yours."

At Eubie Blake's, he greeted the doorman, tipped him and got a front-row table facing the band. Sipping coffee and apparently lost in the music, Heather didn't pull away from him holding her hand. He marveled that she seemed to accept that they would have a relationship of some kind so easily.

They spent an hour at the jazz house. As he walked with her from the elevator to the door of her apartment, he wondered what she'd do if he hugged her good-night. He didn't dare attempt to kiss her. He wasn't in awe of her status. How could he be after spending several hours gazing at the outline of her beautiful breasts and the print of her nipples against the soft fabric of the dress she wore? He'd walked behind her wondering if her lovely hips would move in unison with his. No, it wasn't awe that stopped him. It was respect.

"May I have your key?"

She handed it to him without the slightest hesitancy and stood aside while he opened the door. "Call me when you get home," she said, and as if she read his mind, she added, "I'm not urging you off. I want to know that you got home safely. You don't have to talk. Give it two rings and hang up."

Impulsively he brought her into his arms and hugged her. The feel of her soft and pliant body stirred something inside of him, and he released her at once. When she looked at him with an inquiring expression, he explained.

"I'd still be holding you, but I don't want to lose any points with you."

She reached up and stroked his left cheek with the back of her hand. "You have some points in reserve. Thanks for a really lovely evening, and get home safely."

Several thoughts lodged in his mind as he walked away. Had she been telling him that she liked it when he hugged her, that he could have kissed her, or that she would have forgiven him because he'd showed signs of decency?

"Oh, heck!" he said between his teeth. "Why hadn't she just come out and said it? Getting to know a woman is so damned difficult. I wish they weren't so mysterious."

Later, he walked into his apartment and called her. She had his office and cell phone numbers, and he wanted her to know how to reach him on his home phone. The number would register on her phone.

He nearly laughed when she answered on the second ring. "Hi. This is Judson. I'm home without mishap."

"I'll thank the Lord when I say my prayers. Good night."

"You're a sweet woman. Good night."

"I'm getting involved with this man," Heather said to herself the next morning, thinking of her evening with Judson and still uncertain as to the wisdom of it. She enjoyed his company, and he fit well into her comfort zone with no effort. It seemed natural to be with him.

As she entered the elevator she encountered Scott at the State Department. "How's it going?" he asked as usual.

"Some good and some bad, Scott. With me, you know nothing ever goes perfectly."

"No? What about you and Judson? Have you seen him yet?"

"Yes, but… We had dinner together last night."

They stepped off the elevator, and he gently grabbed her left arm. "I don't get it. I'd have sworn that you two were perfect for each other. Don't you get along?"

"Stop worrying about us, Scott. He's… What do I know? I haven't had enough experience to judge whether it's right to feel so comfortable with a man you hardly know. I mean, I don't even bother to put up my guard when I'm with Judson, and that isn't my style at all."

"Why shouldn't you feel comfortable with him? Besides, the real reason you're comfortable with him is because you trust him."

"Yes. You may be right. I guess what I've needed was a brother."

A grin spread over his face. "You've got a brother. What am I supposed to be?"

She didn't know whether to laugh or cry. "Scott, that's the nicest thing you've said to me in all the time I've known you. If you ever need a sister remember that you have one in me. And if the people on this floor wouldn't get the wrong idea, I'd hug you."

He winked at her. "Hug accepted. Save the real ones for Judson."

"I will," she said and headed for her office, her steps quick and light. Sitting at her desk, she saw in her in-box a letter, the return address of which told her that this was what she had awaited all of her professional career. With trembling fingers and eyes tightly closed, she pried open the flap of the envelope. And after she forced her eyelids to open, she read that she should make an appointment with her superior for an interview the following morning. Her boss was preparing to appoint an ambassador to Albania.

She wanted the promotion, and it was due, but she did not want to go all the way to Albania. She told Judson as much when he called her a few minutes before noon.

"At least they're not sending you to Calcutta," he said. "It could be much worse."

"It isn't an appointment. It's only my first query. They have an opening, and they want to know whether I have the potential to serve as a full ambassador. I definitely do not plan to spend an important chunk of my life in a place that doesn't have a first-class symphony orchestra," she complained.

He couldn't help laughing. "You'll have to start small, though. At any rate, I'm glad that you're being recognized."

"Thanks. So am I. What are you planning for today?" she asked him.

"I have some interviews in connection with that medical malpractice suit. What time do you think you'll get home tomorrow?"

"Sometime late in the afternoon. Maybe around five-thirty or six."

"Could we have dinner together at about seven?"

She hadn't expected him to want to see her again so soon. "I'd like that. Come by for me at six-thirty." She suspected that she had a lot to learn about Judson. She told herself to be home by five-thirty.

"Thanks. See you at six-thirty. Good luck with your interview tomorrow." They hung up.

Heather knew that she had no plans to accept a post in Albania, neither then nor ever. Let them give that post to a deserving political junkie. She was a career diplomat, and she had earned their more thoughtful consideration. And if she didn't get it, she certainly had other, good options.

"I can always practice law," she said to herself, "or, for that matter, I can teach."

But the idea of giving up on her dream, as so many of her colleagues had been forced to do, dampened her spirits.

"I'm going to have to postpone our court date," Judson told Curtis Heywood. "Two of your witnesses don't want to be involved, and I'll have to find others. Meanwhile, see if you can locate more evidence. I'll put my research staff on it, and if there's evidence of culpability beyond what we have, they'll find it."

He put the phone back in its cradle, leaned back in his chair and made a pyramid of his ten fingers. The case didn't bother him. He knew he'd win it. The problem was to get additional evidence so that it wouldn't drag on while the defense lawyer manufactured one cockamamy scenario after another.

His thoughts centered on Heather. Her news that she could be sent to Albania didn't cheer him. Their relationship was too new to withstand a lengthy separation. It was one more reason why he had to get his life in order, beginning with his identity. He left the office an hour earlier than usual, went home and headed for his mother's bedroom. He'd start there, but, if necessary, he'd search every centimeter of the house and its contents from the basement to the attic. He threw his jacket across a chair, rolled up his sleeves and opened the closet door.

Again, he found nothing of relevance in his mother's room other than the mysterious birth announcement and the birth and death certificates of the infant who succumbed not long before his parents adopted him. At least that was his impression based on what he knew of the timing of his adoption. He would have to go to Hagerstown and begin the search there.

"I'm going to Hagerstown tomorrow," he told Heather the next evening as they dined at Chiapparelli's in Baltimore's Little Italy. "I hope I have as much luck as you did today."

"So do I. If you can get one lead, you're on your way."

"Will they offer you an ambassadorship if you go to Albania?" He held his breath until he had her answer.

"Probably, but I have the right to refuse any post."

"Would you really refuse? I'm not sure that would be a good career move, Heather."

She stopped eating and stared at him. "Are you trying to get rid of me? If you are, I can always make it easy for you."

"I'm trying not to be selfish. And on the chance that you appreciate my judgment, I'm being as truthful as I can be."

An expression of pain spread across her face, and she briefly closed her eyes. "Oh, Judson, I'm so sorry. I do trust you, and I trust your judgment. I'm so used to—"

"It's all right. I imagine that in the world you work in, you always have to watch your back."

"Yes, indeed. And look what it's doing to me," she said as if she'd just realized it.

"How about dessert?" he said. "I think I'll have a

slice of sour lime pie," he added, glad to be able to change the subject. "What would you like?"

"I can't sit here and watch you eat it, so I'll have the same." Suddenly, she reached across the table and covered his hand with her own. "If you can be patient, we'll get there." The waiter took their orders, and refreshed their water, smiled at Heather, then left the table.

"Do you mean that?" he asked her once the waiter had gone.

"I didn't plan to say it, but it's the truth." She smiled. "I'll always tell you the truth, Judson, even if it makes me look bad, and I hope I can count on the same from you."

He enveloped her hand with his own. "Of course you can. If you never believe anything else, believe that."

The waiter brought their dessert, and they savored it without speaking. Later, while they sat sipping espresso, she looked at him and said, "I have to thank Scott for introducing me to you. He's anxious to find out whether we get along and whether we will see each other."

He imagined that the facial expression he thought was a grin was more feral than friendly. "Don't tell him a thing," he said. "Let him worry."

"How could you? He means well."

"Sure he does. Jails are full of well-meaning people. It isn't often that I'm one up on Scott, so please humor me."

He held her hand while they walked to his car, and it felt good.

Ten minutes later, he parked in front of her building,

walked around and helped her in getting out of the car and accompanied her to her apartment. She gave him her door key without his asking. He opened the door.

"May I come in for a few minutes?"

She didn't answer, but walked in and flicked on the light.

He didn't want to sit down and talk. They had talked during dinner. He wanted her in his arms. When he remained near the door, she turned, walked back to him and smiled.

"What's the matter? Do you want a hug or a kiss? Which is it?"

He'd never met a woman so lacking in guile. "Both," he said and opened his arms. She went to him with arms raised and lips slightly parted. And the feel of her warm and womanly body as she held him to her almost made him dizzy. He bent his head, brushed her lips with his own and she pulled his tongue into her mouth. He couldn't stifle the groan that erupted from deep inside of him, and with the rush of blood to his groin preparing him for a massive erection, he tried to step back from her. But she seemed oblivious to his movement. He lifted her and set her away from him. She stared at him, wide-eyed.

"I'm sorry, sweetheart," he said, "but I don't want to push you too far, too fast."

She frowned, and then she wrapped her arms around him and hugged him. "I've never met a man like you. I *am* going to thank Scott for introducing us."

"Are the two of you close friends?"

Her eyes twinkled. "We haven't drunk each other's blood, but we've pledged to be brother and sister."

"How is it that you were never attracted to each other?"

"My dad asked me the same question. Scott and I would kill each other. Actually, we nearly did when we first began working together. We backed off because we had to cooperate, and after a short while we realized that we're both too similar. So we began supporting each other, and it's been great for both of us. What time will you leave for Hagerstown tomorrow? If you need to contact a newspaper, try the *Herald-Mail* first."

"Thanks. I will.'

"Don't get your hopes up too high, Judson, and don't be disappointed if you come back empty-handed. This is just the first try. Remember you have my support."

"And that means everything to me. I know it's going to be a long, hard trek, but I'm prepared for it."

Chapter 3

Judson parked beside the Washington County Free Library at a quarter of eleven, went inside and asked the reference librarian for the microfilm room.

"If you can't find what you're looking for," she said, "maybe I can help you."

"Thank you. Where's the reading room?"

She told him and added, "I'll be glad to help if you think I can."

He thanked her again and went to the microfilm room. He found the newspaper with the birth announcement that listed the family name Motens. He went to the library's computer and began copying the names, addresses and telephone numbers for the name Moten. By the time he finished, his stomach was growling. He didn't feel inclined to seek out the helpful librarian. He pocketed his notes and left.

Sitting in the far corner of a restaurant eating a hamburger, French fries and coleslaw, he read over the names he'd recorded. None of the names were listed in his parents' papers, and he couldn't interview or even hope to locate all of them. He finished his lunch, and decided to put a classified ad in the newspaper. He found the office of the *Herald-Mail*, placed the order and headed back to Baltimore.

When he got home shortly before six o'clock that evening, he found his answering machine blinking. "I'll deal with that later," he said to himself. He had to work out a plan in case no one answered his ad. Adoption papers were sealed, but there was always a way.

Suddenly, he bolted upright. The adoption papers were not among those he had found in his mother's closet. She had stashed them somewhere else, but where? Did she have a secret hiding place? *Calm down, man. As Heather said, "you've just started."*

He went to the refrigerator for a can of beer and took it outside on his terrace. Where could he search next if no one answered his ad? He had a sudden inspiration. *The churches!* Most churches kept baptismal records. He let out a deep sigh of relief, rested his feet on the edge of the ceramic flowerpot beside him and closed his eyes as a sense of peace washed over him.

He answered his cell phone. "Philips. What may I do for you?"

"This is Curtis. Is that laboratory's attorney allowed to get in touch with me directly?"

"What? That's a no-no. Did you happen to record it?"

"You bet I did. He wanted to know what I was prepared to settle for. I told him I'd let him know, because I wanted him to continue talking. I'll make a copy of the tape and send it to you tomorrow by messenger."

So they wanted to be sneaky. That only strengthened his hand. He wondered how dirty they'd get.

Two days later while Judson sat on the grass in the sculpture garden of the National Gallery, soaking up the sunshine and eating his lunch, his cell phone rang. He didn't recognize the name on the ID screen, so he used his formal response.

"This is Judson Philips. How may I help you?"

"Mr. Philips, my name is Cissy Henry, and I'm from Hagerstown. I think I may have some information for you."

He nearly choked on his food. "Are you referring to my ad in the *Herald-Mail?*"

"Yes, sir. My daughter-in-law told me you were asking if anybody knew Beverly Moten. Well, I used to know her, but she left here well nigh thirty years ago. Her father was my brother."

He'd forgotten his lunch and was standing. "Do you mind if I come to see you and talk with you?"

"No. I don't mind a bit. Nobody's interested in what we old people have to say. Where are you, and when do you want us to talk?"

"I live in Baltimore, and I can be at your place

tomorrow morning at about eleven. What's your address?"

She gave it to him. "I know you young folks are busy, so you come anytime you want to. I'll be right here. I can fix us a real nice lunch, and we can talk. Judson Philips, you say your name is? You come on. I'll be here."

"Thank you, Mrs. Henry. I'll see you tomorrow morning."

"Well now, seems to me you ought to call me Aunt Cissy. Everybody else does."

His face broke into a smile. "Thank you, Aunt Cissy. I'm looking forward to meeting you. See you tomorrow."

Maybe he would finally know. He told himself that because the woman knew the Motens was not reason to think she knew the circumstances of his adoption. But he couldn't help hoping. He'd needed to know so badly and for so long.

Heather read the letter a third time. As she stared at the bold signature of the Secretary of State, she knew that her next move could determine her foreign service career. She was not going to Albania. In that post, a diplomat was no more than a special envoy, and everybody knew that. She needed to talk with someone about it, and she reasoned that it wouldn't be fair to discuss it with Scott.

She heard a knock on her door. "Come in."

"How's it going?" Scott asked her. "I thought we had a lunch date. What happened?"

What else had she forgotten while she digested the letter? She picked up the letter and handed it to him. "This was not what I expected, Scott."

He glanced over it. "You're turning it down, of course."

"That's what I had in mind. My problem is how to do it. I don't want to shoot myself in the foot."

"You know, Pete is separating from his wife. He said a minute ago that he wants an overseas assignment, any assignment anywhere. He wants a change."

"Goodness! Is he still in love with her?"

"Quite the contrary. They've been miserable for some time. Tell you what—if you want me to, I can drop a hint that he wants out of here, and you don't want to leave. That job is not a promotion for you, and you could be stuck there for maybe four years, but at least two."

"You can drop that hint, and I'm going to tell the Secretary that although I'm due a promotion, this doesn't seem to me to be the one. I've received perfect scores on all of my evaluations, so I'll assume that by exercising my right of refusal, I haven't adversely affected my career."

"Sounds good to me," he said, "but be very careful of your choice of words. What did Judson say about this?"

"I haven't had a chance to tell him."

"Let's go eat. I'm starving."

"Scott, do you mind if we cancel today? I don't much feel like eating. I need to go someplace and blow off steam."

"Heather, this is your first disappointment here. Let

me tell you that you'll have to learn to take the lumps and still walk as if you just won a presidential election. By tomorrow, everybody will have heard about this. Half of the staff will think you got what you deserved. The other half will know you didn't. But not one will ever say anything to that effect. Some people are ignorant, some are cowards, and the others just don't give a damn." Scott turned to the door. "See you later."

"I'd better do this before I lose my nerve." She wrote the letter, read it once, printed it out, signed it and called for a messenger. *It's what I believe is right, and I'm going with it. I'll take the consequences.*

She'd just begun to outline a plan designed to introduce self-help programs to women in sub-Saharan Africa when her cell phone rang.

"Hello, sweetheart." His deep velvet voice had the ability to comfort her. Somehow, hearing it made everything right. "I have the most wonderful news."

"You found something?"

"No, but I found someone." She listened to his tale about Cissy Henry. "That's wonderful. Judson, I'm so happy for you. The pieces will all come together. I know they will. When are you going there?"

"Tomorrow morning. If I thought you'd be free, I'd invite you to come with me."

"That probably wouldn't be a good idea. She'll speak less freely if another person is present. I have some news, too. I've been offered a post in Albania, and I just signed a letter turning it down. Well, not in precisely those words."

"Congratulations. And since you don't want the

post, congratulations for having the courage to turn it down. I'll be anxious to see you when I get back from Hagerstown tomorrow, so can we have dinner together?"

"Yes. Do you think you can come to dinner at my place? I'm a fair cook."

"I'd love that. What should I bring? Do you have wine?"

"Yes, but bring whatever you like to drink. Seven o'clock."

"All right. I'm...I'm anxious to see you. I'll have to work tonight. Otherwise, I'd suggest that we get together this evening."

"Call me and tell me good-night."

"I'll do that. Bye for now."

"Bye."

Cissy Henry stood at her front door when Judson parked in front of her house, a white, green-shuttered bungalow with a well-manicured lawn. A profusion of seasonal flowers marked the property lines.

He strode up the walk to the steps and stopped. "Come on up," she said. "You must be Judson Philips 'cause don't nobody around here dress up this good on a Saturday. How'd you do?"

He shook hands with her. "I'm fine, ma'am. How are you? I can't tell you how much I appreciate your agreeing to see me." It surprised him that she seemed so youthful and fit. He indicated as much.

"I'm eighty-four. All my life I ate right, never smoked or drank. Went to bed early, got up early and said my prayers every morning and every night. Why shouldn't I look well?" And certainly she had her mental faculties in order, too, he observed.

"Let's sit out on the back porch where it's nice and cool. I don't turn on the air conditioning till around three o'clock. Money don't grow on trees."

He sat beside her on the swing in the screened-in porch, and gazed at the irises, peonies, roses, daisies and other flowers that beautified and perfumed the garden. "This place is enchanting," he said.

"I'm happy here, Judson. Now, tell me what I can do for you."

"My adoptive mother passed on about a month ago. It's been a terrible blow to me, especially since my dad died a couple of years ago."

Cissy's eyebrows eased up. "Who was your dad?"

"Louis Philips. He was a wonderful father, and I still miss him."

"I imagine you do. What do you need to know?"

"As I told you, I'm adopted. I'd like to know who my birth parents were. I never asked my parents, because I didn't want them to think I was unhappy. I wasn't. They gave me far more than my share. However, I need to know who I am."

"You look like a prosperous man, and the way you talk tells me you're educated. What kind of work do you do?"

"I'm a lawyer, and I have a degree in law from Harvard."

"Good, then I know you'll know how to handle what I'm going to tell you. I don't know how it applies to you, but this is what I know about Beverly Moten. She had a baby out of wedlock when she was, oh, I don't know, twenty-two or twenty-three. She was going around with this man, but she never married him. After she had the baby, she left the boy here with her mother and moved to Baltimore."

"It was a boy?" She nodded. He started adding. Twenty-two or twenty-three. He was thirty-four, and his adoptive mother was fifty-seven when she died. Was that the other child? He shrugged.

"That's not the end of it," she went on. "When the child was about three, I guess, she married and she came back and got the child from her mama. After that, she never returned here."

His adrenaline shot up, and he could barely manage to remain seated. "Who was the man who fathered that child?"

"Well, you know, that's not something anybody can swear to, but I remember she was in love with the man, an architect, who designed and built the Americana Hotel. They can tell you his name. It wasn't a common name. My daughter-in-law might remember it. I'll recognize it if I hear it. A lot of our young girls were after him, because he was one good-looking man, tall and… If I'd a been single, I'd a gone after him, too." She laughed. "A bit older than Beverly, but that didn't seem to bother her."

He wanted to know about the man's character, in case he was on the right track. "Did he date all those girls?"

"Not to my knowledge. It looked like he was as crazy

about Beverly as she was about him. Nobody ever could say why they didn't get married. Come on in here while I get our lunch together. I hope you like home-cooked food."

"I certainly do, and I haven't had any since my mom got sick." He took a bottle of perfume out of his coat pocket and gave it to her. "I didn't know what to bring you, but I figured every woman likes this."

Her eyes rounded to twice their size. "This woman certainly does. This is quite a gift. Thank you so much. I don't know when I last had any perfume." She handed him the bottle. "Would you please open it? I'll just put on a little dab of it. I always used to put it on my handkerchief, but nowadays it's so dear." She put some on her index finger, sniffed and a wide smile covered her face. "This is just the kind of scent I love."

She put the food on the kitchen table, turned on the air conditioner and handed him a face towel. "You can wash up right around there."

Cissy said grace holding his hand and then passed him a platter that contained barbecued baby back ribs, broiled lamb chops and grilled pork loin. "Help yourself. There's plenty more."

His gaze took in a pan of baked corn bread, string beans, rice, sliced tomatoes and pickled beets. "I know I'm a big guy, Aunt Cissy, but this is enough food right here for six people."

"Oh, go on. Who cooks for you?"

"I'm thinking about getting a cook, but right now, I do. I also eat out a lot."

"And you take home a lot of pizzas and beer. Right?"

"Bad, huh?"

"Yes, sirree. Do you have a nice girl?"

"I met someone recently, and I think she may be the one. I'm not sure."

"Of course you're not sure if you haven't known her longer than that. Anyway, finding the right person is part luck. What does she do?"

He told her.

"That's a good fit for you. You willing to live wherever she goes?"

He liked that question. Aunt Cissy was a modern woman, her age notwithstanding. "If it gets to that point, we'll have to strike a deal. I haven't looked that far ahead."

"Well, you better. It's those surprises up ahead that throw a monkey wrench into the sweetest relationships. You be careful."

"Yes, ma'am. I generally stay alert to what's going on in my life."

After lunch, they sat in the cool living room, and he shared with her his fondest memories of his mother.

"She raised a fine man. No matter what happens and what you find out, always remember that."

"Yes, ma'am. I'd better move on, Aunt Cissy. I want to get to the Americana Hotel. Is it far?"

"Nothing's far here, son. Drive to the corner, turn left and drive till you see the hotel. It's about ten blocks."

She walked to the door with him, and he gazed down at her with mixed feelings. There were so many things he wanted to ask her that he knew she hadn't told him, and he wanted to stay longer. But the answer he sought could be ten blocks away. It was only a slim chance, but he wanted to know for certain.

"Thanks for that wonderful lunch and for receiving me so kindly. I won't forget it. If you need anything ever, you know how to reach me."

"Thank you, son, and thanks for my lovely perfume."

Fifteen minutes later, he walked into the Americana Hotel, presented his card to the receptionist and asked to speak with the manager. A short, formally dressed man appeared at once. "Is there a problem?" the manager asked him.

"No, there isn't a problem, sir," he said and shook hands with the manager. "I'm Judson Philips, and I wonder if you can tell me who designed and built this lovely hotel."

The manager beamed. "It is a fine one, isn't it? Just a minute. Have a seat."

Judson wasn't in the habit of perspiring so profusely, but as he waited for the manager to return, the sweat soaked his shirt in spite of the comfortable air-conditioning. The manager returned after what seemed like hours, though only twelve minutes had elapsed.

"I'm delighted to tell you, Mr. Philips, that one of Maryland's most famous architects designed and built our hotel. His name was Fentriss Sparkman, and here is the original brochure that commemorates the dedication. I hope you will come back and stay with us very soon."

Accepting the brochure with trembling fingers, Judson thanked the man, promised to return and headed for Baltimore. Something was missing, but he'd get to the bottom of it, no matter what. He had to go through his mother's personal belongings. He hadn't done it, because he hadn't expected to find anything among her intimate things. Now, he realized that the woman he had always believed was his adoptive mother may have kept things from his father, secrets she hadn't wanted him to know about, including the child she bore out of wedlock. And that child was most likely him.

He walked into his house ready to renew his search through his mother's things and stopped short as if a bomb had dropped. He'd forgotten to check Fentriss Sparkman's name with Aunt Cissy. He sat on the nearest dining room chair and telephoned her.

"Aunt Cissy, this is Judson."

"Did you go to the hotel?"

"Yes, ma'am. That's why I'm calling you. The man's name is Fentriss Sparkman, and the hotel's manager gave me a brochure that proves it. Do you recognize that name?"

"I sure do. He's the only person I ever heard of with a first name like that one. I hope you learn something good from all this. You let me know what happens, you hear?"

"Yes, ma'am. You and I are linked from now on, Aunt Cissy."

"You come to see me. I have a nice guest room, and you're welcome to use it whenever you want to."

"Thank you, ma'am. I appreciate that."

Fentriss Sparkman. His mother had never mentioned the man to him. "I hope I don't discover something I'd rather not know," he said to himself and ran up the stairs to continue his search. Three hours later, tired and hungry, he looked at his watch and considered having some food delivered. He went to the phone, then suddenly remembered that he hadn't called Heather to give her his news or started getting ready for dinner at her place.

He dashed to the bathroom, taking off his clothes as he went, got a quick shower, shaved and dressed. He had less than an hour, and he had to drive past DeLong's Florist to get some calla lilies. He adjusted the gray-and-yellow paisley tie and checked his image in a flawless suit and light gray shirt. With no time to go to the liquor store, he chose two bottles of wine from his wine rack, locked his door and gave thanks that he'd remembered Heather had invited him to dinner at her home.

The florist had only yellow and white calla lilies, so he bought six of each and had them wrapped in clear cellophane paper tied with yellow and white ribbons. Fortunately, the building in which she lived had valet parking, and he didn't have to waste time looking for a parking space. At three minutes of seven, he rang her doorbell. She opened the door and surprised him with a quick kiss on the mouth.

"I could get used to a greeting like that. How are you?"

"I'm fine." She seemed to study him. "And I think you've got something to tell me. Is it good?"

He smiled at that evidence that she made an effort to understand him. "Yeah." He ran his right hand over his hair. "A lot has happened." He handed her the flowers.

"Judson, these are beautiful." She hugged the flowers. "You're spoiling me, and I like it. I really do." She stepped closer to him, put her free arm around his shoulder, parted her lips and took him into her mouth.

He stopped kissing her and grinned. "Honey, you have to be careful about lighting these fires."

"I'm not even going to pretend to know what you're talking about. That was a sweet little kiss."

"Yeah. If you say so. This wine isn't cold."

She took it from him. "I'll chill it. Have a seat some-place."

Heather arranged the flowers in a crystal vase and put it on the table between two silver candlesticks, gifts to herself when she moved into the apartment. She lit the twelve-inch beeswax candles, stepped back and admired the beautiful place settings.

With that setup, the food had better be good. She took the hors d'oeuvres out of the oven, placed cheese puffs, tiny quiches and grilled mini-franks on a serving dish and walked back to the living room where Judson sat on the sofa looking ill at ease. She put the platter on the coffee table. "You don't seem comfortable. What's the matter?"

"I'm comfortable," he said brightly. "Too comfortable. Suppose you got an assignment to say, Luxembourg, and you were engaged to get married. What would you do?" Her lower lip dropped. He held up his hand to ward off a less than thoughtful answer. "And suppose your husband-to-be couldn't get a job in his field in Luxembourg? What would you do?"

What a question! Heather thought. She controlled her hands before they locked to her hip bones, because she didn't want to give the impression that his questions had surprised her.

"You have a right to know what you'd be in for if we get engaged. I'm way ahead of you, and I don't think that scenario could sustain a marriage or even a live-in relationship. According to my dad, a man's work, his woman and his children—in that order—define him, and he's only happy if he finds pleasure and contentment in all three. Cheer up, and eat your hors d'oeuvres before they get cold. What would you like to drink?"

It pleased her that he smiled. "You didn't answer my question," he said. "But I'm also a lawyer, so I got enough out of that long reply to corner you if I ever have to. I'm driving, so I'd better stick to wine. Most any kind would be nice."

She didn't rush him but allowed him to take his time with telling his "good news," because she sensed in him a new kind of peacefulness. "Let's eat now," she said after he finished a glass of wine and several of the hors d'oeuvres. "I hope you like what I prepared."

He tasted the cold, sour cherry soup. "This is delicious. I have a feeling I'm going to be sorry I ate so many hors d'oeuvres with the wine."

The meal continued with filet mignon, sautéed cremini mushrooms, asparagus and dauphin potatoes, a green salad and assorted cheeses, and ended with raspberry sauce over vanilla ice cream.

"I didn't have time to make a complicated dessert today," she told him.

"Please, don't apologize, Heather. I love ice cream, and raspberries are one of my favorite fruits. This combination is delightful."

After sipping his second cup of espresso, he said, "You told me you were a fair cook. That was an understatement. This was a wonderful meal. Let's clean the kitchen. Then we can talk."

After they cleaned the kitchen, he took her hand and walked with her to the living room. "Heather, I have an awful suspicion. After today, I not only have to find out who my birth father is, but I have to find proof that my adoptive mother is really my birth mother."

"What? Are you serious? What do you mean?"

"The woman with whom I spent this morning in Hagerstown was Mom's aunt. Cissy is her father's youngest sister. She stated Mom had a baby boy when she was twenty-two or twenty-three years old, left the child with her mother and then moved away from Hagerstown. When the boy was three, she had married and came back for the child. Her aunt didn't know her exact age when the child was born, but I believe she guessed right. I'm thirty-four and when Mom died, she was fifty-seven. You can add as well as I can.

"Aunt Cissy—Cissy Henry is the woman's name— gave me enough information to identify the father of that child. He was an architect, and I have a brochure printed two weeks before I was born that's proof he designed and built a hotel that still stands in Hagerstown."

"Which one? Not the Americana?"

He lurched forward. "That's the one."

"We can ask my father if he knew him."

"I have his name. Now I have to find out what the relationship was between him and my mom. Aunt Cissy says they were lovers. My question is, am I the product of that union?"

"Too bad you don't have your birth certificate."

"No, but I'll get it."

"Mind if I ask… You seem, well, not merely pleased, but in some kind of peaceful mood. That's unusual for you, at least the times I've been with you. When you came in here tonight, I actually thought you had found the answer. Explain this to me."

He leaned forward and braced his elbows on his thighs. "This dilemma has troubled me since I was seven years old, and the older I got the more it haunted me. Today, for the first time, I took steps to get the answer. It isn't in my nature to do nothing about a situation. When I have a problem, I get to work on it."

"What's your next move?"

"When I get home tonight, I'll continue my search, but I'll be looking in unlikely places. Mom had something to hide, and I suspect that Dad didn't know her secret. Where would you hide things from someone who had the run of the house, including your bedroom?" He took a small pad from his inside coat pocket.

"Probably with my lingerie, jewelry, toiletries, the most personal things. If she had shoe bags, search them, even her shoes. Check the house for books with hidden storage. Look in the jackets of records and under mattresses."

He glanced toward the ceiling. "I'd decided to check the lingerie drawers, but I hadn't considered those other places. Thanks, and keep thinking. If I don't find what I want in any of those places, I'll ask you again for suggestions. I'd better go, because I know I won't go to sleep until I've searched every one of those places."

"Tomorrow is another day, Judson. If I'd known this could keep you up all night, I wouldn't have mentioned them."

He stood to leave. "Do you mind if I leave now?"

It was only ten o'clock. "Please don't ask me questions like that if you want a truthful answer."

He stared at her as if she'd surprised him. "You don't want me to leave?"

That was a loaded question, and they both knew it. She shot from the hip. "Of course not. It's early. That doesn't mean I want you to spend the night, but I am enjoying your company. I know you want to find the answer to this…this mystery as soon as you can. So it's okay," she said with a laugh.

Throughout her answer, she'd had his rapt attention. "Kiss me good-night, and let me get out of here."

As she walked toward him, she knew he was trying to read the expression on her face. With her hands on his shoulders, she asked him, "What degree of heat do you want?"

His gaze didn't betray his feelings. But she got his message when he said, "Play with me, will you? I'll give you heat." His arms tightened around her, and his fingers dented the curve of her breasts. He enveloped her, and with one hand on her buttocks and the other at the back of her head, he shoved his tongue into her mouth. Though she fought for it, he dipped in and out telling her what he wanted to do to her. Then he lifted her until they were chest to breast and belly to belly. She couldn't get enough of him. Heat plowed through her, and she could feel drops of moisture in the valley between her aching breasts. He let the wall take his weight and, still holding her buttocks, he stroked her left breast with the other hand until she began to undulate against him. His tongue darted around in her mouth, and his hand stroked her breast. Warm moisture dampened her, and she moaned in frustration and pressed his hand against her breast. He put his hand inside the bodice of her dress, released her breast and bent to it.

She held her breath, until his warm tongue touched her nipple. "Stop playing with me. I want to feel your mouth on me."

He sucked the nipple into his mouth, and she let out a cry and pressed his head to increase the pressure. When she bucked against him, simulating the dance of love, he stopped her and looked in her eyes.

"You didn't intend for it to go this far, and I'm not sure I did, but if I don't leave here now, I'll take you to bed."

"I started it, but I'm not sorry about this, Judson, and don't you be. There'll be another time. Get home safely."

"I'll call you later. Good night, sweetheart."

She closed the door and locked it. Deep in thought, she walked to the living room and dropped herself into a chair. She was falling for Judson Philips. *I've known him less than two months. I'm too well-educated, too old and too experienced. This is crazy!*

Judson wanted Heather to believe that he cared for her, but he did not want her to realize the power she had over him. Not yet. He'd jerked away from her seconds before his powerful erection would have given her evidence of it. He didn't believe in playing games with a woman. But he didn't think it wise at present to show his hand.

He walked into his house and didn't pause until he got to his mother's bedroom. She loved to read, so he started with her bookcase and opened each book hoping to find a note, a letter or the directions to something else. Lost in his search, he hardly heard the wind shaking the window. When it became louder, he went to the window, looked out and saw that the sky was still clear, and the full moon shone brightly. Deciding that a storm was not imminent, he resumed his search, but immediately the rattling commenced again. He went to the window to secure the latch, braced his left hand against the heavy valance that hung across the top of the window and jerked it back.

He felt something. He turned up the hem of the valance and saw a small, letter-size envelope secured to the valance with a safety pin. He opened it and stared at a two-and-a-half-inch metal key in his hand that he knew without a doubt fit a safe deposit box. He looked inside the envelope and found the box number and the address of the bank. He put the key back into the envelope and placed the envelope in the pocket of his jacket. He reached for the light to turn it off and realized that the window had stopped rattling.

With a broad smile, he looked upward. "Thanks."

The next morning, he put the notarized copy of his mother's will into his briefcase and headed for the bank. As executor of the will, he was entitled to open her safe deposit box. But the closer he got to the bank, the more uneasy he became. What if he didn't like what he found and wished he'd let sleeping dogs lie? He parked around the corner from the bank and forced himself to get on with it.

He asked for the manager and presented the will. Minutes later, he had in his hands what he knew would be the secrets of his mother's life. He put the bundle of letters into his brief case, ran his hand back to the part of the safe deposit box that he couldn't see and retrieved a bundle of Series E bonds, a gold-and-diamond bracelet, a gold OMEGA watch and a gray cameo set in gold. He phoned his secretary and told her to refer important calls to his cell phone. He locked the box and went home.

Hours later, he still hadn't finished the letters between Beverly Moten and Fentriss Sparkman. He learned that, six months after they had met, they began a torrid love affair that Beverly's family vigorously opposed. But their letters expressed a profound love for each other. He gave her elegant and expensive gifts, which she hid from her family. Her mother discovered her pregnancy, considered her a disgrace to the family and confined her to the house. Beverly sneaked out at night and mailed letters to Fentriss, but they were returned unanswered.

Fentriss's last letter to Beverly stated that he would be working in Atlanta for a few months but would return for the dedication of the hotel. After the child was born, her mother sent her to Baltimore and kept the child. He found no more letters from Fentriss and suspected that Beverly's mother confiscated them. No one had to tell him that the expensive watch, bracelet and cameo were gifts to Beverly from Fentriss Sparkman. He counted the Series E bonds which she had registered jointly in her name and Judson's, and found that they added up to forty-five thousand dollars plus accrued interest. He decided that the money would be a gift to his firstborn child.

He still hadn't satisfied himself that he had the answer until he opened the last set of papers. In the small packet, he found his adoption papers and realized that Beverly and Louis Philips adopted him when he was three years old, six months after the death of their younger child. He had a lot of useful information, but competent lawyer that he was, he realized that he didn't have a shred of proof.

"I have to find Fentriss Sparkman."

Chapter 4

"Can you tolerate my company for lunch?" Judson asked Scott minutes after deciding to find Fentriss Sparkman.

"Sure thing. Where do you want to meet?"

"I don't want to make it a long one, so how about Frank's for some pulled-pork barbecue?" They agreed on a time.

Judson put his mother's jewelry and government bonds in his safe, locked it and left to meet Scott. He hadn't shared with Heather what he'd learned, but he would, later that day. When they could be alone.

Besides the barbecue, to Judson's way of thinking, the garden in back of the restaurant was the only reason to eat at Frank's. But on that day, the heat forced him to eat inside in the air-conditioned restaurant. Scott, who was sitting at a back-corner table when he arrived, stood and they exchanged a fist bump.

"What's up?" Scott asked him.

He didn't have time for preliminaries. "I found the key to Mom's safe deposit box. I didn't even know she had one." Scott lurched toward him. "It contained a huge bundle of love letters exchanged with a man I suspect was my father."

"What? Wait a minute."

Judson explained the basis for his suspicion. "I have to find that man, and if I can't find that child Mom had when she was twenty-three, or incontrovertible evidence of what happened to him, then I'm that child. She and Dad adopted me when I was three. Aunt Cissy said Mom came back for the child when he was about three. So there you have it."

"Whoa, man. What does that prove?"

Scott rubbed the back of his neck. "Judson, do you actually think Aunt Bev let you believe she was your adoptive mother when she was actually your real mother? Man, that sounds cruel as hell to me. I don't want to think that about her."

"Well, if it's true, you have to credit her with finding a way to take me to live with her and not letting relatives or strangers raise me. If there's a culprit in this, it's probably her mother. It won't be the first time that face-saving got in the way of parental love."

"Yeah. I guess not."

They finished the barbecued pork sandwiches and promised to meet the following weekend for a game of tennis to help rid them of the calories they'd just gained. "I'll be in touch," he said to Scott and got into his car.

At four-thirty, he telephoned Heather. "Hi, sweetheart. I've got plenty to tell you, but first, I want to know how things are going with you."

"I have to attend a White House black-tie reception Thursday after next, and since the invitation is for me and a guest, will you be my guest?"

"I'll be delighted to accompany you," he answered.

"I need to talk to you in person, if possible. I don't think I can cook a meal this evening, so I'd like us to eat at a restaurant, if you don't have any plans."

"Okay. What time?"

"Be at my place at seven."

"Is what you have to tell me going to make me happy or sad?"

"I'm making good progress, but I need to process some of this stuff through a brain other than mine. I have most of what I've been looking for and the key to the rest, but the most difficult may be ahead of me."

"I'm with you, no matter what."

He supposed that was why he'd called her, to know that she was there for him. He was reaching a point in his search where he could stumble or, worse, get more than he'd bargained for.

Heather questioned the wisdom of leaving the country at a time when Judson could be facing a critical point in his life. She had to put a cork in the trouble brewing in Colombia, and a trip there within the next few days seemed in order. She hoped Judson hadn't bitten off more than he was willing to chew. It had been her experience that when you dug into the past, you could uncover truths best left alone. She hoped he was willing to acknowledge that. She had already realized that his gentle, laid-back manner camouflaged a strong and tenacious personality and a toughness to match that of any man. But he could falter, because he was dealing with uncertain emotions. She was prepared to see him through some of the pain, if necessary. She had already learned to take the bumps in stride.

She didn't know where he'd take her, so she put on an avocado-colored, lightweight silk suit with a yellow silk blouse. If the place required something dressier, she would merely remove the jacket. And probably freeze. She wore her hair down, attached small gold hoops to her ears, and hurried down the hall guessing that she would barely make it to the door by the time he rang the bell.

She opened the door, and he stepped in, hugged her and stepped back as if to get a good look. "You look better to me every time I see you," he said. His eyes sparkled, though she knew they reflected his happiness that he'd made progress in his search for his birth parents.

She'd been careful not to compliment him on his looks, because he had certainly heard enough of that. But he looked so great in that navy blue suit that she reached up, kissed him on the mouth and said, "Remaining objective about you is practically a full-time job, and tonight, it's impossible."

"Why?"

"Because you look great, and you're interfering with my good judgment."

"Trust me, sweetheart, you're interfering with more than my judgment. I found a great little Hungarian restaurant. It has terrific food, a wonderful décor and live gypsy music. I walked in there one day to get out of a torrential rain, and decided to sample the food. It's really good. But if you'd rather—"

"I can already taste it. Besides, I like gypsy music. It's schmaltzy and romantic."

"This was wonderful," she said to Judson as they sipped espresso after their dinner. The musicians strolled among the patrons taking requests and filling the restaurant with the kind of music that stirs fantasies.

The lead violinist asked Judson, "What would you like to here?"

"'Just One Girl in All the World,'" he said, and explained to Heather that he had once heard the song while sitting alone in a Hungarian café in Vienna, Austria. "You can't imagine how lonely I felt that night."

She reached for his hand, closed her eyes and let the music wash over her. One didn't need the words to know that it was a song for lovers. The musicians moved on to the next table and, as if the song had opened up a place inside of him, Judson began to talk.

"Aunt Cissy said the boy was three years old when Beverly Moten came back to Hagerstown and took him away, and the adoption papers I found stated that I was three at the time of adoption. Now I'm going to find Fentriss Sparkman."

"But where?"

"I'll start with the organizations that architects and builders belong to to see if he's a member, and whether his address is listed. Aunt Cissy said he's a very prominent builder, and he must be if he designed that beautiful hotel."

"Tell you what. I have to visit Annie and my father. Bring your laptop, I'll bring mine, and we can work at this together."

"I'd like that, but what will your dad say about your bringing me to his house? I mean, won't he reach the wrong conclusion?"

She could hardly restrain her laughter. "Seeing me with you would please him, but he might start asking you questions."

"When did you last bring a man to your dad's house?"

"Hmm. Not since I was a teenager."

"There's your answer. I've been introduced to several fathers and their response to me was the same—*What are your intentions?* If I'm lucky enough to have a daughter, that will also be my reaction to any man I see her with. And if I asked, not a one would tell me the truth."

She lowered her lashes. "What if I asked, would you tell me the truth?"

A grin spread over his face, and his large eyes sparkled, sending her heart into a tizzy. He stared at her. "What is it?"

"Nothing," she said. "At times, you take some getting used to. You didn't answer my question."

"Oh, that! If I tell you the truth, you won't play by the rules. I'm not stupid, sweetheart.

"If I go to Hagerstown and don't stay with my aunt Cissy, she'll be hurt. I suggest that you stay with your dad, and I'll stay with my aunt, and we'll meet at the hotel and do our research there."

"Nope. You come to my dad's place. We can work in the living room, the dining room, Dad's den or on the enclosed, air-conditioned back porch. I'm not sitting in a hotel working when I can kick off my shoes and work at home. Period."

"If you had phrased that differently, say, like a suggestion or a request rather than an order, I'd say that's a great idea."

She spent so much of her working day telling people what to do that she'd slipped up. But she figured she'd better not buckle at the first sign of battle. "Point taken. What do you say instead?"

"I'd say it's a good idea."

"I apologize. I'm so used to giving orders at work that I slipped. I'll be more careful."

"Can we leave Friday afternoon after work? I'll call Aunt Cissy and tell her to expect me. Do you want to come back Saturday or Sunday? Or shall we play it by ear?"

"My father won't want me to leave before Sunday." She looked out the window. "Look at that, will you? I didn't know it was supposed to rain. It looks as if the clouds burst wide open. Well, we'll just sit here."

After another round of espresso and two more tips to the musicians to play "Golden Earrings" and "Vienna, City of My Dreams," he seemed to tire of the schmaltz. "I'll get my car. Wait inside here."

"Why should you get wet? I'm—"

He interrupted her. "Will I be drier if you go with me to get the car than if I went alone? Wait by the door."

As he walked away, she considered the evening. She would have to remember to leave foreign service officer Tatum at the office, where she'd been cracking the whip, as it were, all day.

Judson drove up and parked. She was about to open the door when she saw him get out of the car, open an umbrella and walk to the door where she stood. She waited until he opened it and walked with him the few steps to the car.

She sat in the car, completely dry, and when he opened the door on the driver's side and got in, she saw that he was drenched. "When you take me home," she said, "I'm going to kiss you and we'll stop when *I'm* ready."

"If past experience is a yardstick, it's gonna be a long evening. I can't wait." Was he being facetious?

"And I can't wait for you to eat those words."

"Uh-huh. I know."

She tried to see his face. "You're playing with me."

"Would I do a mean thing like that?" He parked in front of her building, cut the motor and turned to her. "Should I let the valet park this car?"

While she looked him in the eye, she put a hand on the door handle as if prepared to open it. "You can do that, or you can find a parking space around here somewhere."

She was about to push the door open when his hand shot out and pulled her toward him. He bent over her. "Some things aren't amusing. You know I want you, that I'm practically going out of my mind wanting you."

Stunned by his outburst, she didn't think. Instead, she put her hand behind his head, parted her lips and brought his mouth to hers. "I'm not playing with you. Kiss me."

She had expected a fierce, passionate and demanding kiss, but his lips barely touched hers. His tongue flicked over the seam of her lips and withdrew. His lips brushed her eyes, her cheeks and her throat. He stopped and looked at her.

"Do you understand?" he asked her, his voice soft and urgent.

"Yes," she whispered.

He stared into her eyes until tremors seemed to surge through her, beginning with her limbs and then throughout her body. She felt herself shake, and he wrapped her in his arms. "There's nothing casual about this for me, Heather. If you can walk away and not look back, tell me now, and I won't get out of this car."

"This is not casual or ordinary for me, Judson. I'm in uncharted waters, and I'm scared to death that I might drown."

His kiss barely touched her mouth, but it shook her from her head to her toes. He got out, went around and opened the door for her. "Say, there's a parking spot," she said when a car moved away from the curb. He looked at her for a moment, and she knew the second that he made up his mind. He got back into his car and parked in the vacant spot, came back, took her hand and walked into the building.

Inside her apartment, he closed the door, took her hand and walked with her to the living room. "Sit here beside me," he said. "Heather, from the time my mother died until the first time you kissed me, I couldn't shake the feeling of being totally alone. It didn't depress me, but it was unpleasant and I felt a terrible loss. As you and I have grown closer, I have only fleetingly felt that loneliness.

"When I eat something that's delicious, I want to share it with you. If I see something interesting, beautiful or funny, I almost always think of you and wish you were with me.

"I can think of several reasons why you may want to break off our relationship. If not now, eventually. If you and I make love, breaking up would cause deep pain. I've thought about this a good deal. If you haven't, this is your opportunity to back away."

"I know that feeling of loneliness, of being by myself even when surrounded by friends and colleagues, and of having no one with whom to share an intimate experience," she said. "You know my story. From the time I was ten, I've had Annie and my father. Now, your nightly and sometime early-morning calls are the moments I live for. I haven't dissected this thing, but I know what you mean to me. I don't care who your parents are or what your heritage is. It produced you, and that's more than good enough for me."

He stood and held out his hand to her. "Thank you. That means more than you can imagine." She tried to read the fierce expression in his eyes. It wasn't passion. Could it be determination?

"When we take the next step, there will be no turning back, at least not for me. You're not that certain yet. So walk with me to the door."

He read her reaction, put his arms around her and said, "We shouldn't make love because one of us decides that it's time, but because we both decide. I believe we're closer right now than we've ever been, and if we treat with care the growing feelings, you'll be happy that we did. Do you understand?"

She nodded. "I think I do." She wanted so badly to ask him if he loved her. But if she did that, she'd be admitting that she cared for him.

"I'm beginning to realize that you are wiser in matters of the heart than I am."

A grin spread over his face. "'Matters of the heart?' Sweetheart, don't candy-coat this. It's okay to call it what it is."

"And what is that?" she asked, looking at him with lowered lashes.

"Intimacy between a man and a woman. Love-making. Anything but matters of the heart. That sounds too vague." He grinned at her, and lights danced in his eyes. "Sometimes I wonder if you're a natural flirt."

"Me? A flirt? Me?"

"Yeah. And a damned good one at that. Walk with me to the door."

"What time do we leave for Hagerstown?"

"You'll find me parked in front of your office building at four-fifteen."

"Great. We'll be there before dark."

He tipped up her chin with his index finger. "Are you disappointed?"

"In a way, but I learned more tonight that I've learned before."

"Our day will come, sweetheart, and it will be magical." He gathered her close to him and spread gentle kisses over her face before running his tongue over her lips. She opened, pulled his tongue into her mouth and caught fire. He broke the kiss, gazed down at her for a long moment and left.

"Our day will come," she said aloud, "and brother, you'd better be ready." But she knew he was right. An hour earlier as they sat in his car in front of the building, he'd given her tenderness, showing her the difference between love and passion.

He'd told her earlier that he wanted her badly, and she would have made love to him then and there. Now she suspected that it was her emotions ruling her, and she needed sexual fulfillment. So why not? After thinking for a while, it hit her that he could get sex anywhere and at anytime. But he saw her as a potential mate and intended to move with great care. One more reason why she admired him.

When Judson left Heather, questions danced across his mind. He told himself that he was not a masochist. So why had he walked away from what he wanted so badly? With the snap of a finger, he could have been ready to exhaust himself inside of her. But he didn't want it as a result of a tease or any ploy. He realized for the first time that he was playing for the highest stakes, that if they found that they loved each other and were sexually compatible, he'd want her for life.

He parked in front of the State Department building at precisely four-fifteen and saw Heather walk out of the revolving door carrying a red leather overnight case. He got out, met her, put the case in the trunk of his car. He got in the car, leaned over and kissed her.

"I like a lot of things about you," he told her, "and they include your punctuality. You never keep me waiting, and you're the only woman I've dated that I can say that about. You're considerate, and I appreciate that."

He hadn't said it to please her, but he could see that it did. "Thank you. My father demanded that. When I was a teenager, I considered punctuality an inconvenience, to put it mildly. Nowadays, I thank him for it. He wanted to know why you aren't staying with us, and I told him you wanted to stay with your aunt."

"What was his reaction to that?" They hadn't talked much about her family, though she'd told him that she grew up without her mother.

"A grunt would best describe it."

"You never told me what kind of work your father did."

"He taught history at Morgan State. He deluged me with so much history that I won't read anything that remotely resembles a history book."

"You certainly studied legal history."

"In those days, Daddy was still drilling me about historical facts." She patted his knee. "It took me a little while last night to understand how you could leave the way you did. At first I was prepared to be annoyed, then hurt. You were right. One day, I'll tell you why I'm so sure you were right."

He slowed down to allow a speeding driver to safely pass. "I'll look forward to that. I want to share anything that will help me know and understand you. That was not an easy thing for me to do. I felt like a cross between a saint and a masochist walking out of that door. If we treat our feelings for each other casually, we'll lose something precious. So let's be honest with each other, and that includes in bed."

She turned on the radio, and Billie Holiday's sultry voice crooned with a hot rendition of "Them There Eyes."

"That's what got me," he said. "Your elegance hit me before I got to you, but those big brown eyes of yours made marbles dance in my stomach."

Her mind's eye gave her a good picture of that scene, and laughter poured out of her. "Judson, your eyes put the stars to shame, so let's not talk about the power of eyes."

"Woman, you're crazy. I never heard of such a thing." He had to laugh. "When it comes to metaphors, that one was hard to top."

Some time later, he passed the sign that read Welcome to Hagerstown and slowed down to conform with the speed limit. "I'll take you to your father's house, and then I'll check in with Aunt Cissy." At her direction, he drove into a broad, tree-lined street and parked in front of a yellow, two-story Cape Cod house.

Immediately, a woman of about fifty or so opened the front door and rushed out to the car. Heather jumped out of the car as he opened his own door, embraced the woman in a tight hug and turned to him. "Annie, this is Judson Philips. Judson, this is Annie Archer, my dear friend and surrogate mother."

He liked how Annie treated Heather, and her penetrating perusal did not escape him. Deciding to throw her off balance and destroy what he believed was her conclusion that he was a handsome stud, he put an arm around her and hugged her in a tender and gentle manner.

"Heather has told me of your role in her life, and I'm glad to meet you."

Annie brushed her hands down the front of her dress as if pressing out some wrinkles and looked hard at him. He resisted grinning, for that would be impolite. "I'm glad to meet you, Judson. Heather hasn't said one word to me about you, and I'm going to take her to task for it."

She locked her hands to her hips and continued to look at him. He could see that she'd already given up her ill-considered assessment of him. "I didn't know such men existed," she said cryptically. "Come on in. Heather, your father is very excited that you're coming, and he's in a really good mood today."

"Thank the Lord for that," she said, her face alight with happiness. With her fingers on his arm, she urged him to go with her to see her father. He doubted the wisdom of it, but the choice was hers.

Franklin Tatum sat in a big, comfortable leather chair facing a window that overlooked beautiful flower and vegetable gardens "Hello, Daddy. How are you?" Heather said to him, then hugged him and kissed his cheek. His hands stroked her back in a feeble gesture of affection. "I brought a friend to meet you," she said. "Come in, Judson.

"Daddy, this is Judson Philips. He's an attorney."

Franklin Tatum braced himself on the arms of the chair and, with great effort, stood and extended a hand. "It's good of you to come. I'm happy to meet you."

He looked at the man, tall and gaunt and probably a mere shadow of his former self, but his dignity was fully intact. "I'm honored to meet you, sir. Please sit."

"Thank you, Mr. Philips. Standing for any length of time has become a chore. I hope you'll join us for supper. Annie tells me that you have an aunt here with whom you plan to stay, but you're welcome to stay here. We have plenty of room."

"I appreciate your offer, sir, but I haven't been to see my aunt yet, and I don't know what she's planned. When I get there, I'll phone Heather and compare notes."

"You're an orderly man, and that's an admirable trait."

"Thank you, sir. I'd better leave now." He walked over to Heather. "I'll be in touch shortly."

He reached Cissy's house ten minutes later, got out of his car and rang the doorbell. The full moon flooded the earth with light, but Cissy turned on the porch light nonetheless.

"Judson. Son, I've been scared to death that something happened to you."

He bent down and hugged her. "Why? I didn't say what time I'd be here."

"That's right, you didn't. Supper's ready. Where's your bag?"

Just as he'd suspected, and not for anything would he have disappointed her. He got his bag from the trunk of his car and went inside. Except for the wallpaper of yellow and red roses, which he preferred not to see, his room couldn't have been more comfortable or more pleasant.

He telephoned Heather. "Sweetheart, as I suspected, Aunt Cissy waited supper for me. She's given me a very nice room and private bath, and she's as proprietary as my mom would be in the circumstances. I'll call you after dinner, and please tell your father that I'll see him tomorrow. Consider yourself kissed."

"And you do the same. Bye."

He looked at the table and the food arrayed on it. "Aunt Cissy, who else is eating?"

"Nobody. Why?"

"Well," he began, sitting down, "you're not fat, and I don't plan to get fat, so what do we do with the leftovers?" She didn't see the problem, so he primed himself to eat as much as he could and not think about what was left.

"Now, tell me, son, what have you found out about your parents?"

"As I told you, I discovered that Mom had a safe deposit box. I opened it and found her letters to Fentriss Sparkman, my adoption papers, the death certificate of a child who died a few months before I was adopted, some other papers and some fine jewelry that was obviously a gift from Fentriss Sparkman. You were right. They were serious lovers, and I think Mom's mother intercepted Sparkman's letters after he left Hagerstown. I suppose you knew that her mother confined her to the house after she got pregnant, and she had no way of contacting Sparkman. She didn't answer his letters and I suppose he eventually stopped writing. Unless I find him, we'll never know."

"Did you say you plan to find him?"

"Absolutely. I suspect she was my mother and that he's my father." He told her how the rattling window was responsible for his finding the key to the safe deposit box.

"You go 'way from here. She wanted you to find it. That's as clear as the nose on your face."

"Where do you think I should start my search for Fentriss Sparkman?"

"Well, that hotel's as old as you are, so it's not likely they'll be able to help you."

"I know. Tomorrow, I'll see if he's listed as a member of the Society of American Registered Architects. They would have a contact for him. I also want to know whether he was a member of a local church or social organization, where he went to college and if he was a member of a fraternity. Since this is the only place I know of that he lived, I have to start here."

"You're a smart man, Judson. Oh, and don't forget the local library. Hagerstown is proud of that hotel, so the library will probably have information on Fentriss."

"Thanks for your help, Aunt Cissy. Let's get this kitchen cleaned." He took the dishes and utensils to the kitchen, rinsed them and put them in the dishwasher. "Where do we put this food?"

"I'll do that. Some woman is going to get a sweetheart of a man. You told me you'd met someone. How is that coming along?"

"Nicely, I think. She's here. You'll meet her to-morrow."

"She's here. In Hagerstown? You're not telling me she lives here. There's nobody here for you."

"No, ma'am. She came with me. Remember, she's a lawyer and an ambassador. She's helping me with this search." He put an arm around her shoulder and hugged her. "I brought her with me. She's my girl, and she's staying at her father's house, but I wanted to stay with you."

"Of course you did. Who's her father?"

"Franklin Tatum."

"Really? He's been a respected citizen in this town. He taught my daughter over in Baltimore. I hear he's not too well these days."

"No, he isn't. If you'll excuse me, Aunt Cissy, I have to phone Heather."

"That's right, son. Let her know she can depend on you. I don't remember her, but everybody in town knows her father."

* * *

The next day, he and Heather had breakfast at her father's house, then left to buy a copy of the *Herald-Mail*. They perused it for possible leads but found none. At the library, they checked newspaper articles online but couldn't find the name Fentriss Sparkman.

"Maybe he's moved," she said.

"Yes, or deceased. We need to find a listing of local architects for, say, five years ago.

"Let's take alternating years," he suggested. "You check one year earlier and I'll check two years earlier until we find him."

"Eureka," she said a few minutes later. "Here he is in Frederick, Maryland. That's five years ago. What do you think?"

"He's probably retired, or worse. Any leads?"

"He built several buildings there. The last one was dedicated a little more than three years ago. We should be able to learn something there. I think we can stop looking," she said.

"I'd like to check out the churches to see if he belonged to any of them. Some of his fellow church members might still be in contact with him."

"Good idea," she said and went online and began writing the names of local churches, the ministers and phone numbers.

"We can check those after lunch," he told her and phoned Cissy. "This is Judson. Are we late for lunch? If we are—"

"You come right on and bring that young lady. I want to meet her. Lunch will be ready when you get here."

"Can't I go home and freshen up?" Heather asked Judson.

"Why? You want to put on an evening gown? You're wearing a white pantsuit and a yellow blouse, your hair is perfect, and you look beautiful, at least to me."

"But she's the only one of your relatives I'll meet, and…"

He stood, took her briefcase and his in one hand and her hand in his other one. "Stop worrying. Come on. You're going to get a wonderful lunch."

He put the briefcases in the trunk of his car and drove them to Cissy's house. They found her sitting on the front porch cooling herself with a church fan. When he parked, she got up and met them as they walked up the path to her steps.

After hugging Judson, she smiled at Heather and then hugged her. "There's a lot Judson didn't tell me about you, but now that I've met you, I can guess half of it. He's too smart to pass up a woman who's both talented *and* beautiful."

Heather's pleasure showed on her face. "Thank you, ma'am."

"Aunt Cissy, this is Heather Tatum." Without thinking about it, he eased an arm around Heather's waist. "Heather, this is my aunt Cissy."

"Yes," Cissy said. "He left out a lot, but he's very proud of you, Heather. He told me you're a lawyer and a roving ambassador. Congratulations. I love to see our young women step up to the plate, educate themselves and do important things."

"Thank you, Aunt Cissy. I appreciate your good

wishes. Getting the education was the easy part. The rest has been like walking barefoot on hot coals."

"I'm sure of that. Anytime a woman gets into a man's world, the menfolk do their best to kick her right back into the kitchen. Till I got a job teaching math at the local high school, only men taught math and science here. For the next thirty-five years, the boys tried to put me back in my place, but I never gave in. You can freshen up in the powder room right there." She pointed to a door off the living room. "I made sure to get the place nice and cool."

They finished a meal of baked ham, corn fritters, butter beans, coleslaw, pickled beets, lemonade and apple pie à la mode. Heather looked at Cissy and Judson, patted her belly and said, "I could go to sleep right this minute. That was wonderful."

"You can't sleep now," he told her, "because we have to call these churches and find out whether Fentriss Sparkman belonged to one of them."

"Okay." She opened her pocketbook. "Here's the list."

"Let me see," Cissy said. She glanced over it. "He might have gone to Mt. Bethel or Shiloh Baptist, but not any of these other ones, unless he was Catholic. If he was Catholic, he was sinning up a blue streak and probably not going to church. I'd start with Bethel and Shiloh. Didn't you make any headway this morning?"

"We found him listed as being in Frederick, Maryland, five years ago, but we don't have anything on him after that. So my next search will be in Frederick."

Sitting in Cissy's living room, he dialed Mt. Bethel

AME Church. "This is attorney Judson Philips. I'm trying to reach Fentriss Sparkman. Could he have been a member of your church?"

"No, sir. I've been preaching here for almost forty years, and I never heard of him."

Judson thanked the man and made the next call. He dialed with shaky fingers, aware that the effort could move him toward success in his search or prove a waste of time.

"He used to come here years ago," the minister of Shiloh Baptist Church told Judson. "I mean that was a *long* time ago. I was a young assistant minister. As I remember, he wasn't active in the church, just attended something like one or two times a month. Tomorrow morning I'll ask if anybody knows his whereabouts. Call me around three o'clock."

"Thank you, sir. I'll do that. You've been very helpful."

He told Heather and Cissy what he'd learned. "I'm wondering if it would make sense to go over to Frederick today. It would probably take us at least an hour to get there, and I don't have any leads."

Cissy poured them each a glass of homemade lemonade. "Frederick's a big city. You could go there and waste a lot of time."

"I know," Judson said, "but I'll have some leads by next weekend. Still, it's as if I got to a brick wall and don't have a way to climb over it."

Chapter 5

"Are you taking anyone to the White House reception?" Scott asked Heather the next Monday morning as they drank coffee in the coffee closet, the staff's name for the little room.

"Judson is my escort."

"That's great. So you finally broke down and decided not to go alone and be a renegade."

"This is the first time I had a man I was proud to go with."

Scott pressed his right hand to the left side of his chest and covered his face with a hurt expression. "You wound me."

"No such thing. I couldn't attend with a colleague. Besides, you never asked *me*. What happened to the woman you took to that last reception?"

"It was nothing serious—you remember."

"That's a good thing. She wasn't right for you. Any tips on that situation in Colombia? I know you're dealing with Mexico, but I see some similar threads in these problems."

"You're right. There are several, and they may be more closely connected than we think. I'll send you my notes on what I've figured out about problems in Mexico. When are you leaving?"

"Saturday morning. I want to speak with a few strategic contacts before I get down to business the following Monday."

"Great idea but watch your back. Say, how are things going with you and Judson? My so-called friend doesn't tell me much."

"He requires a lot of understanding, but I'm getting there, and we're slowly getting on the same page."

"I was hoping for more than that. He's one hell of a guy, and he's decent-looking. What's the holdup?"

"Decent-looking, did you say? That's a laugh! Judson charts his own course. If I had my way, it would move faster because I'm always impatient. But in this case, it probably wouldn't last. To say the least, I'm learning something important, and I'm glad for it."

"Don't waste it, friend. The postman does not always ring twice."

She went back to her office thinking about Scott's advice. The more she was with Judson, the more she wanted to be with him and the more she admired him. He'd known the eight-four-year-old aunt of his adoptive mother for less than one month, and he'd taken her into his life. It had astonished her to see that he regarded Cissy with genuine affection, which the woman truly reciprocated.

"He's like that with her," she said to herself. "Imagine what he'd be like if he loved a woman." She stopped walking when she realized that she badly wanted to be that woman. *When did I fall in love with him? I was being so careful and so clever. It happened anyway.*

Thursday arrived, and Judson was at Heather's apartment at seven-thirty that morning for the drive to Washington, although they usually made the commute separately and by train. Because they planned to stay in Washington and not risk a late-night drive after a day of work and partying, they had arranged to stay at a hotel.

"Do you want connecting rooms?" the registration clerk at the Willard Hotel asked.

"No," they said simultaneously.

He handed them their keys. "I'll send your bags up. Enjoy your stay."

"Thank you," Judson said.

"He was fresh," she said to Judson as they walked to the elevator. "Twenty years old and fresh."

"I remember when I was that age. I spent a lot of time imagining what it was to have sex all the time. Don't think too unkindly of him. That is definitely not the age of wisdom."

"Girls think of moonlight and roses, a guy kissing you at sunset beside a running brook, whether your dad's going to let you out of the house the next evening so you can see him, getting to the next party, stuff like that. Oh yes, we do think about sex and imagine that one day a guy will make the earth move."

"That is definitely not what guys are thinking." He laughed. "I'm in 618. Where are you?"

"Six nineteen. We're in rooms facing each other."

"I'll meet you at the desk downstairs at five-thirty," Judson promised.

She looked up at him. "I don't suppose I could get a kiss here in the corridor?"

He kissed her quickly on the mouth. "I'm not risking one of your sizzling sessions. A lot's facing me today. If we meet at five-thirty, that should give us plenty of time," he said. "We have to be there at a quarter of seven latest. The car will be here at a quarter of six, and the traffic from these few blocks to the White House will be horrendous."

Heather left the office early and returned to the hotel at a quarter of three. Official functions could be as grueling as they were glamorous, and she wanted time to rest. She headed for the elevator and stopped. Judson walked out of the hotel's business center reading a paper and nearly walked into her. Shocked at the near collision, he reached out to her, then leaned down and kissed her cheek. "See you later," he said, barely taking his eyes from the paper he'd been reading. "Don't oversleep."

She caressed his cheek. "Don't *you* oversleep." In her room, she inspected her dress and, satisfied that she would look her best, she put her underwear, evening shoes, gloves and bag on a chair. After a leisurely, scented bath, she dried and powdered her body, checked her nails, rolled up her hair and crawled into bed. Remembering that she had to be ready in two hours, she asked for a wake-up call and went to sleep.

He'd fought with the idea of wearing a cummerbund, decided that it was inappropriate with his navy tux. He didn't spend a lot of time fussing with clothes, but when it came to women and formal attire, he'd learned that you'd better get it right. He leaned against the reception desk waiting for Heather, impatient, not because he minded the wait; he didn't. But because he simply could not wait to be with her, and he knew that no matter what she wore, she would suit him. She turned the corner from the bank of elevators and he glanced at his watch. Precisely on time. A smile lit her face the minute she saw him, and his heart fluttered. He stepped away from the desk and went to meet her, a vision in an elegant dark pink gown and silver accessories.

"Heather, you're so beautiful and so elegant," he said. "You take my breath away."

"Thank you." Her radiant smile seemed to bless him. "I'm glad you like the way I look. I'll be lucky to leave that reception with you."

"Why so?"

"Because I won't be the only woman there, and I'm sure some of those women will recognize the Lord's perfect handiwork. You look magnificent."

He hoped his expanding chest wouldn't pop one of the buttons on his shirt. "I wanted to please you."

* * *

He observed her throughout the evening as she introduced him with a show of pride. She didn't work the room during the cocktails prior to dinner, but moved to people with whom she seemed well-acquainted.

"I thought you'd be in Albania about now," a senator said to her.

"I speak several languages, Dirk, but not that one. I don't see how one can serve effectively if one is saddled with an interpreter."

"I couldn't agree with you more," he said. She shook hands with the man and, with a finger at his elbow, she signaled to Judson to move on. He appreciated that; she never left him to trail behind her.

After dinner, he was ready to leave. He had met and spoken to the president and the first lady, and he'd had the company of the most desirable, elegant and beautiful woman there. And he was leaving with her.

"Do you want to stay and dance, or should we leave now?" she asked him. "It's been a long day."

"I want to spend what's left of the evening with you."

Something quickened in her eyes, and her hand reached out and grasped his arm. Her lips moved, but no words came. "Are you ready to leave?" he asked her.

She nodded, and as if she feared losing what she saw in his eyes, she didn't shift her gaze from his. He led her to the cloakroom, for he guessed that a ladies' room would be nearby. As he suspected, she asked to be excused and went in. He pulled out his cell phone, phoned the hotel and placed an order to be sent to his room. Luck was with him, and he ended the call seconds before she came out of the women's room. He'd confirm the order when they returned to the hotel.

"If what you're going to do this weekend has a potential for danger, don't tell me," he said.

"It doesn't have, though it has great potential for failure. We have an official ambassador there and two advisers, but the problem remains. Not that they aren't competent. They are. But if you have to socialize with people they sometimes don't take you as seriously as they should in business matters. I won't have a single drink with anybody."

He stared at her.

"What is it, Judson?"

"I've just now realized that your work can be dangerous and that the thought unsettles me."

"Don't worry, I get plenty of protection, more than I want, in fact. You may rest easily. But thank you for caring."

"Of course I care!"

Their car arrived, and they settled into its luxurious comfort. He put his arms around her. "This is something I've wanted to do since you appeared in the lobby at five-thirty this afternoon," he said and bent to her lips.

She melted into him as quickly as if she had been longing for him to possess her, parted her lips, took him in and feasted on his tongue, sucking on it, giving him unmistakable evidence that she wanted him. He sensed the car slowing down, guessed that it approached the hotel and broke the kiss as gently as he could

"Sweetheart, we're almost there," he explained.

The car stopped, he got out and assisted her, tipped the driver, and they headed to the door as news cameras flashed. "Who is the lovely lady you're with?" one man asked, microphone and pen in hand.

"We're nobody special," he said and attempted to pass.

"Come on, Mr. Philips. Introduce your lady friend. 'Nobodies' do not get invited to White House receptions." He looked to Heather hoping she'd speak up, but she clung to him as if she hadn't heard the man's question.

"Good night, gentlemen," he said and, holding Heather's hand, plowed through the mass of reporters. He stopped at the receptionist's desk and confirmed that he had ordered refreshments to be sent to his room.

"We may have to leave here separately tomorrow," he said, as they got in the elevator. "A five dollar tip to a receptionist and Google will tell a reporter who you are. I'm sorry."

She handed him her key card. "Would you like to come in?"

He opened the door, walked in with her and closed it behind him. "And thank you for inviting me to accompany you tonight. It was my first time in the White House, and I'll never forget the experience."

"Judson, I've been to all kinds of formals and receptions, but I knew tonight was the first one I'd ever enjoy, so much the first in which I felt at ease and as if

I belonged. Being with you made it so special. I was so proud to be with you."

"I'm the one who was proud. I had the cream of the crop. I knew it and so did every man there."

She reached up, caressed the side of his face and, as if that weren't sufficient, she clasped his nape and brought his lips to hers. She sucked his bottom lip into her mouth, and fire shot through him. He heard her small silver purse hit the chair, realized that she'd tossed it away to gain full use of both hands, and he had a rush of excitement. Her right hand loosened a shirt button, stole inside his shirt and caressed his chest, the first time he'd felt her hand on his bare body.

He held her away from him. "Do you know what you're doing?"

"Probably not," she said, "but I'll take my chances."

He stared down at her. She was not an innocent. A virgin wouldn't kiss the way she did. But she was in some respects naive about male-female relations, and he'd better be careful.

She peeled off his jacket and laid it across the back of a chair. She removed her earrings, dropped them on the desk and placed her hands on his shoulders. "Kiss me as if you mean it."

Watching her unskilled seduction efforts had already heated his libido to fever point, and he wanted to take over and love her senseless, but he knew that by letting her do it in her slow and almost torturous way, he'd be the winner in the end.

He brushed his lips gently over hers, teasing and testing until she seemed exasperated. "Stop teasing me. Give it to me," she said, parting her lips and he shoved it into her mouth. He knew how she wanted it, and he obliged, lifting her to fit him and with one hand on her buttocks and the other at the back of her head, he held her. When she began to moan softly, he increased the pressure of his hands on her buttocks, rubbing and stroking. She raised her dress, wrapped her legs around his hips, rocked against him and he jumped to full readiness. She tightened her legs around him and pressed his buttocks as if to fasten him to her.

"Kiss me," she whispered. "You know I want you to kiss me."

He increased his passion.

"I want your mouth on my breast," she said, her voice urgent.

He released the part of her left breast that wasn't visible, sucked it into his mouth and enjoyed the sound of her cry. He loved the sweetness of her flesh, and he suckled her as if he'd never get enough. She began to undulate wildly.

"Do you want me? Do you?" he asked her. "Tell me."

"Yes. Yes. Don't walk away from me this time. I couldn't bear it. I need you."

He settled her on her feet, unzipped her dress, threw it across a chair, turned to lift her and gaped. She stood before him in the tiniest pink bra and string bikini. "My Lord, you're beautiful."

"Put me in the bed," she said. Adulation was not what she wanted. She wanted *him*.

"Don't worry." He walked over to the bed, threw back the cover, lifted her and laid her on it. He pulled off her shoes, leaned over and kissed her knees, and she could hardly control the movements of her body. He got out of his clothes with breakneck speed. She looked up at him standing above her nude but for the G-string that cupped him, pulled it off him, spread her legs and opened her arms. Like a drunken man, he stumbled into them and wrapped her tightly to his body.

"Tell me you're mine," he said. "I don't want any other man near you."

"I don't want anyone but you. Love me. I need to know who I am in your arms."

He kissed her eyes, her ears, spread kisses over her face, tender and loving kisses. At last she had his tongue in her mouth, but no sooner had she begun to enjoy it than he moved to her neck. She held her breath, waiting for the moment when she'd feel his moist tongue brush over her nipple.

"You're teasing. You know what I want, and you won't give it to me," she pouted.

"Be patient, love. Before I leave you tonight, you'll have every experience with me that you can think of." He sucked her nipple into his mouth and began to suckle it feverishly while he rubbed her other nipple between his thumb and forefinger. She didn't try to hold back the moans.

"I want you in me. I need you." He pulled off her panties and kissed her belly. She thought the feeling of his tongue sliding along the inside of her thighs would incinerate her. "Please, honey," she said, frantic for relief. He slipped his finger into her and teased until he found the spot. Then he hooked her legs over his shoulders, kissed her and then let her feel the thrust of his tongue. She moaned. She couldn't help it. She needed that, but it was a tease. She wanted more. He stilled her undulating hips, sucked, nipped and kissed until heat flooded her feet. He suddenly stopped.

"You can't leave me like this," she cried.

"I'm not." He kissed his way up her body, looked down into her face and smiled a smile so beautiful that she thought she would melt.

"Take me in your hands, sweetheart." She did. "Now look at me. This is something we can only experience together." She brought his penis to her vagina, he touched her, and she imagined that her eyes grew bigger. "We'll take it slowly…"

Before he could complete the sentence, she grabbed his buttocks, swung herself up to him and forced his entry. "Easy, sweetheart." Slowly, he moved. "How do you feel?"

"Fine," she gasped. "Why does it take so long to get started?" she said, pulling him closer. He sucked her nipple into his mouth and stroked her clitoris until she released. Seconds later, he was thundering inside of her, around her, under her, over her, everywhere. She saw stars, moons and a kaleidoscope of images as he took her to another world. Suddenly the pumping, squeezing began in her vagina. Her legs and thighs trembled uncontrollably. He increased the power of his strokes, then slackened, increased them again. Each time she thought that at long last she'd reached the summit, he denied her.

"Honey, I can't stand this. I want to burst. Don't stop."

"Shh. I won't. Give yourself to me. Do you feel me? I mean is it different from this?" he asked. He stroked in another way.

"Yes," she screamed. "Right there." He poured his power into every stroke, and like a slowly revving engine, it came upon her until her entire body shook. She felt herself clutching him and squeezing him.

"That's it, sweetheart. Ah, yes." He tightened his hold on her, stroked rapidly and she screamed in relief.

"Yes, yes. Oh, Judson, honey, I love you. I love you."

"And you're mine. Do you hear me? Ah, sweetheart! Baby, I love you," he said and collapsed in her arms.

After long minutes, she stroked his back. "That was wonderful. You were wonderful. I never dreamed that I was missing something so precious."

"Whether it's precious depends on who you experience it with and, especially, how you feel about that person. It can be plain sex, taking care of your needs and feeling nothing but release or, if you love each other, it can be wonderful."

"Uh…was it the same for you as for me?" she asked him.

He rose up and looked at her. "It was the most precious experience I ever had with a woman. You're perfect for me, and I suspected that you would be. Were you telling me that it never worked for you before?"

"I made love the first time because I was nineteen and the only girl I knew who was a virgin at that age. It didn't work at all. I did that the next time because my libido suggested it. But that didn't work either, and I decided I was not cut out for it. I've never been in love, and never needed anyone until now. I liked one man a lot, but he let me down. I didn't have girl friends with whom to gossip and learn. One day I'll figure out why. Annie shies away from intimate matters, and my dad would have had a trauma if he'd known I was interested in sex. Scott was my first real buddy, and I wouldn't consider discussing such things with him."

"Now, you don't need to," he said and kissed her left breast. "Hey, what's this?" he asked her when he felt in her a series of weak contractions.

"Is that normal?" she asked.

"Absolutely," he said. He knew her now and knew her body. He shifted his hips and, like a bee to stamen, he hit the mark and took them on a fast trip to ecstasy.

"Where are you going?" she asked him minutes later when he swung his legs off the bed and reached for his pants.

"Across the hall to my room. I'll be back in a minute." He put on his shirt, buttoned every other button and grinned at her. "We shouldn't have been so quick to tell that guy on the registration desk that we didn't want connecting rooms."

"I was thinking the same thing. Bring your toothbrush."

He stopped. "Unless you don't want to," she said quickly.

"Don't be shy, sweetheart. It's what I want, too. And after what we've experienced here, I think it's natural for you to want us to be together. Be right back."

She got out of bed, went to the bathroom, freshened up and got back in bed seconds before he knocked and walked in. "What's that?" she asked him.

"I ordered some refreshments and snacks, but I didn't want to be so presumptuous as to have them sent to your room. The wine is still cold. We have some little sandwiches and some sweets. Would you like some? No, stay there. Don't get up. I plan to get back in that bed and eat there."

She'd never done that. "What about the crumbs?"

"What crumbs? You may be messy, but I'm not." He put his pants and shirt on the chair and got into bed. At least he's wearing shorts, she thought.

As if he'd read her mind, he said, "I usually sleep nude, but I put these on to appease your modesty."

"How did you know what I was thinking?" she asked him.

"Another one of my clever traits. Here. Have some of these."

She ate the little ham sandwich, resting her head on his shoulder as she savored it. "What will you do this weekend?" she asked him. "Are you going to Frederick?"

"Absolutely. I intended to suggest that we leave here tomorrow morning at eight o'clock. I'll take you home. Then, I'll go home, check my mail, pack a few things for overnight and be on the road to Frederick by ten o'clock."

"I wish I was going with you."

"So do I." He drained his wineglass, covered the tray of sandwiches, gathered her to his side and turned out the light.

"Are you tired?" she heard herself say, though she wasn't sure she had planned to.

"Not one bit." He leaned over her. She locked her hands behind his head, parted her lips for his kiss and took him in. Minutes later, he began their dance and soon swept them both into an ecstatic oblivion. Later, with one hand on her breasts and the other below her belly, he nestled her in front of him, and she slept in his arms.

The next morning, he asked her, "Are you happy?"

"Oh, yes. I feel as if I want to stand on top of this building and shout it to the world."

He held her close.

Later, alone in her Baltimore apartment, tears trickled down her cheeks. Nothing that wonderful could last. She had opened herself to the possibility of great pain. She'd let her happiness depend on the love of a man. She thought about her father and his twenty years of loneliness. *Please God, don't let me be sorry.*

She walked into the embassy in Bogota, Colombia, at five o'clock that Saturday afternoon. "We've arranged a reception for you at eight this evening," the ambassador told her. "I hope you can get through to these guys. They seem hell-bent on destroying themselves and everybody else."

"Yeah," she said, not hiding her contempt for the matter. "If we could make it inconvenient and unprofitable, they'd cooperate in a minute. The problem is that it's making them filthy rich."

"I know, and making it less profitable is pretty close to impossible."

"Putting them in jail won't make it less possible—they do business from their cells. Getting good-paying jobs for the men who grow and harvest the stuff will make them unavailable to the drug barons who exploit them. They would rather have good, legal jobs, make a living for themselves and their families and not have to stay on the run to escape or pay off the police. So let's start there."

The ambassador appraised her with respect. She was used to that, and it didn't impress her. "There are some people in the government who agree with you. We'll get them here Monday morning. This time, we may make some progress. There's a mineral miner here who may be willing to support a good project."

"I want to meet him," she said. "See you at the reception."

Judson was about to leave home for Frederick that Saturday morning when his cell phone rang. "Mr. Philips, this is Hank Fields in Hagerstown. My pastor spoke to me and said you were looking for Fentriss Sparkman. Is that right?"

He leaned against the front doorjamb and braced himself. "That's right. Do you know his where-abouts?"

"I worked with him for nearly ten years. He built a number of buildings in Frederick, and did a lot of work with some boys, getting them in school and that kind of thing. The police credited him with breaking up those street gangs. If you run into him, give him my regards. He's a good man."

"I'm in your debt, Mr. Fields. I can't tell you how much I appreciate this."

"Well, I hope you find him."

"Thanks. So do I."

He made the fifty miles from Baltimore to Frederick in a little less than an hour and made the *News-Post* his first stop. He handed his card to the receptionist. "I'd like to speak with the managing editor. It's very important."

She scrutinized him thoroughly, and he could see her making up her mind about him. He'd taken that into account when he'd dressed in a lightweight suit. If you wanted to be taken seriously, you had to look serious.

"Have a seat, sir." She spoke into an intercom. "An Attorney Judson Philips of Baltimore is here and he'd like to see you. Yes, I think so." She turned to him. "Mr. Rawls will see you in two or three minutes."

He thanked the receptionist and, minutes later, followed her to Jack Rawls's office. "Mr. Rawls, this is Mr. Philips."

He shook hands with the man. "Thanks for seeing me without an appointment."

"You're welcome. Baltimore lawyers don't show up here every day. What may I do for you?"

"I'm looking for Fentriss Sparkman, an architect and

builder who I'm told lived and worked in this area for a number of years."

Rawls leaned back and looked hard at Judson. "Mind if I ask why you're looking for Sparkman?"

Deciding that if he told the truth he was more likely to get what he was after, he said, "Not at all. I was adopted when I was three. Both of my adoptive parents are gone. My mother died recently. I'm an only child, as far as I know, and I want to know who my birth parents are. From my research so far, I suspect that my adoptive mother was actually my birth mother, and from letters I found in her safe deposit box, I suspect Fentriss Sparkman was my father."

Rawls was sitting forward now, his hands on his knees. "Whew! That's a helluva load. Well, I can tell you this much—Sparkman died about three years ago. But that shouldn't end your search. The Harrington brothers arranged a fine funeral and burial for Sparkman. I used to wonder why, but since you've told me that, I think I have a clue."

"What do you mean?"

"When you walked in here, if Layla hadn't introduced you, I'd have sworn that I was looking at Drake Harrington. You could almost be his twin."

Judson stood up. "Wait a minute. Are you suggesting that Sparkman was that man's father?"

Rawls held up both hands palms out. "No. No. No. As I recall, the funeral notice said Sparkman left three nephews. That would be the Harrington brothers."

"Do you know anything about them?"

"Sure. Everybody in these parts knows them. They

own a real estate development firm. Among the three, you have the builder, an architect and an architectural engineer."

"Are they here in Frederick?"

"They're in Eagle Park, about fifteen miles from here." He wrote something on a piece of paper. "Something tells me your search is about over, Mr. Philips. It can't be an accident that you look so much like Drake Harrington. I wish you luck and Godspeed."

Judson shook hands with the man. "I don't know how to thank you. I've wanted an answer to this question since I was a child. Thank you again." He checked his guidebook, located the nearest restaurant and went there. He was too excited to eat, but he ordered a sandwich and coffee, because he didn't know what he'd find at 10 John Brown Drive in Eagle Park, Maryland. He knew he'd have to deal with three men, one of whom was his spitting image. He prayed that they would at least be friendly. He simply wanted to find out if Fentriss Sparkman was his father.

He telephoned Scott and told him what he had accomplished in Frederick. "The only other time I remember feeling like this was the day before the provost handed me my J.D. diploma. I can't imagine what I'll find when I get there, but I'm about certain that I'll find the truth."

"Good luck, buddy. If you need me, I'm only forty-five minutes away."

"That is, if you're breaking the speed limit. I'll be fine. I'll call you."

He hung up, bit into the ham-and-egg sandwich,

decided that it wasn't too bad and finished it. Considering that he probably wouldn't find working men at home midday, he explored Frederick, a major crossroads during the Civil War when armies from both North and South marched through its territory, and its citizens split their loyalty.

He remembered to call his aunt Cissy. Staring at the number he'd punched in on his cell phone, he wondered when he had accepted that Beverly Moten was his birth mother and that Cissy Henry was therefore his great-aunt. He could be wrong, but he didn't think so. He remembered how his mother hadn't wanted him out of her sight. He'd thought it normal, albeit annoying, but now he suspected that she'd had a guilty feeling about having left him with relatives for the first three years of his life.

He had been unruly at times, but he wouldn't have been if he hadn't had to fight so hard for his independence, his right to grow up as a boy, taking the tumbles and scrapes as they came. He'd had to fight to get a skateboard, tricycle and bicycle long after every boy his age had had them. And money had not been the problem. His parents had lavished everything on him except what he wanted.

He amended that. They hadn't hesitated to give him the books and music that he had wanted. He'd studied piano and violin for fourteen years, from his fourth birthday until he had left home to go to college. From that time on, he hadn't studied music and had rarely touched a piano or a violin, although a Steinway grand, a Julian Britain violin and a Chet Atkins guitar occupied permanent places in his living room. They had loved him deeply.

"Hello. This is Cissy."

"How are you, Aunt Cissy? This is Judson. I'm in Frederick, and I'm sure I'm on the right track." He told her what he had learned that morning.

"Well, son. If his nephews buried him, that means he didn't have a wife and children. Looks like he never married. What a pity! We shouldn't mess in other people's lives. We think we know best, but...well, I don't know. You going there now? Eagle Park. That's a place I never heard of. Well, you be careful. If you need me for anything, I'm here. If you have to go to court, you do that. I'll testify for ya." He thanked her and hung up.

At five-fifteen that afternoon, he parked his Buick behind a BMW in the semicircle at 10 John Brown Drive in Eagle Park and looked up at the elegant mansion. He hadn't expected that, but, if necessary, he could deal with it. The house bespoke more than elegance. It was old. It had class, and it represented wealth. He strode up to the front door, lifted the heavy brass knocker, let it fall and heard Debussy's magical "Clair de Lune."

Chapter 6

The door opened. He looked down and saw a beautiful little girl of about seven or eight who looked up at him and smiled. "Hello," she said. "That was me playing "Clair de Lune" when you knocked. Did you like it?"

Shock didn't quite cover his reaction, but he was more than surprised. "I certainly did," he said, completely enchanted. "That was beautiful, and one of my favorite piano pieces. Is your father at home?"

"No, but Mr. Henry is here. My mommy is upstairs with my little brother."

"Who is it, Tara?" came a voice from behind her.

"I don't know, Mr. Henry. He wants to see my dad."

Judson glanced at the note Rawls had given him and read: "Telford Harrington, head of the Harrington clan.

10 John Brown Drive, Eagle Park. First exit off Route 340 will take you straight there."

The slim, older man approached and gazed up at him with a curious expression on his face.

"Good afternoon, sir. I'm Judson Philips, and I want to see Telford Harrington."

The man seemed even more perplexed. "You've come to the right place. Is he expecting you?"

"No, he isn't. If that's a problem, I'll wait outside in my car."

"Mr. Henry, doesn't Mr. Philips look like Uncle Drake?" asked Tara.

"Yep. I was thinking the same," Henry said. "Go upstairs and ask your mother to come down. Come in, Mr. Philips. Tel will be home any minute."

After a few minutes, the little girl came back downstairs. "Would you like to sit down in here?" she asked, pointing to a room off the hallway.

He looked from Henry to the girl. "Come on," she said. "My mommy said you should have a seat in the family room. It's very hot. Would you like some water or some lemonade?"

He didn't know what to make of the girl. He'd never seen a child that age who seemed so completely at ease with an adult she didn't know. "I'd love a glass of lemonade, Tara, if you'll join me in having one."

"Okay. I'll be right back."

She returned in a few minutes with a pitcher of lemonade, two glasses and a plate of oatmeal raisin cookies. "Mr. Henry and I made the cookies this afternoon. They're still hot." She poured lemonade in each of the glasses and passed the plate of cookies to him. "These are my favorites," she said, "and they're good, too."

He bit into one. "They are indeed good. How old are you, Tara?"

"I'll be eight October the tenth. My dad and I have the same birthday. Oh, I hear my mommy coming down the stairs."

A tall, beautiful woman glided into the room with her hand already outstretched. "Welcome, Mr. Philips. I hope my daughter made you comfortable. I'm Alexis Harrington, Telford Harrington's wife. Please have a seat."

"I'm delighted to meet you, Mrs. Harrington. Your daughter has indeed looked after me as well as any adult could. I confess that I am enchanted with her."

"Excuse me, Mr. Philips," Tara said and left the room.

"Tara is very comfortable with adults, and especially if they're male," Alexis said with a twinkle in her eyes. "At one time, there were four men living here, and she twisted all of them around her finger."

"Those relationships didn't hurt her," he said, "although I'd be a bit nervous if she opened the door to a strange man and began a conversation with him."

"Thank you. I'll have a talk with her about that." She paused. "You bear a striking resemblance to one of my husband's brothers."

"You're the fourth person to tell me that today. The editor of the paper in Frederick, your daughter and Mr. Henry remarked on it. I'm looking forward to judging that for myself. My reason for being here, Mrs. Harrington, is in some ways connected with it. I'm trying to find out as much as I can about Fentriss Sparkman. My long search has led me here." He could see that his remarks revved up her adrenaline when she sat forward, alert and ready, no longer laid-back and at ease.

"Is there a problem?"

"Oh, no. Nothing unpleasant. I'm only seeking information for my personal edification."

"Mommy, Mommy. Daddy is here," Tara called from the hall.

Alexis stood. "Please excuse me for a minute."

He watched as the man's wife and daughter greeted Telford Harrington as if he were king of their world. Harrington walked into the family room with his wife holding one hand and his daughter holding the other one.

"Greetings, Mr. Philips. I'm Telford Harrington. I'm sorry I wasn't present when you arrived. Welcome. If you'll let me freshen up a bit, I'll be with you in ten minutes."

"Thank you. I'm very happy to meet you, Mr. Harrington." He sat down. Flabbergasted at his resemblance to Telford Harrington in looks, height and build. He could hardly contain himself. A glance at his watch told him that it was six o'clock and possibly close to the Harrington family's dinner hour. Perhaps he should offer to come back another time. But his excitement at seeing his physical resemblance to a Harrington was such that he could hardly wait to begin unraveling the mystery.

"I sense that something is bothering you, Mr. Philips," Alexis said as her husband left to change, "but if we can help you with it, we certainly will. Where do you live?"

He liked her immensely. She knew that his business was with her husband, so she didn't ask him why he was there. Instead, she attempted to put him at ease. "In Baltimore. And yes, something has bothered me—a question that I've lived with since I was about seven, and the fact that I may soon know the answer is almost more than I can handle."

Telford appeared dressed more casually in an open-collared shirt but with a jacket. "What would you like to drink, Mr. Philips? I have the makings of just about anything you'd like."

"Thank you. I'm driving, so I'll settle for a glass of white wine or a vodka Collins with a lot of ice, whichever is easiest for you."

"Vodka Collins it is. What would you like, sweet-heart?"

"Ginger ale, thanks." She looked at Judson. "Alcohol isn't good for the baby, and I'm still nursing."

"Tara said you were with her little brother. How old is your son?"

"He's six months old and a real busybody."

"I hope you have the success with him that you have had with your daughter. What a delightful little girl."

"Thank you," the couple said in unison. Telford brought the drinks. "Excuse me while I find some snacks," Alexis said, giving him the opportunity to speak with her husband alone.

Telford raised his glass. "Cheers. Mind if we use first names? I suspect we'll be doing that for some time to come. Is it an accident that you resemble my brother Drake? And me, too, for that matter?" Telford said. "My curiosity is about to get the better of me."

"I didn't know about the resemblance until Jack Rawls, editor of the *Frederick News-Post*, mentioned it. It was he who told me to look you up. I was adopted when I was three years old."

Telford put his glass on the table with a loud thud. "Go on."

He relayed his story.

"The only thing I want from you, Telford, is any evidence you can give me that he was my father. I've only heard good things about him. If it's true, I'll be a proud man. You and your brothers didn't bury a stranger. What was Fentriss Sparkman to you?"

"I can give you some evidence one way or the other. Fentriss Sparkman was my father's half-brother. My grandfather did not marry Fentriss's mother, because he was a social climber. Fentriss never forgave him or my father."

"You're telling me that he was your uncle?"

"He was, and he was a brilliant man. That's why you look so much like Drake, and to a slightly lesser extent, like Russ and me. I know that's not proof, and that's what you're looking for. But it's too close to ignore. We'll do everything possible to help you, Judson. My brothers live not too far. I'll see if they can come over after dinner. Can you stay for dinner?"

Telford had stood to refill his drink, but he sat back down. "Tell me a little about yourself."

It was a reasonable request, and he was pleased to comply. "I'm a lawyer with a J.D. from Harvard." Telford's eyebrows shot up. "I am founder and senior partner of Philips, Marshall & Higgins, Attorneys at Law in Washington, D.C. I live in Baltimore. My business is mostly corporate law, but I'll take damage suits for individuals only if they have particular merit. I'm single, but I'm in a committed relationship. I don't have any children. I've traveled abroad. I love music and play a couple of instruments. As far as I know, I'm in good health."

"Thanks. That's a commendable résumé," he said, clearly impressed. "By the way, what instruments do you play?"

"Piano and violin rather well, guitar in my fashion."

"Interesting. I play the piano and violin rather well. Guitar in my fashion.

"My brothers and I own Harrington, Inc., Architects, Engineers and Builders." He said as introduction. "I'm the builder. Russ is the architect and Drake is the architectural engineer. We work together, and you'll find any number of our buildings in this region and as far away as Barbados and Accra, Ghana. From here up to Wells Road and to the other side of the river is Harrington property. We inherited the land and this house from our father and grandfather, but Russ and Drake built their own houses as you'll see."

"So this is the ancestral home?"

"Yes. I'm the eldest. I married first, and my brothers lived here until a few months before they married. My father died when Drake, the youngest, was sixteen. My mother died a year later. She was never much of a mother, and our father, worked all the time. Henry raised us. I put Drake and Russ through school. It wasn't easy, but we did it."

"What a story! I'm anxious to meet your brothers. Is Henry a relative?"

"My mother hired Henry and his wife as cook and housekeeper. His wife's been dead so long I hardly remember her. Henry's like a father to us, and we treat him that way. He refuses to retire, because he'd be lonely doing nothing. We built him a house between here and the river, but he only sleeps there sometimes. He does as he pleases, and that's fine with us."

The two enjoyed a hearty laugh. "I see the two of you are getting on well," Alexis said, walking into the room and placing a tray of hot hors d'oeuvres on the glass coffee table.

"Indeed, we are," Telford said. He summarized what Judson had told him about his search for the identity of his birth parents. "I strongly suspect that Judson is our first cousin. All evidence points that way, and we're going to work at getting the proof. Can you and Henry feed another person at dinner? I'd like Judson to join us."

"I thought something like that. Of course he can join us for dinner. Henry cooked a big pork roast."

"Good. I'll phone Russ and Drake and see if they can come over after dinner."

He had not known what to expect when he knocked on Telford Harrington's door. Certainly not the generous welcome he had received and the ready acceptance that Fentriss Sparkman could have been his father. Plus Telford's declaration that he and his family would assist Judson in proving whether Fentriss Sparkman was his father astonished him.

Alexis looked at Judson. "You will have dinner with us, won't you? We're happy to have you. I imagine this issue has been a private kind of hell for you, and I hope it will soon be over."

"Thank you. You know, I've had some wonderful experiences in my life, but the graciousness with which you and your family have received me makes this a special moment for me. I am very grateful."

"It's nice of you to say that, Judson. May I call you Judson? I'm Alexis."

"Of course. Telford and I have already settled on that."

"If you'll come with me, you can wash up. We eat at seven." She showed him to a lavatory near a wide staircase, and he could see that the house was as elegant inside as its facade suggested. He washed up, brushed his teeth and shaved with the electric shaver that he always carried in his briefcase. He looked at his watch. Three minutes to seven, and he suspected that when she said seven she meant exactly that.

He tried to place a call to Heather at the United States Embassy in Colombia, but couldn't get through. Frustrated, he leaned against the wall and looked toward the ceiling. Judson wasn't very religious, but with his need for her bearing heavily on him, he said a word of prayer for her safety.

He stepped out of the bathroom, closed the door and saw Tara coming toward him. "My mommy said you're having dinner with us. She doesn't like it when you're late." She took his hand. "You can come with me to the dining room so you won't get lost."

"Thank you, Tara. I like to be punctual. What grade are you in school?"

"I'm in the third grade, but I have advanced classes in reading, geography and arithmetic."

"You also play the piano. You're a very busy little girl."

"I like school," she said, "because I make very good grades."

"I'm sure you do."

They sat down to a beautifully set table, and he bowed his head when the others did. "I say the grace, Mr. Philips," Tara explained, "except when Uncle Russ is here. He can't stand my grace, because it's too long. I'll make it short for you tonight."

He wanted to laugh, but he wasn't sure whether it would be appreciated. "Thanks. I can't tell you how much I appreciate that." Much to his relief, everyone at the table laughed, including Tara.

Henry brought a tureen of soup to the table, sat down

and said, "Soup doesn't taste worth a thing when it's cold, Tara." She giggled and said the grace.

"I made it short for Mr. Philips."

Telford raised his wineglass. "Welcome to our table, Judson. Henry Wooten, this is Judson Philips. Judson may be my first cousin. We'll find out for sure."

"I wouldn't be a bit surprised," Henry said. "When I first looked at him, I figured he was closer kin than that. But your daddy and Sparkman looked almost like twins when they were younger. They were some fine-looking men, and the women loved them."

"Want some more turnip greens, Mr. Philips?" Tara asked him as she passed the dish of greens around. "If you don't eat some of everything twice, Mr. Henry may get insulted. Then, he'll give us cabbage stew, and I hate cabbage stew."

"Pshaw!" Henry said. "I never cook cabbage stew unless one of you gets on me nerves."

Tara beamed at the old man. "I know that, and I don't do it."

"No problem, Tara," Judson assured the child. "I like turnips, I like cabbage, and I can swear that Mr. Henry is a terrific cook."

"My mommy is, too. Daddy, is Mr. Philips going to have time to hear me play?"

"Better ask him, Tara. If he doesn't want to drive to Baltimore, he's welcome to spend the night. In fact I suggest it."

"I play real good, Mr. Philips, and I just learned to play Schumann's *Waltz in A minor.*"

Judson looked around at the people he hoped would

one day be his close relatives and had a catch in his throat. A short while earlier, he'd had no one. Now, he had Heather and his aunt Cissy and, God willing, the Harrington brothers and their families. If only the other two brothers proved to be as gracious and as hospitable as Telford.

They completed what was, to him, a tasty meal topped off with warm cherry cobbler and black-cherry ice cream. He raised his glass to Henry. "This was a delicious meal. Thank you."

"Especially the ice cream," Tara said. "Mr. Henry always keeps it in the refrigerator for me."

Judson looked at the little girl and smiled because she made him feel good. "I hope that one day I'm lucky enough to have a wonderful little girl like you," he told her.

"Let's have coffee in the family room," Alexis said. "Russ will be here soon, and he'll want a cup."

Judson tried to explain to himself his contentment, his comfortable feeling of being at home with total strangers. He didn't want to take advantage of Telford Harrington's hospitality, but he believed the man was sincere, and he considered himself a good judge of people. He didn't reply to Telford's suggestion that he spend the night. He'd decide after meeting Russ and Drake.

He didn't have to wait long. The doorbell rang seconds after he took a seat in the family room. Tara dashed to the door. "Wait, Tara," he heard Telford say. "I'll open the door."

"I was waiting for you," he heard Tara say. "We have company, and Uncle Drake, you're going to get a surprise."

"How's my girl?" He heard the happy giggles.

The doorbell rang again. "Hi, Uncle Russ. We have company. Did you bring my kite?"

"Hi, sweetheart. You bet I did."

As Judson had begun to expect, he'd encountered a warm and loving, closely knit family. He stood as the three men entered the room. Shock spread throughout his nervous system. He didn't have to be told that he was looking at Drake Harrington. The man's similarity to himself was so stunning that he had to check himself to avoid gaping.

He gathered his aplomb and extended his hand to Russ Harrington, who stepped in front of his younger brother. "I'm Russ, and I'm sure you are as surprised at your resemblance to us as we are. I'm glad you found us."

"This is almost overwhelming, Russ. Fortunately, I'm a sober man. If I wasn't, I'd consider it appropriate to get stoned." He reached out to Drake. "If I have to look like another man, I'm certainly glad you're the one." They all laughed at that.

"Thanks," Drake said. "You don't happen to be an architectural engineer, do you?"

"Good Lord, no. I'm an attorney."

"Thank God for that. At least I still have my identity," Drake commented drily and brought laughter to everyone present.

"Yep," Henry said. "When I first saw Judson here, I thought Mr. Josh had slipped up somewhere."

"Our father was named Josh," Drake explained to Judson.

Judson nodded and sipped his drink. "I gathered as much."

Alexis stood and took Tara by the hand. "I may be back later. Judson, feel free to stay the night with us. We have plenty of room."

He stood, thanked her, bent down and kissed Tara's cheek. To his surprise, she kissed him back. "Good night, Mr. Philips. I hope you're here when I get up in the morning."

Judson stood and looked at Telford. "That little girl is the reason why a man ought to get married. But duplicating her would be impossible."

"Thank you," Telford said. "My brothers and Henry have had a lot to do with the way she's developed. She was never spoiled, but she got a lot of love. Well, here's where we are." He summarized for them what Judson had told him earlier. "Our father had no sisters and no other brother, and it's clear from all he's told me and from his stunning resemblance to us that Uncle Fentriss was his father. But he wants proof and so do we."

"What more proof do you need?" Drake asked Judson.

"I've never seen my birth certificate. For nearly all my life, I've longed to know. I don't want to guess or suppose. Can you understand that?"

"I certainly can," Russ said. "You want to know not only for yourself, but for your children's sake. I can imagine that not knowing is a terrible weight on you. Not to worry. We'll do everything we can to help."

They talked long into the night, telling tales of their youth, comparing experiences, attitudes and ideas. "When I was small, I consoled myself with the thought that I was probably better off with my adoptive parents than I would have been with my birth parents," Judson said. "But as much as I loved my father, sitting here with the three of you tells me I would have been a different man growing up with Fentriss Sparkman. I must look very much as he did at my age."

"I imagine you do," Telford said. "Henry can tell you about that."

"I have to start early for Philadelphia Monday morning," Drake said, standing. He looked at Judson. "We're putting the finishing touches on some housing units that we're dedicating to our father and Uncle Fentriss. We have another one, the Josh Harrington/ Fentriss Sparkman Houses, in South Baltimore. Drive over to Pickney and turn north on Trainer. You'll be there."

"It's late to be driving back to Baltimore," Russ said. "Why don't you stay here?"

"You beat me to it," Telford said. "Unless you have a pressing reason to be back in Baltimore in the morning, we can go over what you've done in Hagerstown and figure out what else we can accomplish there. So stay. You may have our guest room down the hall, or you can stay upstairs with us."

"Take the guest room," Drake said. "If you like the

water cold, you can step outside and skinny-dip, but I warn you Henry's up at five-thirty."

"I'm not concerned about Henry's innocence. What time do the ladies get up?"

"Alexis gets up at seven, and Tara gets up when we drag her out of the bed," Telford told him.

"Thanks. I'll take the guest room, but I'd rather not take a chance. Do you have a pair of bathing shorts I could borrow?"

"You bet. I'll walk you down there."

"Do you happen to have a washer and dryer?"

"Right down those steps. If you need anything else, let me know." He showed him the guest room, came back a few minutes later with a selection of swim trunks and said good-night.

Judson looked around the large and elegantly furnished room, then walked into the smaller sitting room that adjoined it. A door to what proved to be a bathroom revealed a shower stall, Jacuzzi tub and a room-length marble-top counter with two porcelain sinks, all in beige, brown and yellow. He looked out the window. In the bright moonlight, he could easily see the Olympic-size swimming pool. Telford Harrington lived well, and he imagined that his brothers did, too.

He laundered his underwear and dried it in the dryer. Then he put on Telford's swim trunks and the white terry-cloth robe he found in a closet, opened the door and stepped barefoot on the lawn. Seconds later, he threw off the robe, filled his lungs with the clean, late-night air and dived into the pool. After swimming three laps, he put the robe back on and went inside. There, he took a quick shower, dried off and got into bed. What he wanted most right then was to talk with Heather and share with her the joy he felt and the feeling he couldn't shake that at last he'd found people who were his own flesh and blood and with whom he belonged.

He awoke the next morning after a comparatively short but restful sleep, dressed and found his way to the kitchen where Henry mixed biscuit dough. "Good morning, sir. I'm up, so what can I do to help you? I'm a firm believer in the principle that a man eats, therefore he should cook."

"It's a principle worth following," Henry said. "You telling me you know how to cook?"

"I can't pull off the kind of meal you cooked last night, but I'll never starve for want of a cook. What can I do?"

"You can fry up some bacon and sage sausage, if you want to."

"Sage sausage, eh? Are you going to cook grits?"

Henry stared at him. "Unless I want Tel to get a hangdog look and keep it for the rest of the day, I will. You like grits and sausage?"

Judson nodded. "You bet I do. I could eat it at every meal."

"Then cook about a pound and a half of sausage and two cups of grits, provided you can do that without getting lumps in 'em."

"I can do that, friend." He put the sausage on a griddle pan to cook, measured the grits and water in a saucepan, found a wooden spoon and leaned against the kitchen counter.

"You knew my father. Am I so much like him?"

"The spitting image of him at the age you are now." He cocked his head to the side and let his gaze travel over Judson. "Yep. Ain't no way he could've disowned you."

"What can you tell me about him?"

"I expect you know he was an architect and builder. He designed and built buildings throughout this region to me knowledge. When Tel, Russ and Drake finished college and got into the building business, Sparkman saw 'em as rivals and he did everything he could to put them out of business."

He didn't like the sound of that. "Are you serious? Then why are they so nice to me?"

"Telford and the boys always played fair, even when they nearly killed themselves getting the better of Sparkman. They didn't even know that he was their uncle, but I had always suspected it. Tel beat him on the last job they fought over, and Sparkman congratulated him. He got terribly ill and revealed everything. It didn't cost much imagination to believe the man, because he still looked just like Mr. Josh. The boys rallied around him, and when he passed on, they were on great terms with him. He was one smart man. Hard-working and generous. His father had refused to marry his mother, thinking she wasn't high-class enough, and Fentriss suffered for it. He had a hard time till he was out of college. Josh didn't, because he had his father behind him. But when Fentriss Sparkman left this world, he had everybody's respect. Better turn those sausages."

"I did that a minute ago, sir. I just can't get over the way Telford and his brothers have received me."

"I taught me boys to be gentlemen, and to respect and care for other human beings. They're all good judges of character, and especially Drake. He can spot a phony a mile away."

"I gathered that Russ is retiring, Drake is outgoing and Telford, the leader, is somewhere in between."

"Looks like you're a fine judge of people yerself. And you're to quit calling me sir and Mr. Henry. Me neck is getting tired of looking around to see who else is in here. You're to call me Henry." He put a big pan of biscuits in the oven.

"Thanks, Henry. I'll do that if you'll call me Judson."

"Good morning, Henry, Judson," Alexis said, walking into the kitchen. "I hope you rested well last night, Judson."

"I did indeed. After three laps in that pool, I wasn't fit for anything but sleep."

He couldn't believe his eyes. How could Alexis look like a beauty queen at seven o'clock in the morning? "She looks as if she's ready to go dancing," he said to Henry. "I wish I could manage that. It takes me a good fifteen minutes to open my eyes, and another forty-five to get my mental adrenaline flowing."

"She's been like that since I first laid me eyes on her," Henry said in Alexis's presence. "She never stresses about anything, drinks hardly any alcohol—none while she's nursing—and gets eight or nine hours' sleep as often as the sun goes down. That'll keep you good and fresh."

"I don't drink much because I'm usually driving in the evening, but I'll start work on an important problem at eleven o'clock and work till an hour or so past midnight."

"I know you're a busy man, but if you don't get yer rest, you won't be busy long. Mark me word."

"I'm listening. Can I set the table? For how many people?"

"Alexis is setting the table. You can start the grits now."

He put the sausages and bacon on paper towels to drain, got a spoon and prepared to stir grits.

"What can I do, Henry?" Alexis asked.

"Pour some milk for Tara and as soon as she and Tel get down here, this'll be ready. Judson here is stirring the grits. He's already cooked the sausage and bacon. There's a bowl of mixed fruit in the refrigerator, and I'll scramble some eggs as soon as you all sit down."

"Can I have a bowl for these grits?" Judson asked Henry as Telford and Tara entered the kitchen.

"Good morning," Telford said. "Henry, you mean to tell me Judson is cooking?"

"That he is, and he's good at it. Where's Tara? We're ready as soon as these eggs cook."

"Here I am, Mr. Henry. Hi, Mr. Judson. I was quiet 'cause my mommy said I talk too much."

He couldn't help laughing at that. After breakfast, Telford drove Judson around his property, and as he drove, he talked. "When can you and I visit your aunt Cissy?"

"I'll call her this morning. What's a convenient time for you?"

"Saturday afternoon is probably best, although there isn't much else we can accomplish in Hagerstown on a weekend." He opened his appointment book and studied it. "I could meet you there Friday around noon. Would that work for you?" Telford asked.

"Of course. I'll make it work." He went back to the Harrington house with Telford, said goodbye to Henry, Alexis and Tara and got into his car. "Give my regards and thanks to Russ and Drake," he said to Telford, "and please accept my gratitude for your uncommon graciousness to me. See you Friday." He headed for Baltimore and home.

Two hours later, he walked into his house, threw his jacket across the nearest chair, sat down and dialed the United States Embassy in Bogota, Colombia.

Heather's mission to Colombia had not proceeded as smoothly as Judson's trip to Eagle Park. She had little patience for the exchange of genteel smiles and gentlemanly handshakes with adversaries who had as their primary goal the wreckage of her efforts and all the work she'd done for the previous twelve months.

"But you can't lower the boom on him," her local counterpart had argued. "He's from one of the best families here."

"Yes," she'd said, "and where does their wealth come from?" Her guess was that he'd taken the job to protect his family. She sprawled out on the floor, raised her knees, clasped her hands around them and tried to figure out what to do next. That man was a part of the problem, and he had to go. "They can lay the blame on me," she said aloud, "but tomorrow will be his last day working here."

At the sound of distant thunder, she rushed to the windows and closed them. The ringing phone startled her, because she hadn't heard that loud, almost onerous sound before.

"Hello."

"Dr. Tatum, a Mr. Philips is on the line. Do you want to speak with him?"

"Yes. Thank you." With her heart pounding like the hooves of a runaway horse, she dropped down on the bed and wiped the perspiration that formed on her brow. "Hello, Judson. I'm so glad to hear from you. How are you, and how is your search going?"

"It's going better than I could have imagined. I have so much to tell you. I've met Sparkman's nephews, and I look just like them from head to foot."

"You're kidding me. Really? This is wonderful."

"There's more, but it will have to wait. How are things going there?"

"I'm scheduled to leave here late tomorrow afternoon. All is well." It wasn't, of course, but she dare not say so, for she was aware that the operator hadn't hung up. "I'll phone you when the plane lands."

"Thanks. I'll be waiting for your call. I won't keep you longer, because I know you must be busy. Till tomorrow."

"Right. Thanks so much for your call."

She hung up hoping she'd managed to communicate to him that she was happy he'd called. He'd figure out that the line wasn't private. The operators considered it their right to listen in on anyone's call, and she suspected that, on more than one occasion, they'd been privy to sensitive information. Energized by Judson's call, she dressed for her appointment with the ambassador with more enthusiasm than she'd felt earlier.

"Maybe getting all this behind me will raise my spirits. Another two days in this place, and I'd be fit for a case of depression. How can these people be so satisfied with this situation?"

She gave the ambassador a summary of her report and thanked him for his helpfulness. He had been helpful, she reflected later, but he trusted the wrong people.

When leaving the embassy en route to the airport the next day, she feigned surprise that the man she'd found to be at the root of the problem had been fired. "What a pity!" she said.

"Yes. He knew a lot about a lot of things," the driver replied cryptically.

Chapter 7

Judson checked the incoming flights from Bogota, looking for Heather's flight number. He had arrived at the Baltimore-Washington Thurgood Marshall International Airport minutes before the plane bringing Heather had landed. She had texted him as she'd said she would, but he didn't tell her that he was already at the airport. A little more than forty minutes after the plane landed, he saw her walking into the waiting area and looking around.

"Heather!"

She stopped. Her gaze landed on him, and the most beautiful smile he'd ever seen brightened her face. He opened his arms, and when she walked into them as if she belonged there, he pressed a quick kiss to her lips.

"You devil," she said, gripping him in a fierce hug. "You didn't tell me you were already here to meet me."

He handed her a dozen multicolored calla lilies. "You didn't think I'd let you struggle to get a taxi after that long flight, did you? Have you had anything to eat?"

"Some, but I slept through some of the serving." She smelled the flowers. "When you travel first-class, those guys don't let you get hungry. Thank you. These are so beautiful, and I love them so much."

They walked arm in arm to the garage where he'd parked the car. "I'm anxious to know how things went with you in Bogota," he said. "Did you have to be the hatchet man?"

"It amounted to that, although it wasn't what I'd planned. I'm beginning to think we'll never wipe out those drug cartels. They're like an old house that leaks. You plug up one hole, and another spouts even more water. You hire a guy to combat the problem only to discover that he applied for the job in order to make certain that you never find the root of the problem. We're straight now, but who knows for how long?"

"I didn't realize that you dealt with the problem of drugs," Judson said, concern lacing his voice.

"I don't, but one of our attaché's down there does. I suspected that he wasn't doing his job. He wasn't." She looked brightly into his face. "Now—tell me about you."

"There's so much to tell. Let's stop by a good take-out shop, get some food and go to your place. I know you're tired, and I promise not to stay too long."

"Sounds good to me."

He bought leek soup, two veal Marsala dinners, lemon chiffon pie and two bottles of white wine. "Whether you're hungry or not," he said when he returned to the car, "I've got you covered."

He parked in front of her building. "You take the food, and I'll bring your luggage." He took her two big suitcases out of the trunk of his car. "Why do women travel with so much more stuff than we men do?" he said, though he didn't expect an answer.

She gave him one. "Because guys will wear the same suit every day. We women don't do that."

"Yeah, but we change everything else every day. Gals compete with each other as to who looks best. Men don't do that."

"Whatever you say." She handed him her door key. "Thanks for meeting me. You make life wonderful."

He stopped in the act of closing the door. "Don't say such things to me unless you mean them."

"I meant that from the bottom of my heart."

He closed the door, stepped closer to her and took her into his arms. "And you illumine my life. Don't ever forget it. I need you the way I need air to breathe." He brushed her lips with his, and when she opened to him, he slipped into her and let her possess him. Overwhelmed by a sense of belonging to her, a feeling he'd never had until he loved her, he broke the kiss and stared down at her. Was a man foolish to give one person so much power over his well-being?

"What is it, Judson? What happened?"

"When we're together like this, many things flash

through my mind, not the least of which is amazement that I have you in my life."

She tucked herself into him, tightened her arms around him and seemed to relax. "I'm happy, too."

More than anything, he wanted to believe in what they'd found in each other, but he'd had too many disappointments to believe in miracles. Maybe if his search for his parentage panned out… He didn't let himself finish the thought.

"I'm going out of my mind waiting for you to tell me what you've discovered," she said, walking him to the living room. "Let's sit here."

He brought her up to date, beginning with his visit to Jack Rawls, managing editor of the *Frederick News-Post*, and ending with his goodbye kiss to Telford Harrington's daughter, Tara.

"That's the most remarkable story I ever heard," Heather said. "It's got to be true. Nobody's ever heard of a coincidence that great."

"That's what I feel, but because it's so phenomenal, I need absolute proof. As I said, I've got a lot more work to do. The Harrington brothers seem inclined to accept me as their cousin, but they also agreed that we need proof. I'm going with Telford on Friday morning to see Aunt Cissy. I'm at the center of this, and he's only marginally involved, so perhaps he can come up with a question or an angle that hasn't occurred to me."

"And you're sure he's on the up-and-up?"

"If you meet that man, his family and his brothers and spend an evening with them, you'll trust him. If

I'm wrong on this, I'll have to reassess my ability to trust my judgment of people."

Telford Harrington had no misgivings about Judson. He sat with his brothers in the office of Harrington, Inc., Architects, Engineers and Builders, situated on the top floor of the warehouse they'd built on the Harrington estate. They'd come together that morning to discuss their obligation to Judson in the event that there was incontrovertible proof of his blood relationship to them.

"Let's look at it this way," Russ, the least benevolent of the three, began. "There's no doubt that Judson Philips was sired by a descendant of our grandfather, and that man seems to have been Uncle Fentriss. I don't believe in such coincidences. You could almost mistake him for Drake. I watched him closely. How could he be so much like us and not be our cousin unless Uncle Fentriss was his father?"

"I agree with all that," Drake said, "but for what I'm thinking, we need solid proof. He has letters from Uncle Fentriss to his adoptive mother acknowledging their affair, and circumstantial evidence that she was actually his mother, but that is not proof."

"All right," Telford said. "I'm willing to take a DNA test if Judson asks me to do it, but I'm not sure that will satisfy him."

"That goes without saying," Russ said. "If he gives me proof, he deserves a share of Uncle Fentriss's estate, and as executor of Uncle Fentriss's will, I couldn't in good conscience refuse to do it."

"We won't argue about that," Drake said. "Right is right."

Telford loved his brothers and not the least because he could always count on their sense of decency and their insistence on doing what was right. As they talked, he came to an important conclusion. "I see that we're in this together and that we're thinking along the same lines. If we get solid proof that Uncle Fentriss was Judson's father, I suggest we give Judson something that we inherited from Uncle Fentriss. What do you say?"

Drake stood, rubbed the back of his neck and walked to the window that overlooked the driveway and the swaying trees that lined it. "Something you said last night is jumping around in my head, Telford, and I can't place it. But I know it's important. It's something you told us about Judson's background. Let's see. His adoptive mother had a baby out of wedlock, left it with her own mother and moved to Baltimore." He repeated it several times. "That wasn't it, but I'll get it."

"Then we're agreed that if we get what we regard as proof—"

Russ interrupted Telford. "By proof, I mean a birth certificate and DNA tests."

"Right," Drake said. "What about you, Telford?"

"I'd accept less, but I'll go along with the two of you. Is it agreed that we'll do all we can to help Judson solve this to *his* satisfaction?"

"Right," Russ and Drake said in unison.

"I'm anxious to welcome him to our family," Drake said, "because already I like him a lot. I searched for him on Google—he's an impressive and seemingly honorable man."

"I agree," Telford said.

Russ stood, stretched expansively and said, "Me, too. I don't like the idea of a stranger looking that much like us. I'd rather have him as a confirmed relative." His brothers laughed at his dry humor, but they knew that Russ had never been more serious.

As they walked down the stairs, Telford patted Russ on his shoulder. "I suggest that we keep this conversation strictly to ourselves. I don't even plan to tell Alexis." Russ and Drake agreed not to divulge their decision to share their uncle's wealth with Judson in the event that doing so proved inappropriate.

Judson was not surprised to receive a call from Telford that Thursday afternoon. "How are you, Telford? I was expecting to hear from you, to confirm our meeting with Aunt Cissy."

"That's mainly why I'm calling. My brothers and I are looking forward to getting this all cleared up, and we're hoping that as a result, we'll welcome you as a member of our family. What is your aunt Cissy's address?"

He gave Telford the address.

"Thanks. As agreed, I'll meet you there at noon on Friday."

"I'm looking forward to it," Judson said and told him goodbye.

He rescheduled his Friday appointments and called Lon Marshall, the partner second to him, and told him he wouldn't be in the office on Friday. "If you need me, you may reach me on my cell."

"Right."

He arrived at Cissy's house at around eleven-thirty and, as usual, she came down the walkway and met him at her gate. "Something tells me you're closing in on this, Judson. Am I going to like this man who's coming here to talk with me?"

"I'd be truly surprised if you didn't. He and his brothers impressed me as being honorable. You may have a shock. I look a lot like him."

"And well you should if he's your first cousin."

"That remains to be proved, Aunt Cissy."

"I've been discussing Fentriss Sparkman with some of our relatives because I wanted to refresh my own memory. He was quite a man, and from what everybody remembers, he would have married Beverly if he'd had a chance. But after Beverly got pregnant, she was under her mother's foot and, with Sparkman in Atlanta, there wasn't a thing Beverly could do.

"We can have lunch as soon as Mr. Harrington gets here. He's built some buildings around here, too. Not as many as Sparkman, but he and his brothers are known around here." A smile floated over her face. "I bought a beef tenderloin. I want that big shot to know your other relatives got class, too."

He hugged her. Cissy Henry had come to her own conclusions about his parentage and obviously had decided that further proof wasn't necessary. "I wish Mom hadn't put such a distance between herself and

Hagerstown. She must have lived in perpetual fear that dad would discover her duplicity. What an awful way to live!"

"So you're convinced, too!"

"I can add, Aunt Cissy."

"Don't judge her too harshly, son. She must have paid heavily for it. Imagine your own child thinks somebody else is his mother. Come on in here while I put this roast in the oven. You can't keep a beef tenderloin roasting more than forty minutes at best." She tried to open a cabinet door. "This thing gon' drive me crazy. Half the time I feel like yanking it off its hinges."

He examined the door, opened it and sat down. "I'll fix it before I leave. Is there a hardware store around here?"

"Yes. 'Bout three blocks over." The doorbell rang.

"I'll get it, Aunt Cissy. You take care of that filet mignon roast. I can taste it already."

At the door, he greeted Telford.

"Hi. You're right on time. I hope you didn't stop to eat. Aunt Cissy is preparing to show off her culinary talent, and believe me, she has some talent to display."

Cissy came into the hallway wiping her hands on her apron. "Come on in, Mr. Harrington. Welcome. Judson has spoken so highly of you and your brothers that… My goodness! The resemblance sure is strong."

"Aunt Cissy, this is Telford Harrington. Telford, my aunt, Cissy Henry. I realize that this was probably unnecessary, but it isn't easy to ignore one's training."

Telford extended his hand. "Thank you for receiving me, Mrs. Henry. This is as important to me as it is to

Judson. If a man looks this much like you, you want to know why."

"You're right," she said. "I sure would try to get to the bottom of it. Come on back here. Lunch'll be done in a bit. We can sit out there on the back porch. The living room is too far from the kitchen, and I have to check the oven and things."

She opened the refrigerator, got a pitcher of lemonade and handed it to Judson. "Take that and some glasses outside, please, Judson. I bought some beer, in case you and Mr. Harrington would rather have that. I don't have a taste for beer."

"Thanks," Telford said, "but I'll take the lemonade. I don't drink when I have to drive."

"Well, it won't spoil. We gon' eat first and talk business later. I don't like for things to get in the way of my meals. I only eat at mealtime, and I do love to enjoy my food. I never get indigestion, 'cause I don't mix eating with anything else."

"That's a good policy," Telford said. "How long have you lived here, Mrs. Henry?"

"I want you to call me Aunt Cissy. My husband built this house and brought me here the day we married. That was sixty-three years ago. It's been renovated and modernized, and now I guess it needs work again."

"Looks pretty sound to me," Telford said, "and it's situated on a choice piece of property."

"I know. Several of these real estate people been after me to sell it, but I'll never do it."

"I doubt they would offer you a third of what it's worth."

She got up and went into the kitchen. A few minutes later she called to them. "Judson, show Telford where he can wash his hands, if he wants to."

Telford laughed. "I want to."

A half hour later, they finished a meal of beef tenderloin, lemon-roasted potatoes, string beans, stuffed squash, baked corn bread and a dessert of caramel cake and vanilla ice cream. "I'm too full to talk sensibly," Telford joked when they moved back to the porch.

"What y'all need is some coffee," Cissy said. "I'm by myself most all the time, and when I have somebody to cook for, it makes my day." She poured the coffee and sat down.

"Well, Telford. It's quite a story. Judson has told you much of it. I just learned from my husband's cousin that Fentriss Sparkman came back here many times asking for Beverly." Judson noticed that Telford reacted as if something had stunned him, though he quickly covered it up.

"He said the last time Sparkman came here asking if anyone knew her whereabouts must've been a little over three years ago. Seems like he never gave up on her. Was he married when he died?"

Telford shook his head. "We've searched his tax records, his insurance records and the registrar of deeds in Frederick, and it seems that he never married."

"When he was here back then, he lived as a single man."

"Do you know where he lived, Aunt Cissy?" Telford asked her.

"He had an apartment in that house on the corner, the one with the brick front."

"I know that one."

"My husband's cousin said Beverly once disappeared for over a week after Mr. Sparkman went to Atlanta."

"I'd love to know what he was building in Atlanta," Judson said.

"Not to worry. I'll find out. You've been more helpful than you can imagine, Aunt Cissy," Telford said. "Next time I'm in Hagerstown, I'll drop by to see you."

"Let me know you're coming, and we can have a meal." She showed him her guest room. "Don't stay at no hotel when you come here."

Judson walked to the gate with Telford. "I'll find out what Uncle Fentriss was doing in Atlanta around thirty-three to thirty-four years ago, Judson. It shouldn't be too difficult. By the way, what did you say your adoptive mother's name was?"

"Beverly Moten Philips."

"I'll call you as soon as I get a lead. Incidentally, we're celebrating Henry's seventieth birthday next weekend, and we'd love for you to come and be with us. You said there's a woman in your life. She's welcome, too."

"Thank you. I'll ask her if she can come. If she doesn't have a travel assignment, I imagine she'd be delighted to come."

"What does she do?"

"She's a lawyer with the same degree that I have, only she got hers at Yale, and she's a roving ambassador for the State Department."

Telford released a sharp whistle. "How exciting! I'm anxious to meet her."

"She's a wonderful person."

Telford's grin implied a tease. "Of course she is. As hard as we work to avoid getting hooked, only an exceptional woman can manage it."

Judson stared at Telford for a second and then released a guffaw. "Tell me about it. I didn't know that was standard."

Telford slapped him on the back. "For us, it certainly is. See you in a week." To his surprise, Telford embraced him as if he were a brother before getting in his car and driving off.

Telford drove directly to the house on the corner of Peel and Broad, and when he left, he had the building superintendent's word that Fentriss Sparkman had indeed lived there and that, over the course of a year, Beverly Moten had spent many nights there with him. As he drove home, he added the pieces of information he had together, including that his uncle Fentriss had given his big apartment building the name of the woman he loved. He didn't have to be an Einstein to figure out that Judson Philips was the son of Fentriss Sparkman. But, as he and his brothers had agreed, proof was what they needed.

He phoned Judson. "Uncle Fentriss lived in an apartment in that building just as Aunt Cissy said and, according to the building superintendent, who's about seventy or so, for about a year, Beverly Moten spent many nights there with him. I'm headed back to Eagle Park."

"Thanks for calling and letting me know. I appreciate it. Regards to your family and Henry. See you Friday."

Before going home, Telford stopped at Russ's big redbrick house about half a mile up the hill from his own and walked around to the back gate. He knew he'd find Velma and Russ barbecuing on the deck and enjoying the air.

He told them what he'd discovered and what he suspected, omitting mention of Beverly Moten's first name. "We're on the right track, but we don't have proof. I've invited him and his girl to Henry's birthday celebration. He knocked me for a loop when he said she has an J.D. from Yale and that she's a roving ambassador for our State Department. I expect we'll enjoy having her here."

"Yeah," Russ said. "He'd have been the joy of Uncle Fentriss's life."

"How can you be so sure of that?" Velma asked.

"When you see him, you'll realize that the question is superfluous," Russ said. "It's almost unbelievable."

Velma leaned back against her husband's thigh. "I can't wait for next weekend."

He wanted to talk with Drake, but he knew that Drake was in Philadelphia again, so he turned the big Buick toward John Brown Drive and headed home to the family that he loved. His cell phone rang, and when he saw that the call was from Drake, he broke his rule against using that phone while driving.

"Hi. What's up, Drake?"

"I've just remembered what I was trying to recall the other night. Uncle Fentriss named that apartment building for Judson's adoptive mother. She was his birth mother. I don't have any proof, but I'd swear to it, brother."

"So would I. I'm just getting home from Hagerstown, where I met with Judson and his aunt Cissy. Shortly before Uncle Fentriss died, he went back to Hagerstown to try and locate Beverly Moten. I believe she's the reason why he never married. He went back there a number of times looking for her, but she'd married and cut ties with her relatives there. I guess she did it to protect her secret. There's a good deal more. I'll tell you when we get together. I'm going to Atlanta to see if I can find any clues there. It shouldn't be difficult."

"Right on, brother."

Telford hung up, and a few minutes later parked in the circle in front of his house. Getting home was always the happiest moment of his day.

Judson got back home around six-thirty that evening. Rick, his big German shepherd, met him with tail wagging, jumping up and down as if he hadn't seen him for days. "I know I've neglected you, boy, but I've been so involved with my parentage that I hardly remember to eat." He knelt and rubbed the dog's back. He didn't spend enough time at home to justify having a full-time housekeeper, but at the moment, he wished he had one and the aroma of a delicious, hot meal wafting to him from the kitchen.

He sat down and telephoned Heather. "Hi, love. How are you?"

"I'm fine. How did it go in Hagerstown?"

"Heather, the more I learn, the more certain I am, but these comforting bits of information are not proof. Telford Harrington is a great guy. He wants us to spend next weekend at his place. The Harrington brothers and their families are celebrating the seventieth birthday of Telford's cook and the brothers' surrogate father."

"Both of them?"

It was a reasonable question, but he couldn't help laughing. "The cook and the surrogate father are the same person. Their real father died when Drake, the youngest, was sixteen and Henry helped Telford raise Russ and Drake. Telford put them and himself through college. They're a tight, loving family. Will you come with me?"

"Of course I will. Thank you for asking me. You didn't have to tell them that I existed."

"The night I met Telford, I told him that I was in a committed relationship, so when he asked me to spend the weekend, he asked me to bring you."

"Really? I'll look forward to it. Have you had dinner?"

"No. I walked in here, dropped my briefcase on the floor and telephoned you. I think I ought to get a housekeeper, but that would mean I'd have to come home every evening and eat dinner. Housekeepers are like office wives."

"Not if you don't permit it. I thought of hiring one,

too, but if I do, nice men like you won't come and look after me when I get sick."

"Don't you believe it. As Bacall said to Bogart, 'All you have to do is whistle.'"

"I don't know how," she said in what he suspected was a tease.

"Baby, 'you just put your lips together and blow.'"

She hooted. "For that, I'll cook you something to eat."

"Thanks. I'd like that one evening when you haven't worked all day. I'll bring dinner with me. All I want you to do is set the table. Give me an hour."

"Take all the time you need. I'm not going anywhere."

He didn't feel like rushing. He wasn't tired physically, but with half of his mind on Sparkman, and the remainder split between Heather and his law firm, he was becoming mentally exhausted. Even so, knowing that Telford Harrington and his brothers shared his dilemma and had vowed to help him solve it made the burden seem so much lighter. Still, it had to end and soon.

After a refreshing shower, he dressed and sat on his back deck for a few minutes listening to the night animals. Years, maybe months earlier, he wouldn't have heard them, but knowing and loving Heather seemed to have quickened his senses and elevated his consciousness of nature and all living things. A glance at his watch told him that he risked getting to Heather's apartment later than he had planned. He stopped at a restaurant he favored, bought two lobster dinners and a pint of raspberry ice cream and drove to Heather's place at a faster speed than he thought wise. Realizing that he'd forgotten to buy flowers for her, he stopped at a drug store, bought a bottle of Dior perfume and had it wrapped.

A few minutes later, Heather opened the door and gazed up at him as if seeing him there was a surprise. "Hi. What's the matter?" he asked her.

"I…uh…I'd begun to think you either had some trouble somewhere or you fell asleep and weren't coming."

He looked at his watch. "It's only twenty minutes to eight."

"I know, but it seems like ages since I saw you."

He dropped his packages on the floor, brought her into his arms and held her there. His lips brushed hers. "That's the best greeting you could have given me. The food is hot, but the dessert needs to go into the freezer."

"If you brought ice cream, I'm going to kiss you."

He grinned because happiness suffused him. "You'd kiss me even if I didn't bring you ice cream."

She looked into the bag. "Oh, you're such a tease." Her arms went around him and tightened. "Thanks. You're so sweet."

He reached in his pocket for the perfume but didn't take it out. "Heather, I want you to be careful about saying such things to me. You can joke about the weather, even about Armageddon, but please not about what you feel for me or what you think of me."

She knitted her brow in a dark frown. "Why can't

you accept that I think you're a wonderful man, and that I nearly burst with pride when I think that I'm the woman you love?"

"I can accept that, but I want you to be sure. I've heard similar words before, and there wasn't much truth behind them. I believe in you, but don't put me up so high. I'm only human, and human beings are prone to mistakes."

"You're not planning to let me down, are you?"

"I'll hurt myself before I'll hurt you, and you may carve that in stone. Let's eat before this food cools down." He handed her the small package. "I didn't have time to go to that florist shop."

"Thank you, I used to wear this, and I loved it."

"Really? Why'd you change?"

"I didn't, but Annie gave me a bottle of Cabochard for my birthday, and I liked it, so I'm wearing it."

"I like it, too." She put the ice cream in the freezer and transferred the food from the foam containers to serving dishes. "Lobster! There are times, like now, when I think you can read my mind. I was hoping you'd get a knack for some lobster."

She put a bottle of chardonnay wine on the table, lit the candles and sat down. "Would you please have a seat and say the grace?"

He took her hand and said the words he'd learned when he was two years old. The memory of Tara teasing about the length of the grace she said floated back to him, and he held Heather's hand a little tighter. Family. What would it be like to have his own family? Heather looked at him, and their gazes clung. He didn't want or need passion, but pure love. Unable to resist, he got up from his chair, walked over to her and kissed her lips. As if she understood the measure of his feelings, she stroked the side of his face.

"I love you, too, Judson."

Deeply moved, he struggled to change their moods, sat down and tackled the lobster. She told him the details of her day and of the letters of praise for her work in Bogota that she'd received from her superiors.

"I have some good news, too," he said. "Telford has the word of an eyewitness that, in the course of a year at least, my mom spent many nights with Sparkman at his Hagerstown apartment. Furthermore, he returned to Hagerstown many times trying to find her, but she'd cut ties with relatives there, and no one knew her whereabouts. I'm assuming that she didn't want my dad to know that she'd had a baby out of wedlock. Of course, it's my guess that she had adopted that baby.

"If my conclusions are correct, I can at least enjoy the fact that I was a love child, conceived in love. Fentriss Sparkman was last in Hagerstown looking for Mom between three or four years ago. He's been dead almost that long."

"Wouldn't a DNA test prove paternity?"

"It would prove that I'm related by blood to the Harringtons, but it wouldn't confirm that Sparkman was my father, because he had a brother, and that brother was Telford's father. And don't forget—I look enough like Drake Harrington to be his twin."

Her fork clattered on her plate. "You don't think—?"

He interrupted her. "No, I don't, because I have the letters that Mom and Sparkman wrote each other. Mom kept copies of hers. Besides, Henry said that when Sparkman and Telford's father were young men, they looked almost like twins. What I'm saying is that genuine and undisputable proof is hard come by."

For about an hour after dinner, they sat on the floor playing jazz records. *I'm so comfortable with her,* he thought, more comfortable with her than he had ever been with anyone. A glance at his watch told him that he'd better get a move on.

"Will you be unhappy if I leave now?" he asked her. "I have to write a brief tonight for a discussion with my partners at nine in the morning."

"I mind because I love being with you, but I understand that you were away from your office today, and you have to get your work done. Will you ask Telford to ask his wife about the dress code at their home?"

"Sure, but I can tell you she looks good at dinnertime, not dressed up, but nice."

A grin spread over her face. "In other words, the lady's good-looking to begin with."

"You could say that."

"Ask anyway. I'll walk you to the door."

As much as he wanted to spend the night with Heather, he didn't let his lips linger on hers. Everything in him wanted to lose himself in her. He looked down at her. "You make it hard for a man to use his common sense. If I call you tonight, I won't get that brief written. I'll phone you tomorrow."

Her arms eased around his waist and tightened. "You'll get it done, and you'll be proud of it." She opened the door. "Get out of here while I'm in a good mood."

He worked until two o'clock the following morning, but he was pleased with what he'd done. If he won that class-action suit, his firm would get more cases than it could ever handle. He didn't take hopeless cases, because he didn't like to accept payment from an unsatisfied client. He'd done it once, and from that time, he made it a policy not to accept a case unless he figured he had at least a fifty-fifty chance of winning it.

After the conference with his associates that morning, he called Telford. "What time would you like us to be at your place Friday?" he asked him after they greeted each other.

"Anytime after noon is good, but by five-thirty at least. Dinner's always at seven, and Alexis will want to get you settled in and comfortable and enjoy a couple of drinks before that."

"Good. I'll ask Heather if we can plan to leave Baltimore by four-thirty. Friday afternoon traffic out of Baltimore can be horrendous. By the way, what's the weekend dress code? Since Heather hasn't met Alexis, she asked me about her style."

"We're country casual, but you saw my wife at dinner. That's her style. A pretty street dress or something comparable for Henry's party would probably work. If I've misled you about that, I'll call you back. Women take these things seriously, and I wouldn't like to get you into trouble."

The picture of Heather fuming because he'd given her the wrong information set him to laughing. "I'm single, and I know that much. I laughed because I got a mental picture of Heather's face if she went to dinner wearing slacks and a T-shirt only to find Alexis sitting at the table in that red silk jumpsuit she wore when I was there. I doubt I'd ever live it down."

He hung up. He had to buy Henry a birthday gift, and he had no idea where to begin. Perhaps Heather would have an idea.

Heather sat on the edge of her desk dictating a report to her secretary when her cell phone rang. "Hello." She listened for a second. "Just a minute." She looked up at her secretary. "That's all for now," she said to him and waited till the man left her office, then resumed her call. "Hi. Did you finish it?"

"Hi, sweetheart. I did, indeed, and my partners said I hit a home run."

"I knew you would. Congratulations."

"I won't keep you because I know you're busy. Telford said they dress country casual."

"Thanks. So she's a relaxed person, and she doesn't go to dinner in what she's worn all day. I get it."

"By the way, I need to get us a present for Henry. He'll be seventy. I imagine he doesn't leave Eagle Park except on special occasions or when he goes to do the marketing. They're surrounded by forests, shrubs and their property. The Monocacy River is-a short walk from the house."

"I'd get him a good rod and reel and a digital camera. Even if he doesn't have a computer, the Harringtons certainly have them, and they can print out his pictures. Buy them in Frederick, and he can exchange them easily."

"What a great idea. It's not for nothing that I love you, woman. How about meeting for lunch at twelve-thirty today?"

She realized she'd taken too long to answer and stopped her musing when he asked her, "Are you still there?".

"Uh…yes. I was thinking of reasons why I love you," she said softly.

"And you couldn't think of one?" Uncharacteristically, he'd raised his voice, but she figured she might have annoyed him and that finesse was not on his mind.

"I thought of a few," she said, "but I was trying to decide which was the most important."

"And?"

"I don't know. You interrupted my thinking process." She knew that her voice had carried the sound of laughter and that she'd gotten to him. His next words confirmed that she knew her man.

"Wait till I get you to myself. I'm going to make you scream uncle."

"Really? Lord, I can't wait. See you at lunch."

"Bye, sweetheart."

She hung up, put the cell phone in her purse and

walked over to the window. If she'd ever been so happy, she didn't remember it. She didn't see how she could bear it if her bubble should burst.

Chapter 8

Judson had said that Telford had an seven-year-old daughter. Heather dialed her secretary on the intercom. "Rod, you have little girls. What can I buy for an seven-year-old girl who lives in remote suburbs and whose parents are wealthy?"

"This is my theory, Heather. If her daddy's rich, you can bet her ma's good-looking. Good-looking women wear pretty clothes, and their daughters try to copy them. Buy her a necklace."

Heather clapped her hands. "Take a bow. At last I know how men think. That was deductive reasoning at its best. I'll go to a store for girls and follow your advice."

Before taking care of the gift, she went to meet Judson. She arrived at the restaurant almost simultaneously with him. He greeted her with a quick kiss on the mouth and took her hand. "I don't have anything new to tell you, so let's have a good lunch and enjoy each other's company," he said.

They sat at their favorite table. Her right hand reached out and stroked his arm, and he seemed to know that she was merely verifying that he was real, live flesh and blood. No emotion played on his face as he observed her, but, she let him see what she felt, and the fiery stars that leapt into his eyes gave her his response. Shivers streaked through her, and she had to avert her glance.

He reached for her hand. "If you'll give me a chance, I'll make a new world for you. A world of calm waters, clear skies and soft breezes. A world without loneliness. A world filled with all the love you can tolerate." She squeezed his fingers and wiped the tears that wet the white table cloth.

"Why would you pick a place like this to say that to me," she said, fighting to keep her emotions in check.

"I didn't choose to say it, Heather. It's what I feel with all my heart, and if I had complete privacy with you right now, I'd make love to you, and I wouldn't hold anything back."

"Sometimes when I'm with you, I think I no longer know who I am," she said. "You have a way of showing me a different Heather Tatum. You're something special."

"Do you think I'm the same man who heated soup for you when you were in bed with the flu? I definitely am not. And I'd tell anybody that I like myself better, and not because I've begun to decipher the identity of my birth parents, but because you've given me something that I never had and didn't dream that I needed. You showed me that I'm acceptable for myself no matter who my parents were, and when you made love with me, you told me something else that brought me peace of mind. Someday, I hope to share that with you."

She didn't know what that could have been, but she knew he'd tell her when he considered it appropriate. They didn't talk while they ate lunch, and it amazed her that each seemed content to glance up occasionally and smile, knowing that the other understood. Later, he called a taxi for her as they stood outside the restaurant holding hands.

"I'll get a little gift for Alexis and their daughter," she said. "So get a bottle of something for Telford."

"I will. Be at your place tomorrow afternoon at four. Okay?"

"Yes. I'm excited. Bye for now." His kiss sent shock waves throughout her body. "Do you do that intentionally?" she asked him. A taxi stopped, and he smiled as an answer. Maybe it was just as well, she thought. That man hardly had to lift a finger to set her on fire.

Back at her office, she learned that Annie had called her, and dialed the number at her father's home in Hagerstown. "Hi, Annie. This is Heather. How's Dad?"

"I don't know. He wanted to sit out on the back porch this morning, and when I told him it was too cool, I think he got mad at me. I don't know what to do. Suppose he catches cold out there and develops pneumonia?"

"Why don't you phone the gardener and ask him to install the storm panels, including those on the door? If it warms up, you can remove one of the panels so that he can get fresh air. At this point, I don't see the logic in arguing with him or denying him anything he wants."

"All right. I'll do that right now. Some days he's so contrary, but at other times, he's so…so sweet."

"I know, and I understand."

"I wonder if you do. I don't think anybody does."

"I'd tell you, Annie, but I don't think you want me to."

"Did he tell you anything?"

"Some, but not as much as I told him. I'm a woman, too, Annie, and I have eyes and an ability to understand what goes on with the people I love. I'll see you soon."

Her father loved Annie, and Annie certainly loved him, and it didn't make sense that they had never married. Annie didn't want people to think she'd been "living in sin," and he didn't want a woman who behaved as if she were ashamed of him. What a terrible waste in the lives of two wonderful people!

On the way home after work, she bought two pairs of velvet evening pants, one black and one navy, an elbow-length, billowing-sleeved yellow blouse for the black pants and a dusty rose, long-sleeved silk tunic top for the navy pants. She found a small opal pendant on a white gold chain for the Harrington daughter, and completed her purchases with a Dior sachet set for Alexis. "I don't dare buy perfume for her, but this sachet is wonderful for any woman."

* * *

"I'll be out of town this weekend," she told Scott on Friday morning. "If anybody upstairs wants to send me somewhere, would you mind volunteering? This is very important to me. I'll cover for you sometime."

Scott leaned back in his desk chair and looked hard at her. "Are you spending the weekend with Judson?"

"For goodness' sake, Scott! Good guess. Actually, he and I are guests of the Harrington family in Eagle Park, Maryland."

"He told me about Harrington and his brothers. If he's taking you there, he's sending out a signal, and I hope you're smart enough to catch it. My, my. Things are looking up. Sure, I'll cover for you. And, Heather, wear your hair down and put on some spiked-heel shoes. You're a gorgeous woman, and I wish you'd believe it."

"I like to look feminine, Scott, but damned if I'll break my neck in shoes doing it."

"Then practice at home."

"I don't need to practice. I have a couple of pairs. I've worn them, but believe me I hated every second they were on my feet."

"Grin and bear it if you have to, babe, but wear them. They're sexy."

"Thank goodness Judson isn't as frivolous as you are."

He raised an eyebrow. "Oh, yeah? Judson's a man, and what's sexy to me is sexy to him. You can trust me on that. We grew from kindergarten to manhood together. I repeat—wear your hair down and get some sexy shoes."

"Judson has seen me with my hair down, and—"

A grin spread across his face. "Oh, yeah? The brother's not as slow as he seems."

"Don't make something out of nothing," she said and went back to her office.

He wasn't nervous, and he didn't allow himself to get overly excited about things over which he had no control, Judson reminded himself. So why was his heart pounding like the hooves of a spooked thoroughbred horse? "Want to stop for anything?" he asked Heather. "I don't recall seeing a store within several miles of the place."

"Thanks, but I have everything I need. If you want to stop, please do."

"Thanks, but I'm in good shape. We'll be there in about ten minutes."

Drops of rain spattered the windshield as he drove into the circle at 10 John Brown Drive. "Here we are," he said.

She reached for the door.

"I thought you and I agreed that I open that door for you." He got out, opened the trunk of the car, removed an umbrella and walked around to the passenger door. It got on her nerves, perhaps, but that was the way he wanted it. As soon as he opened the umbrella and the door and she stepped out of the car, a cloud emptied a torrent of rain. He held her close beneath the umbrella.

"Now, aren't you glad you behaved and didn't jump out of the car in a huff?"

"Just because you were right this time doesn't mean you'll forever be right," she said and kissed his lips.

"Come on," he said and sprinted with her to the front door, which seemed to open automatically the minute he touched the bell. "That's Tara playing," he explained of the sound the doorbell made, looked down and saw the little girl standing there with a welcoming smile.

"Come in, Mr. Judson. Mr. Henry opened the door, but he had to run back to the kitchen. Welcome, Miss Heather."

He bent down and hugged Tara. "Thank you for the warm welcome, Tara. Heather, this is Tara Harrington."

She curtsied and shook Heather's hand. "Actually, Mr. Judson, it's Stevenson-Harrington, but I don't use the Stevenson part. It's too long, and anyhow, I don't like it."

"Hello, Judson. Welcome back," Alexis said, striding to the door. "I've been looking forward to meeting your girlfriend."

"Heather, this is Alexis Harrington. Alexis, this is Heather Tatum. Thank you for the warm welcome." The two women greeted each other and then took each other's measure. He'd been anxious for them to like each other, and he could see that they did. He eased an arm around Heather, and when she settled against him, a feeling of contentment washed over him.

"I left our bags in the trunk of the car," he explained to Alexis. "I'll get them when the rain slacks."

Heavy footsteps on the stairs alerted him, and when Telford appeared in the foyer, where they still stood, Judson took a step to meet him. They embraced each other as brothers.

"Heather, this is Telford Harrington. Telford, this is Heather Tatum."

Telford took both of Heather's hands. "I'm so happy to meet you. Welcome to our home."

"Thank you," Heather said. "Judson has spoken so highly of the three of you that I could hardly wait to meet you. I think he's enchanted with Tara."

Judson smiled down at Tara. "I see the rain has let up, so I'll get our bags from the car. Excuse me for a minute."

Telford rested a hand on Judson's shoulder. "I'll go with you." When the door closed behind them, he added, "Heather is a lovely woman, and it's clear that you're special to her. I hope the two of you make a go of it."

"Thanks, Telford. I'm beginning to want that. We'll have to find a way to adjust to her career, but I don't think that will be too big a problem." He opened the trunk of the car.

"I imagine that a Philips and Tatum law firm would do well," Telford said. "And especially if the suggestion came from her."

"I can't afford to be selfish, Telford. I love her, and I want her to be happy."

"If she feels the same way about you, you have nothing to worry about."

Alexis put an arm around Heather's shoulders. "You may share with Judson or you may have your own room. Whatever suits you."

She looked at Alexis and grinned. A sister after her own heart. "Thanks. I'd love to snuggle up with him, but that would be too easy for him."

"You're so right. The harder they work for it, the more they appreciate it. Your room will be down the hall, and he'll be upstairs. Of course, me being a devil, I'll make sure he knows where you are."

A sly perusal of Alexis told Heather that Judson pegged her right. Alexis Harrington had class. Tall and beautiful with an exquisite figure, she could hold her own among any group of women anywhere. Yet, in spite of her obvious polish, she had an engaging, down-to-earth quality.

"When it comes to me, at least, Judson is a genius at maneuvering. I met him at a party, discouraged him in what he considered a put-down, and the next time I saw him, he was standing at my door. I had the flu, and he came over to bring me food and medicine. I don't know where he got the soup he fed me, but it was delicious."

"Hmm. Man after my own heart. I suspect he had a helper."

"Of course he did. We have a mutual friend, Scott,

who's been best friends with Judson since they were in kindergarten. I asked Scott to help me out, and he turned the job over to Judson."

At the end of the hallway, Alexis opened the door to a beautifully furnished room. "You have a small sitting room through that door. There's a garden and a pool through this door," she said walking toward it. "The water's very cool now, but if you want to swim in it, you may. That twelve-foot fence is wired at the top, so you're safe. I warn you, there's been a lot of high-powered love in this room. So watch out."

"Thank you, Alexis. I hope we're going to be good friends."

"I have a feeling we are going to be friends and that in the years to come, we'll see a lot of each other."

"Oh. Do you think Judson will find that Fentriss Sparkman was his father?"

"The evidence is so strong that it can't be ignored, proof or not. Wait till you meet Drake."

"I see a strong enough resemblance between Judson and Telford."

"Drake and Pamela, his wife, will be over soon. You'll see. That must be Telford with your luggage," she said, getting up. "Come in."

The door opened and a hand slid the two bags into the room and closed the door. She looked at Alexis. "Who's hand do you think that was?

"Telford's, of course. Judson would have knocked on the chance he'd get you alone for a minute. Come down the hall around six or six-fifteen. Telford's brothers and their wives will be here and we'll have some drinks before dinner. If you need an iron, there's one in this closet. See you later."

"Thanks for everything. When is the birthday party?"

"Tomorrow. Henry will be seventy."

Heather hung her clothes in the closet, got in the Jacuzzi tub with her Fendi bubble oil, turned on the jets and relaxed. Later, she stretched out on the chaise longue and tuned in the president's speech. "If I was stupid, I'd envy Michelle. That is one gorgeous man," she said to herself and added, "but he doesn't look a bit better than my man."

Her cell phone rang, and she answered it. "Hello." It was Judson.

"How far from me are you?"

"I'm in a guest room someplace."

"Does it open out to the pool?"

"Uh…yes."

"Thanks. Drake's here with his wife, Pamela. How long before you'll be ready? I'm going down there for you."

So he wanted to introduce her. "Ten minutes." She jumped up, slipped on the black velvet pants and yellow blouse and combed out her hair. Thinking that she looked pale, she put a little rouge on her cheeks, slipped on the black sandals, dabbed some Fendi perfume in strategic spots and fastened gold bangles to her ears. Satisfied that she could hold her own in any crowd of glamour girls, she put the two gifts in a small shopping bag, put a handkerchief in a little black purse and waited.

There was a knock at the door and when she opened it, she nearly swallowed her tongue.

"My goodness, you look great in that gray pinstripe."

He blessed her with a smile that spread from ear to ear. "And did you notice my yellow tie that goes with your blouse? You look beautiful, and I want to kiss you."

"What's stopping you?"

"Common sense. If I start that now feeling as I do, the Harringtons won't meet you tonight."

"Oh, I'll have something to say about that."

He took her hand. "Really? Let's go."

She'd never been more proud than when she walked down that hall with Judson to meet the family that he hoped would be his own. When they entered the living room, Drake and Russ Harrington stood and walked toward them.

"Russ, Drake, this is Heather Tatum."

"I'm glad to meet you, Russ, and you, Drake. This is astonishing. Please call me Heather."

They each shook her hand and Russ kissed her cheek. "Come," they said simultaneously.

"Heather Tatum, this is my wife, Velma Harrington," Russ said. The two women embraced and she turned to the woman who was Drake Harrington's wife.

"I'm glad to meet you both," she said after Drake introduced her to Pamela, his wife. Maybe she'd find a close friend in one of the three women.

Pamela embraced her. "I've been looking forward to meeting you and Judson. This is so exciting. We're hoping he joins our family, because it's so clear that he belongs with us."

She liked Pamela at once and decided to cultivate her friendship. The women had in common excellent taste in clothes. Alexis wore a flattering long, green silk shift. Velma wore a long, straight skirt, split up the side to midthigh, and Pamela wore red silk evening pants with a matching jacket, elegant yet not too dressy. "I brought just the right thing," she said to herself.

Tara came into the room, and Heather approached the little girl. "Where is Mr. Henry? I haven't met him yet." She handed Tara the package containing the gift she brought for her.

"This is for me?"

"Yes. Maybe your mother will let you wear it to Mr. Henry's party."

Tara's arms slid around Heather's waist. "Oh, thank you. Can I open it?"

"It might be a better idea for you to wait until you go to your room. Where's Mr. Henry?"

Tara took her hand. "Okay. I'll wait. Gee, thank you. I love presents. Oh. Mr. Henry's in the kitchen. Let's go find him."

They passed through what she imagined was the family room, walked down a short corridor and into a yellow-brick, blue-tiled kitchen. "Mr. Henry, this is Miss Heather, Mr. Judson's girl, and she wanted me to find you so she could meet you," Tara said when they found him. "Her last name is Tatum, and Mommy said she's an ambassador, and she brought me a present in this box."

Henry wiped his hands on his apron and shook her hand. "I'm glad to meet you, Heather. You've got a good man there, and from what I'm seeing in ya, I say he's got fine taste. Welcome."

"Thank you, Mr. Henry. I appreciate that. I understand you raised the Harrington men. Congratulations. It's rare to find three such remarkable men in one town, not to speak of one family."

"Their daddy worked himself to death, and their mother wasn't suited for parenthood. I was all they had, and I did the best I could. Call me Henry. Tara calls me Mr. Henry because she's seven. You're a mite older than that." His eyes twinkled with devilment, and she suppressed the urge to hug him. "My little assistant here and I will be in there in a minute with some eats," he told her.

"You gonna let me help, Mr. Henry?"

"Don't I always?"

She walked back to the living room, and she couldn't believe the stricken look on Judson's face. "Tara took me to meet Henry," she explained. "He was so nice that I didn't hurry back. I like this family."

"So do I. What would you like to drink? I'm having bourbon and soda."

Her eyebrows shot up. "Really? Why?"

"Because I'm not driving. What do you want?"

"I'm not ready to live dangerously, so I'll have a vodka comet."

They sat down to dinner at seven o'clock. Henry entered the dining room bringing a large tureen and took the empty chair at Telford's left. "Am I going to say grace tonight, Uncle Russ?" Tara asked.

"No, you definitely are not. By the time you blessed everybody in the state of Maryland, we'd have died of starvation." Russ said the grace, and Alexis served lobster bisque.

"Tara and Russ have been playing this game ever since Tara was four," Telford told Heather and Judson. "No one ever heard Russ say grace until Tara subjected him to her version of it. Thereafter, he managed to beat her to it every time. Now, she asks, and he says no."

"Uncle Russ is my friend, and Uncle Drake is my best buddy," Tara said. "I love my uncles, and I love my aunties, 'cause they all love me."

Heather observed carefully the interactions among family members. "Are you and Velma blood sisters?" she asked Alexis, having observed a resemblance.

"Yes we are, and Velma is the older."

Russ was the one person there who was taking her measure. She didn't mind if someone studied her. They'd already made up their minds about Judson, and she supposed they figured that if he became a member of their family, she'd probably be a part of the package. She hadn't made up her mind about that, but she already knew she'd suffer if she and Judson separated.

After a scrumptious five-course meal, they gathered in the family room. The Harrington women served espresso and chocolates, Tara served mints and Telford served cognac and liqueurs. "There's nothing so satisfying," Heather said to herself, "as a meal done right."

Judson walked over to her and sat on the arm of the big chair in which she sat. "Hi, beautiful! The brothers and I are going to meet at ten tomorrow, right after breakfast, so I doubt you'll see me at lunchtime. The party for Henry is at the hotel, but we'll all gather here first. A sitter will stay with the baby, but Tara's coming to the party."

"She is?"

"Henry put his foot down. So she's coming. Alexis will tell you that you and the Harrington wives are having lunch at Drake's house, but Tara's taking Henry out to a restaurant for lunch. Telford rented a limousine and driver for them."

"Let me know when I should wake up. These people do things in style."

"Alexis will leave a note on your pillow explaining everything. If you want to make a friend, help in the kitchen in the morning. Henry will be in there cooking breakfast about seven-thirty. If he's in a talking mood, you'll learn a lot about the family."

By ten o'clock, she was exhausted. "Would you mind if I turn in, now?" she asked Alexis. "I've been up since five, and I can hardly keep my eyes open. I've consumed three times the alcohol I usually take in, and I think that's why I'm so sleepy."

"Of course I don't mind. You'll find a note on your bed that'll tell you what we're doing tomorrow and when."

Judson caught her signal that she was leaving the party and took her hand. "Good night, all," she said. "Sleep has overcome me."

With an arm around her waist, he walked with her to her room, stepped inside and took her in his arms. "What do you think of them?"

"So far, I'm enchanted with them. What a wonderful family! They have already embraced you as one of them, and no matter what anyone says, you definitely are one of them. I pray that you find the proof."

"So do I. It's sinking into me. I'd better go back, but believe me, I'm in no mood to leave you." He opened his arms, and she walked into them with her own arms wide and ready to embrace him.

"Take it easy, sweetheart. If you turn it on, I won't be able to walk back into that room." She kissed him without parting her lips. "I didn't say you should forget how to do it." He hugged her. "See you at breakfast."

"Man, you could walk away from that woman so fast?" Drake asked him with raised eyebrows.

"Sure thing," Judson replied, sipping more bourbon and water. "It was leave then or spend the night, and I didn't have her permission to do the latter."

"Yeah," Drake said. "Been there and done that. Life has its crappy moments. Have you made any more progress? We've checked out this region, but we've found nothing more substantial than you've found. Still, that doesn't concern me much. Nobody in this family really doubts that you're Uncle Fentriss's son, but I know that isn't good enough for you."

"As much as I appreciate what you've just said, and in spite of the deep affection I'm developing for you and your families, I need the proof for my own edification."

"I'm sure I'd feel the same way. In any case, we'll all get together tomorrow morning. By the way, I like your girl a lot, and I really hope the two of you make a go of it."

"Thank you. Your sentiments about this mean a lot to me. I saw her and I was hooked. I only needed to learn that she lived up to her notices, and she does, a few times over." He sipped his drink with relish. "There are no shortcomings in this group, either. I've decided that the Harrington women, including Tara, are a superior group."

"Thank you. My brothers and I are fortunate that our wives like each other and that they're good friends. Of course, Alexis and Velma are sisters, but they treat Pamela as if she is, too."

"You're fortunate indeed. Say, where's Henry?"

"Probably sound asleep, either in that room back there or over in his house. He doesn't stay up late, and I guess he's resting up for tomorrow, his big day."

"I think I'd better turn in, too." He shook hands with everyone, said good-night and headed up the stairs to his room. Ten minutes later, he was in bed.

"Well," Telford said to his brothers and their wives, "what do you think?"

"They're a terrific couple," Russ said, "and she's every bit his equal. If he doesn't marry that woman, he's crazy."

"She's warm and friendly, and you don't see that

in many women who are educated, successful *and* beautiful," Velma said. "I think she's perfect for him."

"You don't see many women who're as educated, successful and as beautiful as she is anyway," Pamela said. "I think she stunning, and he appreciates her."

"Just like women to look at that side of it," Telford said with a laugh. "What kind of woman would you expect a man like Judson Philips to have? Same kind of women that we have. Shall we call it a night? Tomorrow will be a long day."

Heather walked into the kitchen minutes after Henry got there. "Happy birthday, Henry," she said. "Nobody should cook his own breakfast on his birthday. You sit somewhere and tell me what to cook. I'm not as much of an expert as you are but, when it comes to breakfast, I'm pretty good."

Henry looked hard at her. "Well, danged if you ain't just like me others. Me wife—God rest her soul—and I weren't blessed with any children, but me boys married women who look to me as me boys do, and they're like daughters to me."

"It isn't accidental," she told him. "Love and caring beget love and caring. Now, what do you usually cook for breakfast?" He told her. "I doubt my biscuits will be as good as yours, but I'll also make some waffles. No." She waved a hand when he started to get up. "You sit there and talk to me. Today is Henry's day."

She hadn't made biscuits in a while, but she knew that if she had self-rising flour and put buttermilk, eggs and enough fat in them, they'd be good. She made a big batch, cut them and put them on trays. "Where's the waffle iron?" Henry put it on the table.

She put on two rings of rope sage sausage and a pound of double-smoked bacon, measured the grits and water in a saucepan and made the batter for the waffles.

"Danged if you're not real handy in a kitchen," Henry said. "I put the oven at four hundred, and you can put the biscuits in now." She did as he suggested, washed strawberries, raspberries and blueberries, and put them in a bowl. Only one hour and ten minutes had passed.

"Where's everybody?" she asked Henry.

He barely raised an eyebrow. "Sleep."

"Well," she said, "they're going to get up. Breakfast will be ready in ten minutes."

Telford walked in and saw Henry sitting in the corner without his apron. "What's the matter, Henry? Are you okay?"

"I'm fine. It's me birthday, and me new daughter over there thought I shouldn't cook me own breakfast. She said it's ready, and she's threatened to wake up everybody."

Telford's facial expression said, "Heaven forbid." His words were, "I'll be right back."

She heard him running up the stairs. Minutes later, he walked into the kitchen. "They'll be down shortly." He sniffed. "I smell biscuits, so I'd better get the table set. I'm surprised that Henry let you cook."

"She told me to sit down and let her cook, because it's me birthday. I didn't realize that she'd know what to do in a kitchen. Judson better know how lucky he is."

"Oh, but I do."

She swung around, and her gaze landed on Judson in a pair of black jeans and a red T-shirt. She wouldn't have been more surprised if all of her hair had dropped on the floor. The man was sex personified.

"Never let a man catch ya with yer guard down, Heather," Henry said, his voice tinged with laughter and his eyes twinkling.

She closed her mouth, went to a drawer that contained eating utensils and looked at Judson. "You and Telford set the table. The knives and forks are in here."

His laughter could be heard over most of that big house. "Yes, ma'am. Come on, Telford. She wasn't joking."

She heard Telford say "You bet she wasn't" just above a whisper. "The sight of you all of a sudden got to her. I take it you don't usually wear casual clothes."

"No. When I see her, I'm usually buttoned down."

"Good morning. I'm sorry I overslept, but Marc—the baby—awakened me twice during the night. I'll set the table," Alexis said, looking as fresh as a soft ocean breeze.

"The boys are doing that," Henry said. "Where's—"

"Hi, everybody," Tara said, entering. "Happy birthday, Mr. Henry. Ooh. I see waffles. Thanks for my necklace, Miss Heather. How did you know it's my birthstone?"

"I didn't. I bought it for you because it looked pretty."

"You can thank Miss Heather for yer breakfast, Tara."

Heather hadn't been in the breakfast room before, and she fell in love with the wall-to-wall, floor-to-ceiling window that let her feel that she was eating in the garden. They gave her kudos for the breakfast, and afterward, Judson and Telford straightened the kitchen and breakfast room. She had four hours until lunch.

"I hate to be away from you this morning," Judson told her as they walked back to her room, "but it's an opportunity to see how far the brothers will go with me in this search. Telford told me last night that he went to Atlanta to trace Sparkman's steps there and discovered that a much younger woman visited him for a week but never came back. That fits with what Aunt Cissy told me. Somehow, somewhere, I'll get what I'm looking for."

"You are so much like them that they're accepting your kinship to them, or at least that's my take on it."

"Mine, too, but I need to prove it. If only my mom had put her name as birth mother on my adoption papers."

"Who's name did she put?"

"I wrote it down, but I knew it was a fabrication. By the time I saw the adoption papers, I suspected that Mom was my birth mother. I'm going to check and ask Aunt Cissy about that name. Have a good time at lunch with the Harrington women. We'll meet this evening."

She opened the door to her bedroom.

"I'm not going in there, sweetheart. Damned if I feel like holding you and gazing at a bed while I do it."

"Oh, honey. You're a master at self-control, and I've

seen you exercising it. So, come on in here. I need a kiss."

He stepped inside, fastened her body to his, and with one hand on her shoulders and the other on her buttocks, he swirled his tongue across the seam of her lips, made his way inside and possessed her, searching and anointing every crevice and every centimeter of her mouth, firing her until she slumped against him.

"It's all right, sweetheart. I came on a little strong there, but that's the way it is with me right now." He hugged her to him, stroked her arms and patted her shoulders as if trying to ease her discomfort.

"It's okay," she said. "See you this evening."

Heather didn't think she'd ever had so much fun as she had with the Harrington women at lunch that day. She had never engaged in girl talk, nor had she an inkling of the amusing takes on men and life that intelligent, mature women could express. Pamela's dry wit and Velma's wicked, sharp tongue contrasted with Alexis's loving appraisal of people and life.

"Don't bother comparing yourself to Alexis," Velma said. "She's a Quaker, and she doesn't even swear when she spills hot coffee on herself."

"Don't tell her that," Alexis said. "She'll think I'm saintly."

"Don't worry," Velma said. "She'll wise up. By the way, Judson Philips is a catch and only a stupid woman would pass him up." She winked at Alexis and Pamela. "Does Heather look stupid to you?"

"Not to me," they said in unison.

"Listen, girl," Velma went on. "He's got the looks, the style, the manners and the profession."

"Right," Pamela put in. "He loves you, and if it swings right in the hay, go for it."

"Don't I have to love him?" Heather asked with laughter in her voice.

"Oh, that's not in question," Alexis said. "We watched the two of you. You're crazy about each other."

"Yeah? I wonder what the men are telling Judson about me," Heather said, letting them know she could hold her own. The women hooted.

"Are you all going formal tonight?" Heather asked.

"Not formal. Just dressy," Alexis said. "A dressy street dress or something on the order of what you wore last night."

"Thanks," Heather replied. "I think I guessed right."

That evening, Heather and Judson arrived at the hotel along with Alexis, Telford, Henry and Tara at a quarter of seven. Silver and blue balloons and streamers, bouquets of red and white roses, and a *Happy Birthday, Henry* banner decorated the room. Judson's hand never left her but was on the ready at her arm, at the small of her back and occasionally around her waist. In a dark blue suit that complemented her navy blue velvet pants and mauve pink velvet tunic, he looked stunning to her.

"You look wonderful," he told her.

"So do you."

Her tongue bathed her top lip, and when something

akin to a fire leapt into his eyes, she realized what she'd done. "Sorry. That was subconscious."

"And all the better for it," he answered. They walked over to the buffet table, which was laden with a great variety of dishes and lined one end of the room. The bar stood at the other end.

By seven-fifteen, the room was crowded. First Telford, then Russ and finally Drake offered testimonials of their love for Henry and their appreciation for his importance in their lives. Then Tara walked over to the piano, announced that Henry gave her her piano and played Brahms's *Waltz in A-flat Major* for him to resounding applause.

"My daddy said everybody can eat now," Tara said when she finished.

"I didn't realize that Tara was going to play the piano," Judson said to Henry.

"She told me she wanted to give me something that her parents didn't buy, and asked could she play for me. I told Tel that if she couldn't come tonight, I wasn't coming either, but I never told him she was going to play the piano."

"She's a wonderful little girl."

"She's me very heart."

Telford stood with Alexis shaking his head as if in awe. Suddenly, he rested his glass of lemonade on a table, put both arms around his wife and kissed her. She took him in, and her face glowed as she kissed the man she loved.

Heather sucked in her breath and looked away, only

to see the passion in Drake's eyes as he gazed at his seemingly hypnotized wife.

"Love doesn't end with marriage," Judson whispered to her and gathered her close and began to dance. "Marriage should make it stronger. I know that, owing to your childhood, you don't really trust it, but I believe it's up to the two people who share it to cultivate it and make it last. What I saw in my mom and dad really was beautiful. Up to the time of his death, he worshipped her, and she soon followed, because she didn't want to live without him."

She made herself look at him. "I hope you're right. They're all lovers. Look at Russ and Velma. All they need is a bed."

"Does it bother you?"

She shook her head. "In one way, it's reassuring. In another, it makes me wonder if I've done the wrong thing with my life. Until I knew you, I put romance on a back burner. We're around the same age. How did they understand life better than I did?"

"Don't think like that. Providence dealt them a good hand, and it will deal you one. You only have to open your eyes and your heart."

Chapter 9

As they prepared to leave the Harrington house that Sunday morning, Heather and Judson stood at Judson's car with Telford, Alexis, Henry and Tara. "It's been many a year since I met people who touched me so much," Henry said, "and I know I speak for the whole family. I can't thank you enough, Judson, for me fishing gear and me camera. As soon as Tara prints them out for me, I'll send you the pictures I took at me party."

Alexis slung an arm around Heather. "You were sweet and so thoughtful to bring Tara that beautiful necklace. She's a good child, but if she hadn't been able to wear that necklace last night, she'd have had a hissy fit. Fortunately for all of us, it went beautifully with her dress. I had to give Velma one of my sachets. She loves Dior as much as I do."

"Are you coming back soon, Miss Heather? Please ask Mr. Judson to bring you back," Tara said.

She hugged Tara. "Thank you, Tara. You made me feel so welcome."

"We'd better get on the road, sweetheart." He turned to the group. "Leaving here isn't easy. I hope to see you all soon." They exchanged hugs and kisses, and Telford grasped Judson in a brotherly embrace.

"Drive safely," Telford said, and they headed back to Baltimore.

Heather waved as they drove off. She'd never had a weekend like that one, and told Judson as much. "It was wonderful," she added. "Pamela and I are meeting for lunch next Thursday. She's a newscaster at WRLR."

"I didn't know that," Judson said. "When is she on?"

"She's on camera live four to four-thirty. They run her taped segments at six o'clock."

"I'm glad she works in Washington, so that the two of you can lunch occasionally and get to know each other."

"Oh, I am, too. Are we going to see each other tonight?" she asked him. "I…uh…I mean—"

He stopped at a gas station, filled the gas tank and got back into the car. "Please don't qualify it," he said. "I need to know when you want to see me, just as you need me to tell you how I feel about you. Knowing that you love me, that you care for me and want me gives life an entirely new meaning. I was going to ask you if we could spend the rest of the day together. We could get some food at one of the take-out places, play some music and enjoy each other's company. I've been looking at you for the past two days, and I've seen a big sign that said 'Be careful about touching. Everybody's watching.'"

She winked at him. "Passion flares highest when you can't do anything about it. When you walked into the Harrington kitchen in those tight black jeans and red shirt, I nearly swallowed my tongue. Unfortunately, both Henry and Telford caught my reaction."

He turned the key, started the motor and drove off. "There was nothing unfortunate about it. Every man likes for other guys to know that his woman wants him."

"I'm not your woman," she joked.

"You're not a woman who can be convinced with words."

"You have other means of convincing me?"

He flashed a wide grin. "Sure I have. Don't you remember?"

"I won't dignify that with an answer."

"The real reason is that you don't have one."

At their favorite take-out shop, they bought enough food for lunch and dinner and went to her house for a leisurely afternoon. "Who takes care of your dog when you're away?"

"I have a dog sitter. Rick doesn't like kennels, so I leave him at home."

They put a tablecloth on the living-room floor, spread the food there and had a picnic while they listened to Buddy Guy play and sing the blues. "I've never done this before," she said. "It's fun."

"Anything I do with you beats what I do with anybody else," he said, and after they ate, he put the food and used utensils in the kitchen, came back and stretched out on the floor with his head on her lap. Absentmindedly, she let her fingers play in his hair and at his nape while they listened to Duke Ellington's "Satin Doll."

He turned on his side, put his arms around her and kissed her belly. He pushed up her T-shirt just enough to kiss her bare flesh. Shudders ricocheted through her as he adored her with the sweet torture of his tongue. She caressed his head, and when his lips drifted lower, heat shot through her, and she shifted her hips because she couldn't help it. As if he didn't know the effect of his kisses, he pushed her T-shirt higher and fondled her breast while his tongue wreaked havoc inches below her belly.

She told herself not to let him see how his maneuvers affected her, but he lifted her hips, spread her legs and buried his face in her center. It was too much. "Judson, stop teasing me."

"What do you want me to do? Don't you want me to love you?"

"Oh, honey. I want you to get inside of me and make me feel the way you make me feel and stop playing with me."

"I'm not playing with you. I adore you. I want to make love to every centimeter of you inside and outside," he said, easing his fingers into her pants and under her bikini panties and letting them dance.

Taking him by surprise, she rolled him over, straddled him and took off his belt. She stared down into his eyes, not sure that she hadn't gone too far, but the hot, shining lights in them encouraged her, and she pulled down his pants and his cup, finished getting out of her own pants and bikini, got back on him and took him into her. She began to move, and he sucked a nipple into his mouth and moved up to her with rapid strokes. Almost at once, the heat started at her feet and moved up her legs until her thighs quivered, the pumping and squeezing in her vagina shook her to the core and she lost control.

"Honey, I can't stand this. It's… I'm going to die."

"You won't. Tell me you love me."

"I love you. I love you so much."

"Tell me that I'm your man."

He slowed down.

"Yes," she conceded. "You are. Honey, give it to me. I need it."

"Who's your man?"

"Oh, Lord. You are. You're my man." Screams erupted from her throat as he turned on the power and she exploded around him.

He'd tried to postpone the moment when she would possess him completely, thrilling him as no woman ever had as she squeezed, pinched and throbbed around his penis. But she exploded so violently around him that he was helpless to hold back.

"Baby, I love you. You're mine. Mine," he moaned and splintered in her arms.

She had her head on his shoulder, but he moved it so that she could see his eyes. "I don't want another man to touch you. Not now. Not ever."

She gazed down at him. "And I don't want you to put your hands on any other woman."

He couldn't help smiling, because he'd known that she'd say that or something like it. "Not to worry, sweetheart. You've hooked me."

She hugged him. "You blackmailed me."

"It was a moment of truth, baby, and you told the truth. You're my woman, and I am your man. Period."

They stayed that way for a long time, not speaking. Holding each other. His belly began to pinch him, and he moved her to his side. "I never thought I'd be happy with my back pressed to the floor," he said, getting up. "I'm getting hungry. Let's see what's left to eat in there." He dressed, went to the kitchen and made sandwiches of the sliced ham, Gruyère cheese, tomatoes and bread.

"Any mayonnaise in here?" he called to her.

He heard her padding to the guest toilet. "Look in the refrigerator. And please fix a lot. I'm starving."

They ate the sandwiches, drank beer and sang along with Ella Fitzgerald, Louis Armstrong and Luther Vandross as the CD changed. "Do you think you could tolerate having me around all the time?" he asked her, taking a last swig of beer with his head resting against her shoulder.

"I don't know. I just started thinking about it."

He sat up straight. Why in hell had he asked her that question? Angry at himself and hurt as well, he retorted, "Well, don't spend too much time on it. Life is short." The words had barely left his mouth when he felt the change in her, and he was sorry. She didn't lash back, didn't say one word. Maybe that was because she realized she'd hurt him. But he didn't think so. For the first time, she'd had a taste of his temper, and she didn't like it. He cleared away the results of their picnic and walked back to the living room where she sat in seemingly deep thought.

"I precipitated that, Judson, but I spoke honestly. Perhaps I shouldn't have. I'm sorry. Let's leave it for now."

He stood gazing down at her. Finally, she looked up at him, but she didn't speak. "For the first time in my life, I'm vulnerable to a woman. I never realized how tender it makes one feel. I imagine it's the same with you. We have to talk about this later. I can't deal with it more right now."

They stood at the door looking at each other until, unable to bear any longer the distance between them, he drew her into his arms and held her for a minute. "I'll call you."

"All right. Drive carefully."

He opened his front door, and Rick jumped all over him "At least you love me," he said to the big German shepherd.

"He's been very unhappy this afternoon, Mr. Philips," the young boy who was Rick's sitter said. "I didn't know what to do, so I put his leash on him, went to the park and sat with him there for an hour. He was much happier after we came back."

"I imagine he was. You're a sucker for Rick's she-nanigans." He paid the boy. "I'll call you in a couple of days. Are you saving your money for school?"

"Yes, sir. I'm going to Morgan State in January."

"Great. If I can help, let me know."

After unpacking and putting his clothes in the laundry bag, he called Scott. "Judson here. You were always a pretty good detective. From what I've told you, what is your guess as to why Mom and Fentriss Sparkman didn't get married?"

"How's it going, man? How was your weekend? I want you to know that I covered for your girl."

Heather hadn't told him she'd asked Scott to do that. "Thanks, buddy. I'll do the same for you."

"Don't be so flippant. I could've been sent to most any place on the planet." Scott's tone turned more serious. "I think your mother's mother got in between them, and I'm just about sure from what you've said that he never knew she was pregnant."

"I'm thinking that, too, because he went back to Hagerstown several times looking for her, the last time not long before he died, according to Telford's calculation."

"You need to see if she left any evidence in Hagerstown. Have you searched your basement?"

"Yes. I'm convinced that she didn't leave any information about her past in our house, because she didn't want my dad to find it."

"I think you're right, Judson. Maybe you need to do some more sleuthing in Hagerstown."

"I'll give that some thought. Hang in there." He hung up and got ready for bed, but he didn't feel right. After what he'd experienced with Heather that afternoon and evening, he didn't feel like passing the night without getting things in order with her. After he got into bed, he phoned her.

She barely had the energy to get out of her clothes. After a haphazard shower, she dried off and crawled into bed. Maybe a man didn't want honesty when the truth hurt his ego. Would he rather that she lied? She loved him. Oh, how she loved him, but he'd better learn that she could teach herself to live without him. He'd made love to her as if she were the most precious thing on earth, and when she could no longer tolerate that, he'd gotten into her and sent her almost out of her mind. And yet…

Wait a minute. Didn't I do the same to him? He felt secure enough to ask me that question, and what did I say? Oh, Lord, why did you make the human male so fragile?

As she reached for the phone, it rang. "Hello."

"Hello, Heather. I can't leave it this way. Your reply hurt me, but you answered honestly, and I…I guess I have to work harder on our relationship. If I've been remiss in any way, tell me. And I apologize for my sharp reply. I'm mature enough to know that striking back only worsens things."

What she'd said to him was true. If she followed her heart, she would never be out of his sight, but she wanted to succeed in her career, and she wanted that badly. But did she want it more than she wanted him? She could count on her brain and her intellectual ability, but could you count on love? Her father had worshipped her mother, and what had she done? Linda Tatum had married Franklin Tatum after breaking off with a good-for-nothing lover. It hadn't worked. In the end, she had left her husband and her daughter and gone back to the man who she had known could ruin her life.

Judson said that his parents loved each other, but his mother deceived her husband every day of their marriage. Was that love?

"When the phone rang, I was reaching for it to call you," she said. "I'm certain of my feelings for you, but you know I come with baggage. My mom left me and my father and went back to her lover. My father thinks I shouldn't blame her, but I do. Please bear with me."

"I also come with problems, sweetheart, but they don't interfere with my love for you and my trust in you and your love for me. I know you may not want to settle for a man who's unsure of his parentage, and—"

She interrupted him. "My goodness! Is that what you think? I don't believe I'm hearing this. Judson, you can't be serious. What I see *in* you far outshines what I see when I look *at* you. Whoever your birth parents were, they gave you more than your share, and your adoptive parents cultivated that beautifully."

"Thank you. What you think of me means more to me than I could begin to tell you. Heather, give us a chance, will you?"

"I will, because I have to. You've changed my life. Since knowing you, I'm a stronger, happier person. Kiss me good-night?"

"I love you, Heather." He made the sound of a kiss, and she reciprocated it.

I've got to stop doubting him and what he means to me. If he ended our relationship, I don't know what I'd do.

* * *

Judson sat in the conference room at his office the next morning with a senior partner discussing Curtis Heywood's case when his secretary buzzed him. "Excuse me."

"Telford Harrington on the phone, sir. Can you speak with him or would you like to return his call and at what time?"

"I'll return his call in half an hour. Get the number where he can be reached."

"This is a tough one," Lon Marshall said. "It's clearly in Heywood's favor, but there are five dentists in that clinic, and they'll lie for each other."

"I know that," Judson replied, "but Heywood has found three other people who had the same problem after going to that clinic, and he developed a liaison with one of the secretaries there. So he got information that he wouldn't otherwise have been privy to."

"All right, but I suggest we call only one of those dentists as a witness."

"My thoughts exactly. Lon, I'd like you to speak with Heywood about this. I want to know if your impression of him is the same as mine."

"Right on. I'll make the appointment today."

Judson left the conference room, went to his office and phoned Telford. "Sorry I couldn't take your call. I was in a conference. How are you?"

"I'm fine. I'm assuming that if you had more news you'd have shared it with me."

"That's right. I would have."

"Judson, I'd like us to go back to see your aunt Cissy,

and instead of us leading her by asking her questions, let's tell her we want her opinions on this matter and just let her talk. Russ thinks she may have overlooked something because we led her on with our questions."

"That's indeed possible. When can you go?"

"Tomorrow."

"All right. I'll call her now. Be in touch." He hung up and dialed Cissy

"Y'all come tomorrow for lunch. You want me to invite my sister-in-law to come over after lunch? She was very close to Beverly's mother. I 'spect if she had a secret, Rose knew as much about it as she."

"Thanks, Aunt Cissy. That could prove useful."

He was parking in front of Cissy's house at noon the next day when Telford drove up. "Man, that's what I call perfect timing," Telford said after they greeted each other with an embrace as had become their custom.

"Y'all planning to stay out there all day?" Cissy asked as she stepped out on the front porch wiping her hands on her apron. She hugged first Judson and then Telford. "Come on in. It's getting cool, but it's my favorite time of year. I picked up some pecans for you to take back, so don't let me forget them."

Judson realized that Cissy loved company, but didn't have it often enough, and that his visits were special to her. She served them roast loin of pork with baked apples, roast lemon potatoes and string beans, with lemon meringue pie for desert.

"If you continue to cook like this for Judson, he'll move out here," Telford said to Cissy.

"Couldn't happen soon enough for me. I'll take him for my son any day."

"Thanks, Aunt Cissy. I'm happy that we found each other."

"Me, too. That must be Rose," she said at the sound of the front door knocker. "Y'all, let's go in the living room." She introduced them to her sister-in-law.

"Glad to meet you, both," Rose said and took a seat. "You don't look a bit like Beverly, Judson, but you're the spitting image of Fentriss Sparkman." She looked at Telford. "Y'all half brothers?"

"His father was Sparkman's brother," Cissy explained.

"I guess Sparkman loved Beverly," Rose said. "He came back here many times looking for her after she left, but nobody knew where she was. He would've married her, I'm sure, if he'd gotten the chance. For some reason, Agnes couldn't stand him. You see, he was Agnes's age, and I always thought she had a crush on Sparkman. She really punished Beverly. Beverly would sneak out at night, and sometimes she'd stay out all night knowing Agnes was gon' knock her 'round when she came home.

"She'd find things Sparkman gave Beverly and take 'em away from her. Nice things. Do you know that man gave Beverly a gold watch and Agnes took it from her? I never could figure out why Beverly didn't leave home. 'Course, Sparkman could've been married."

"He wasn't," Telford said. "He never married."

"Well," Rose went on, "Beverly got pregnant for Sparkman, and Agnes tried to make her get rid of it.

When Beverly refused, that was the first time she ever stood up to Agnes. Agnes was in a rage, claimed Beverly had disgraced the family."

"Where was Uncle Fentriss?" Telford asked her.

"He'd gone to Atlanta to work, and when he came back here for Beverly, Agnes had taken her to Baltimore and left the baby with her mother, Beverly's grandmother. Far as I know, Fentriss never knew nothing about that baby. Agnes came back a couple of months later, but she never said much about Beverly, claimed she didn't know where she was. I remember that she had the baby christened at Shiloh, but there's no telling what kind of lie Agnes put on those christening papers.

"You ought to check that out, though, 'cause sure as my name is Rose Faison, you are Sparkman's child, and he didn't look at another woman but Beverly during the two years he worked here. How old are you? About thirty-four, thirty-five? Beverly had that baby thirty-five years ago this December."

Both men leaned forward. "You don't remember the date, do you?" Judson asked her.

"No, son. My memory's not that good. But I remember it was the first part of December, because it was the day after... Wait a minute. Beverly had that baby the day after Agnes's birthday, and I'm pretty sure Agnes was born on December the first. Everybody knew her birthday, 'cause she wanted the whole town to give her presents. It's in my old date book. I'm sure. I'll check it. Anyway, that will be correct on the christening certificate."

When Judson slumped in the chair, Telford asked him, "When is your birthday?"

"December the second."

Rose leaned back and folded her arms. "I rest my case."

"I don't see why we need more proof than that," Telford said. He stood, put a hand on Judson's shoulder. "Maybe we'd better try to reach the people at Shiloh Church and see if they can locate that christening record."

"Right," Judson said, and as if a boulder weighed on him, he managed to get up with great effort.

"I know it's a blow, son," Cissy said. "Knowing you lived with your mother all those years and she never 'fessed up to you. But I guess she did what she had to do, and at least you can thank her for not letting anybody else raise you." She walked over to him, and he welcomed the comfort of her arms around him.

"I've accepted it for months now, and I thought I'd adjusted to it, Aunt Cissy, but... If I'd known, I would have found my father, and she probably knew that. Too bad she and Fentriss Sparkman lost track of each other through her mother's meddling."

"That's about what happened," Rose said. "Agnes got to face the Lord about her meanness."

"Excuse me a minute," Judson said to Telford, and took Cissy's arm and walked with her into the kitchen. "How are you doing financially? What do you need?"

"God bless you, son. I don't need anything right now."

"Promise me that when you do, you'll tell me at once. I don't want you to want for anything. Is that clear?"

"Bless you. I promise, but all I have on me are taxes, food and utilities, and my pension covers that."

He grinned at her. "If the house springs a leak, call me."

They left Cissy's house and went to the office of Shiloh Baptist Church, but the clerk there could find no record of the christening. He embraced Telford, thanked him for his help, promised to stay in touch and headed back to Baltimore. Happiness suffused him; he was almost certain of his parentage, and he couldn't wait to see Heather and share with her what he'd learned.

Judson couldn't know that Heather was also in Hagerstown visiting her father, roughly a ten-minute drive from Cissy's house. She sat beside her father's chair holding his hand. She knew she wouldn't have him for long and shrank from the knowledge.

"I've been hoping for news that you've been appointed to a full ambassadorship," he said. "I know it's coming, but I want to be able to share it with you."

"I turned down Albania, Dad, and now they've offered me a post in Lithuania, but I'd be so far away, I might as well be in Albania."

"You're young yet. Don't be in such a hurry. You shouldn't take the assignment if you don't want it. You deserve better."

She understood that, although he wanted to see her with that coveted title, he didn't want it at the expense of her career. He patted her hand. "What about Judson

Philips? What are you doing about him? I made a mistake with Annie. I should never have listened to her old-fashioned foolishness. If we'd gotten married, we'd both be happier. But she wouldn't, because then everybody would think we'd been living in sin. So what! I never gave a damn about what people thought. Besides, we sinned, as she put it, a few hundred times these past twenty years.

"Don't be a fool where Philips is concerned. He's a first-rate man, and he's in love with you."

"I know. And I love him. But he's not focused on me right now. If I go to Lithuania, that may finish it, though that's not why I'm turning the offer down. The problem is that a post in Lithuania will also finish my career. Nothing happens there, so State will forget about me, and the next president and his staff won't know or care who I am."

Annie brought tea for Heather and cocoa for her father. He sipped the drink, put the cup down and looked at Heather. "Then why would you consider the post?"

She hugged him. "I love you, Dad."

"I know. And that means everything to me."

At around three that afternoon, she started the drive to Baltimore, hoping to beat the rush-hour traffic. The sound of a siren behind her got her attention and, when she glanced at the side-view mirror, she slowed down on the chance that the state trooper wanted to pass her. He didn't. He signaled for her to pull over and stop.

She hadn't realized that she was speeding and told the trooper as much. When he questioned her, she told him of her visit with her father and how happy she was as a result of it.

He took his book of tickets away. "Enjoy your dad while you have him, miss. But with that kind of driving, you'll be gone before he is. Don't let me catch you again." He returned her license.

"I won't. Thank you, sir." Eighty miles an hour in a fifty-five-mile zone! Was she crazy?

She drove on at a comparative snail's pace. Her cell phone rang, but she didn't even glance toward it. One brush with the law and with fate was sufficient for a day. But when she got home, she found the red light on her house phone blinking. A check of her answering machine revealed a call from Scott and two from Judson.

She phoned Scott first. "Hi. What's up?" she asked after greeting him.

"Nothing. Judson called and asked if I knew your whereabouts. He sounded excited, but you bet he wasn't going to tell me what was going on."

"But aren't the two of you buddies?"

"Sure we are, but he'll tell you first, and if he has any excitement left, then he'll tell me. He cares a lot for you, Heather, and right now he's really vulnerable. You know what I'm saying?"

"I think so. I've been with my dad in Hagerstown and had a wonderful visit with him. He's about as good as could be expected."

"Glad to hear it. You gonna phone Judson?"

"Of course. See you."

She hung up and dialed Judson's cell number. "Hi, honey. You called me?"

"Three times. How are you, sweetheart? I've been at my aunt Cissy's with Telford, Aunt Cissy and Aunt Cissy's sister-in-law, Rose.

"After hearing what Rose had to say, it's crystal clear to me who my birth parents were, but I need the proof. Rose said I look exactly like Sparkman, but that wouldn't stand up in court, and it won't mean anything to my children. They'll want proof of their lineage, and I'm not going to stop until I get that proof."

"Can't say I blame you. Are you upset?"

"Definitely not. Why?"

"While you were with Aunt Cissy, I was at my father's place. He asked about you."

"You mean…I thought of going by to see him, but then I decided it would be presumptuous of me to do that, so I came home. I'm sorry I didn't follow my hunch. Can we see each other for dinner? Nothing lavish because I spent the day in Hagerstown when I should have been working. Suppose we eat in Little Italy? The service is excellent, and the food never disappoints."

"Fine with me."

"See you in thirty minutes."

When she opened the door for him later, he handed her a yellow calla lily. She was neither a crybaby nor any other kind of weakling, but she looked at the flower he held, shifted her gaze to his face and to the love she saw in his eyes and stared at him, speechless, while tears rolled down her cheeks. He closed the door, picked her up and carried her to her bed. An hour later, he dressed, phoned an Italian restaurant that he favored and ordered their dinner.

She dragged herself to the bathroom, showered, put on a pair of jeans and a T-shirt and padded barefoot into the living room where he sat in the dark. "It's too late now," she said to herself. "I'm head over heels in love with him." After switching on a light, she sat beside him and rested her head on his shoulder.

"Will you agree not to see other men?" he asked her. "I need a commitment from you, and I'm willing to give you the same."

"I thought we were already committed."

"Not in the way I mean. I've been holding back because I've needed to know who my parents are. I'm not absolutely positive now, but I feel certain enough to start putting my life in order. If we can work out our problems, such as your career and where we'll live, I want us to get married and start a family."

"It makes sense," she said softly.

"Sense? I need more than that, and please don't tell me you haven't given it any thought."

"I love you, Judson, and I cannot conceive of any other man in my life. Nor do I want any other. Is that good enough for now?"

"No, it isn't. But until I can make it more definite, I'll accept it."

She didn't want to be without him, but how could she commit herself to marriage, knowing how tenuous relationships could be? Yet, she knew he wasn't going to let her string him along. Eventually, she knew it would be marriage or lose him.

* * *

The following day, she made an appointment with her superior, told her that she couldn't leave her terminally ill father and recommended Scott for the ambassadorship to Lithuania.

"I'll miss you," she told Scott, "because you're the first real friend I ever made."

"Thank you for recommending me. You won't be alone, because you have Judson now, so you won't need me. I'm depending on you to see that I don't stay in that outpost for longer than two years."

"I promise, friend."

"Marry him, Heather. He's the best thing that's ever happened to you."

"I know. Too bad you won't be around to make me think straight."

"Not to worry," he said. "We can talk every day. I'm going to try and stay focused on what's important, and you do the same. "

"Just tell me this—in your opinion, is Judson a very vulnerable person?"

"You mean fragile? No, he's got enough self-assurance for three men. With one exception. He has always lacked confidence about his parentage, what kind of stock he comes from and whether he'd be proud of his mother and father."

"He's about to resolve that, because it appears his father was Fentriss Sparkman."

"Yeah, but until he sees proof of that, he'll agonize over it. That's why he's a helluva lawyer."

* * *

Shortly thereafter, Judson phoned Scott for lunch. "It doesn't have to be special, Scott. A barbecue sandwich will suit me. What about you?"

"Man, you know I go for the barbecue every time."

Scott was seated at the table when Judson arrived. "What happened to you?" Judson asked him. "In over thirty years, you didn't go anyplace early. What's up?"

"Heather turned down an appointment to Lithuania, pleaded her father's illness and recommended me in her place. You're looking at the chief diplomat at the U.S. consulate in Lithuania. She didn't have to do it, but she did, and I'll never forget it."

"Well, I'll be. I'd adore her for that if for nothing else. She's a classy woman. I couldn't be happier for you, Scott. But won't she damage her career? That's the second opportunity she turned down."

"Trust me, she hasn't done herself any harm. She has a hell of a record at State, and they owe her a better post. Between you and me only, there could be some reluctance to send a single woman her age to a high post. I'm not sure, but I've thought about it a lot. Don't mention the idea to Heather, man, because she'll freak out."

They placed their orders, and Scott included in his a bottle of beer. "Don't I know it," Judson said. "She'd have a fit."

"What more have you learned about Aunt Bev and Sparkman?"

He recapped the day and the information. "I don't

doubt that Mom was my birth mother and that Sparkman was my father, but I want to see the proof, and I am going to get it. I want to be able to tell my children who their grandparents were. When are you leaving for Lithuania?"

"Two or three weeks. I have to have a lot of briefings, lease my condo and take care of some other personal things. I'll miss you, buddy."

"Same here. It will be the first time we've been separated since we met."

"Yeah," Scott said.

After a moment, Judson broke the silence. "I'd better go. I'm meeting with the D.A. on a case of criminal negligence tomorrow morning, and I have to be on my toes."

"I'll see you before I leave. Remember that Heather isn't as tough as she seems."

"I know that, buddy, probably better than you do. Not to worry. I'll take care of her, if she'll let me."

"She won't want to think that you're taking care of her, Judson, but she needs it. Not where her work and the management of her life are concerned, but she needs caring and she's just realized it."

Judson raised an eyebrow. "Since when?"

"I'd say, six or seven weeks at the most. I suspect she's just now learning that she's not all brain and smarts. You've had a role in that."

"Yeah. I have. But she possesses awesome self-control and determination. I can only hope that she'll decide I'm worth it."

Chapter 10

Judson could hardly contain his surprise when he received a call from Russ Harrington. "We're all going for a spin on my cruiser this weekend, and I'd be delighted if you'd come. We'll spend nights at Drake's house in St. Michaels—and bring Heather."

"That would be wonderful. I'll ask Heather if she'd like to join us. Where is your boat?"

"On the Chesapeake. It's about an hour-and-a-half drive from here, and about fifty minutes from you. We could hook up in Baltimore and drive over together. Telford and Drake will drive their cars. Henry hates big boats, but he's coming because he loves to fish, and he wants to try out the gear you gave him. We'll have a great time."

"After I speak with Heather, I'll phone you. Thanks

so much for thinking of us, Russ. And please give my regards to Velma."

"It's a family outing, Judson, and that automatically includes you."

They said goodbye, and he hung up. He dialed Heather's number and waited, anxious to hear her say she'd go with him on the cruise. When he heard her voice, his heart skipped a beat.

"Hi, sweetheart." Surely that calm voice was not his. He relayed to her Russ's invitation. "I want to go, and I'll be miserably lonely if you don't go with me."

"I'd love to go. Maybe Henry will teach me how to fish."

"Henry, huh! What about me? I'd think you'd look forward to spending a weekend in my company."

"You poor baby. Of course I will." She practically purred.

"Why do you get kittenish when I'm nowhere near you? I'd like to curl up somewhere with you right now."

"But, honey, I'm in my office."

"Don't I know it! If you were at home, I'd be halfway there by now."

"Honey, tone it down. I've got a lot of work to do today."

He sucked in his breath. "At least I get to you the way you get to me."

"I didn't think that was in question," she said.

"It isn't, but when you get fresh with me, I'm never sure how serious your teasing is."

"I'm honest, Judson. You can depend on that."

"I know, and that's important. I'll call you when you get home. In the meantime, I'll let Russ know we're joining him and the family on the cruise."

On Friday afternoon, he picked up Heather at her office and drove her to his house. "Except for the first three years of my life, I've always lived here, and what you see represents my parents' personalities rather than mine."

"It's a beautiful home. You haven't changed anything?"

"Nothing. Since mom died I've been focused on clearing up the matter of my parentage. Eventually, I'll sell it and build one that suits me."

"Are you thinking about the Harringtons for the job?"

"I hadn't, but I've seen Russ's and Drake's homes. They're magnificent. Sure." He looked straight at her, and without any semblance of a smile, he said, "Unless you'd prefer some other architect and builder." The bell rang simultaneously with her gasp. He rushed to open the door.

Judson and Russ greeted each other with a brotherly embrace. "Come in," Judson said. "Heather's in the living room."

Russ greeted Heather with a kiss on the cheek. "We're glad you're coming with us. Imagine Judson all alone among a bunch of lovers."

Heather's grin creased her smooth face, and sparks danced in her eyes. "Why? I thought he got on well with Henry." She turned to Judson. "You did, didn't you?"

"Keep it up," he growled. "I may forget Russ is here."

Both hands went to her hips in a gesture he hadn't previously seen her make. "Really? Honey, I can't wait to see what you'll do."

She challenged him often, but she hadn't previously challenged him in the presence of a man he considered his equal. He took his time getting to her and, as if choreographed to do so, Russ stepped aside to let him pass. He stopped in front of her, stared down at the mischief dancing in her eyes and crushed her to him. Like a robot, her arms went around his shoulders, but he put on his thinking cap and resisted the temptation.

"When I do get you alone, I'm going to make you scream with pleasure, and that's a promise," he whispered in her ear.

Russ whooped. "From the expression on her face, Judson, you may as well have said it aloud. I was going to suggest that you two ride with Velma and me, but I wouldn't like to have my car set on fire."

Judson hugged Heather and kissed her forehead. "Try to behave."

"Don't I always?"

He picked up two of their bags, handed one to Russ and then lifted the one that contained gifts. "Sure you do, and Baltimore borders on Canada."

Velma got out of the car and greeted them. "I'm so glad you could come, Heather. We've been looking forward to seeing you again."

"As I think of it," Russ said, easing away from the curb, "it's not such a good idea, Judson, to have these two women together. My wife's full of pranks and devilment, and challenge is her middle name."

Velma turned so that she could see the backseat. "Don't listen to him, Judson. I'm as innocent as a lamb born today. Nobody ever got away with challenging Russ, and there's no point in trying to argue with him."

"The way to keep a marriage nice and friendly," Russ said, "is to forget about winning arguments. Women love to win. I couldn't care less about that. I say what I think, and that's it."

"I love to win," Heather said. "And I like a good fight so long as it's genteel, clever and is conducted by rules of good conduct. You know…foxy, outwitting your opponent."

"That's why you're a good ambassador," Judson told her. How would she ever give up that goal and settle in Baltimore with him? The thought depressed him.

"That's the trait of a first-class lawyer, too," Russ said. "Life with the two of you should be exciting."

"It is," Heather said. "Judson's a wonderful man."

He reached for her hand, and she moved closer to him and rested her head on his shoulder.

They reached Pinehurst in time to see the sun slip into the bay. Russ walked onto the boat first, looked back and called to Judson. "You all come on. I hired a captain for the weekend because I want to enjoy it. Steering a boat is as much of a responsibility as driving at high speed on a crowded highway. We'll spend the night at Drake's house in St. Michaels. He's got a small boat docked there."

"This is not a small boat."

"No, but I didn't want a second house, so I got a big boat. Velma and I spend weekends on it."

Henry baited his hook and cast out as soon as the boat moved out to deep water. "Come over here," he called to Heather. "You can hold the basket in case I catch anything." Judson looked at Russ in time to see him throw back his head and laugh.

Heather had already planned to marry Judson, but she liked Henry, and she suspected he had a reason for his request. He didn't keep her waiting. "How long is it gonna take you to get Judson's ring on yer finger, Heather? He's a fine man, he loves you and he's lonely."

"He doesn't seem lonely to me, Henry."

"Then you're not as smart as I thought you were. Heather, a first-class man like Judson does not go around with the word *lonely* stuck to his chest. If you love him, you shoulda figured it out just like I did. Here, hold this while I support me back."

"But suppose a fish bites."

"Then you'll hold on tight, 'cause that's me best rod and tackle that Judson gave me."

She heard the pride in his voice. "Isn't the water too deep for fishing?"

"No, and don't change the subject. If you show Judson you need him, he'll get the courage to ask ye to marry him."

"Why would he need courage?"

"Child, there's not a man born who enjoys the word

no coming from a woman and especially if he loves her. Ever hear of the male ego?"

"Gotcha. But, Henry, I think he wants the proof of his parentage first."

"And 'spose he never gets it? Don't you believe that. Look at him standing over there wondering why you'd rather be with me than with him. Go on over there. I can handle me basket when I need to. Don't let it drag too long. You hear?"

"Thanks, Henry. You have a way of endearing yourself to me. Be back later."

She walked over to Judson. "Is he pulling in anything?" Judson asked her.

"Not yet. I thought Telford, Drake and their families would join us. What happened?"

"Telford went directly to Drake's house. Drake dropped Henry off here this morning. He wanted to catch crabs and, according to Russ, he pulled in a couple of bushels. Henry's an expert fisherman."

Judson took her hand and walked with her down to the bar where Velma was putting together snacks. "What do you want to drink, sweetheart?"

"Gin and tonic if I get something to eat along with it."

Russ entered the room, picked up Velma and kissed her. Then he eased her down until her feet touched the floor and kissed her properly. She hung on to him as if her life depended on it. When Velma's breathing accelerated almost to a pant, Heather forced herself to look away. But frissons of heat plowed through her, and she turned to leave the bar. Judson stopped her with a hand on her shoulder and gave her the drink.

"They love each other," he said for her ears only, "and they're free to do whatever they enjoy doing."

She nearly spilled the drink. "I know. Oh, I know."

He set her glass on the bar and pulled her into his arms. "No woman is more precious to a man than you are to me."

She kissed his neck. "Do you really mean that? I want so badly to believe it."

"If you trust me, I'll show you beauty you didn't dream existed. The sun will shine brighter, the moon will shimmer with a silvery glow, and your life will be fuller and sweeter than it's ever been. Give me a chance, and I'll show you a world you've never seen or imagined."

She held him tight and snuggled closer. "If you don't stop it, I may cry. If you give me all that, what can I give you?"

"Yourself is all I want and all I'll need."

What was he saying? Did he even realize what he was saying? She had so many questions and just as many misgivings. She reached for her glass, playing for time, and saw that they were alone in the bar room.

"Our time will come, Judson. At least, I hope so." She looked around. "Where did they go?"

"They saw that we needed privacy."

"I guess. How long have they been married?"

"Around four years, I think. Drake's been married almost three years and Telford, almost four years. Why?"

"They're like lovers, courting," she said, increasingly bemused. This was not her estimation of marriage.

"Why shouldn't they be?" he asked her. "Drake and Pamela are the same. Love and passion do not end with marriage. The feelings should deepen."

"Yes," she said softly and tried to believe it.

"Supper's ready," Velma called. "We'll be at Drake's place in about forty-five minutes or so. Honey, pull Henry in here. He'd stay up there trying to get a fish all night."

"Did you catch anything?" Heather asked Henry after Russ said grace.

"I got meself three good-size croakers and two mackerel. A big flounder got away."

Judson sampled a piece of baked bluefish. "That's quite a haul for a couple of hours, Henry."

"I ain't tired, though. I caught two bushels of crabs earlier, got meself a couple hours of sleep, and now I could fish all night."

"But you won't," Russ said, in a no-nonsense voice. "You're going in that house and go to bed like the rest of us."

Henry looked at Heather. "When I was raising me boys, they never considered talking back to me, but this one here's got to the place where he thinks he's me daddy."

"But you know he loves you," Velma said. She looked at Heather. "I didn't grow up in a loving and peaceful home. You don't want to know what it was like to be around my parents, and especially at night. I never knew what a loving family could be like until I met Russ, his brothers and Henry. They loved each other and they showered love on Alexis and Tara. That's why I love Henry. He planted the seeds for that. Witnessing the genuine affection and love among them changed my life and the way I looked at life.

"When I realized and accepted that Russ really loved me, I saw myself and everything around me differently." She sniffed back the tears. "And it seems like we love each other more every day."

The pressure of Judson's knee against her drew Heather's attention to him. He let his expression say, "Isn't that what I told you?"

She reached for his hand and gave it a gentle squeeze, but what she wanted most was the assurance of his arms around her. If only she could know where she'd be, with whom, and what she'd be doing a year hence. She smiled because he needed it from her.

They finished supper shortly before the captain spoke through the intercom. "We'll be docking in a few minutes. I see Mr. Harrington's signal lights."

"Are we docking at the edge of Drake's property?" Judson asked.

"Exactly," Russ said. "He's got a pier that extends out into the bay. Henry'd sit there all night and fish if we'd let him. You go on, Henry. I'll take your fish and your suitcase in."

"I'll help you with this stuff," Judson told him. When they reached the gangplank, he saw Drake and Telford coming to meet them. "I've finally got some brothers," he said to himself happily.

The brothers embraced him and Heather and took the bags that he carried. "We'll be back for the crabs," Drake called to Russ.

"If there're any mosquitoes," Heather whispered to Judson, "I'm not coming back outside."

"Not to worry, baby. I'll cover you with this spray I bought, and neither the mosquitoes nor I will come within a mile of you."

Pamela met them as they entered the front door and embraced first Henry and then Heather. She put an arm around Heather and walked toward the stairs. "You may share with Judson or have your own room."

"Thanks, but I'll suffer alone."

Pamela laughed. "That's what I figured. Sharing with him would be a mistake, 'cause Henry would give you a tongue-lashing."

"Why? Is he that old-fashioned?"

"Indeed not, but he told me not to make it easy for Judson."

"I guess I'm backward about these things," Heather said. "If he wants the benefits of marriage, he'll have to get married. Making love is one thing, but keeping house for a man goes with a solid commitment and witnesses to that fact. And even then, housekeeping will be a shared activity. Slavery is out."

"My sentiments exactly. Telford and his gang will have the master bedroom. You and Judson will have the two guest bedrooms, Henry will have the other bedroom, and Drake and I will sleep in the den on the Murphy bed. So there's plenty of room."

They walked into a room that faced the bay and which Pamela had decorated in aqua and white for a very feminine effect. "This is beautiful," Heather said. "I love the colors, and it suits this environment." She sat down. "I know you're busy, but I've wanted to ask you something. I'm sure women make a fuss over Drake because they literally throw themselves at Judson, and they're dead ringers for each other. Does it annoy you?"

Pamela sat down and exposed a perfect pair of legs when she crossed her knees. "What used to get to me was the way they ignored my presence. Some would suggest to him that I'd caught *him*. One woman put her arm through his and asked him where he came from. Another one asked me where I found him, but he grinned at her and said, 'I found *her*.' Drake detests that adulation, and he has a sharp-tongued way of putting the women in their place.

"Don't worry about it, and whatever you do, don't be jealous. He could have had any of them, but you're the one he wants and the one he loves. Never forget that, and you'll be happy. Do you want to marry him?"

"We love each other, Pamela, and I haven't loved any other man. But what I saw in my parents' relationship was not conducive to faith in marriage."

"Every marriage is different, Heather," Pamela confessed. "My dad worships the ground my mother walks on, and she doesn't want to be away from him ever. After thirty-five years of marriage against their families' wishes and without their support, they're still passionate about each other. It's an interracial marriage, and they've had a lot of social problems because they live in the South, but I've never heard them say one cross word to each other."

"Which one is African-American?"

"My mother. Her dad didn't speak to her for seven years after she married my father, but they reconciled a good while before he died."

Heather shook her head as if saddened. "My mother just walked off one day when I was ten and never came back. I can't understand how she could leave a nine-year-old child and never look back."

"Maybe she did look back. Sometimes when you close a door, you can't reopen it."

Heather nodded. "I'll think about that. It's an angle I hadn't considered. Let's go down. I haven't greeted Alexis and Tara."

Tara met them on the stairs. "Hi, Miss Heather. I was afraid Mr. Judson didn't bring you."

Heather hunkered in front of the little girl and hugged her. "I'm so glad to see you, Tara."

"Are you going to marry Mr. Judson? If you do, I'll have another auntie. I love my aunties."

"I don't know about that, Tara. Be patient. We'll see."

"Okay. I'll be patient as long as you don't say no." Heather hugged the little girl. So Telford's family had discussed her relationship with Judson, and it seemed as if they wanted Judson to marry her. They must have seen something deep and loving between them.

"There you are."

Heather looked up and saw Alexis reaching toward

her with open arms. "I've been looking forward to seeing you and Judson here. This is always a bang-up weekend for us, and it's probably the last we'll have this year."

She embraced Alexis. "I was wondering how long Drake keeps this house open. I'll bet it would be a beautiful place for Christmas festivities."

"I imagine it would, but everyone gathers around Henry, Telford and the family home at Christmas. I hope you'll be with us this year. We have a wonderful three- or four-day celebration."

"Thank you, Alexis. I confess that I feel happy with this group. Love and affection seem to spill out of everybody."

"It does. We don't go barhopping or night clubbing, and we don't seem to need much entertaining. I guess that's one of the reasons why we're so close to each other.

"Come on, we're having coffee and dessert here. Velma made the dessert, and Drake's in there making the coffee. I think we're having it in the den."

"Where's the baby?"

"Marc's upstairs sound asleep. I'm just having dessert. I don't take in caffeine while I'm nursing. The most difficult adjustment to that wasn't the coffee, but giving up chocolate. I love chocolate."

"Thanks for telling me. The minute I decide to get pregnant—if I ever do—I'm going to pig out on chocolate. So I won't miss it as much."

Alexis let a grin spread over her face. "And start drinking orange juice."

Heather threw up her hands. "I'd better make a list. I always thought that all you had to do was…"

Alexis interrupted her with a big laugh. "Dear Lord, that's *huge!* Honey, that's the least of it."

After dessert, Tara went to her bed, Velma and Drake served espresso and cognac, and Pamela treated them to a rendition of "Climb Every Mountain" because Henry asked her to sing it. Drake played some CDs of Buddy Guy's gut-bucket blues and jazz. It surprised Heather that the brothers immediately paired off with their wives in slow dancing. She didn't look toward Judson, and hoped that Henry would ask her to dance, but instead, he announced that he was going to bed.

"Dance with me?" She looked up at Judson, and shivers soared through her body. Zombielike, she took the hand he held out to her, walked into his arms and let the flow of love and passion possess her. She loved the way he danced and gave herself over to it.

"Unless you want me to find my way to your room tonight, ease up, will you? This atmosphere is sufficient to lull me into a stupor without the lure of your body moving against me," he said.

"I'm sorry, hon. When you're this close, my brain seems to take a vacation."

He rubbed her nose with his index finger and then kissed her mouth. "I know I can't get my birth certificate, because I doubt Mom put my name, hers or Sparkman's name on the certificate filed with the recorder of deeds. But if I can get Aunt Cissy's sister-in-law to file an affidavit that includes the information she gave me, I may be able to get some kind of legal document. At least, I hope so. That, along with DNA tests, should be sufficient. It won't be perfect, but it will be better than what I have now."

She wrapped her arms around him. "Oh, honey. I... want this so much for you."

"Thank you," he said softly. She moved her head from its comfortable place on his shoulder and stopped dancing.

"Judson, we're the only ones here. They've...they left us."

"They didn't want to interrupt whatever we were experiencing. In any case, I doubt they were thinking about us."

"You're right. I sure wasn't thinking about them. Let's sit here for a while. The moon's shining like daylight. If we knew this place better, we could go for a walk."

He locked his arms around her and rested her head against his shoulder. "Maybe we can do that tomorrow night. I love you, woman."

"And I love you. But I'm going to bed, because the temptation to be indiscreet is too compelling. Kiss me good-night."

In a second, he had his tongue inside of her. His fingers plied their magic on her body, roaming until they found her breast. "No," she said. "It would be more than I can tolerate knowing you're sleeping in the room next to mine. I, too, am human, and I've got too good a memory to expose myself to that. Good night, love." She pulled away from him, pulled off her shoes and sashayed up the stairs.

* * *

He walked over to the bottom of the stairs and watched the sight of her swinging hips. He waited until he heard her door close, checked the lock on the front door, extinguished the lights and dragged himself up the stairs.

He wasn't often ill-tempered, but if he gave into his mood right then, he'd send his fist straight through a wall. He stripped, stepped into the shower and turned on the cold water full blast. Thank God his room had its own bath. After a punishing ten minutes, he dried off and crawled into bed.

"A lot of good that cold shower did," he grumbled and started counting sheep.

After an hour of that, he gave up. She'd wanted him as badly as he wanted her, but she left while she could do it gracefully. Funny thing. When they were alone and had privacy, he always had to be the one to stop.

Hours later, the barking of a dog made him want to curse. He opened his eyes, saw streaks of daylight through the blinds and got up. If he'd slept for a single minute, his body didn't feel like it.

Judson dressed, found his way out of the back door, looked around and, seeing a path, headed down it. Jogging. After a half-mile run, he stopped suddenly at the sight of a woman slowly backing up as if afraid to move forward and just as scared to turn and run. He made it a point not to alarm her, but moved closer to determine the nature of the threat. He got close enough to see that the woman was Heather wearing a green jogging suit.

He could also see that one large and three smaller animals blocked the path, and quickly determined that she had intercepted a family of raccoons. He called to her.

"Turn around and walk away, Heather. They won't attack you if you don't threaten them."

As if the sound of his voice was all she needed, she swung around and ran to him. He caught her in his arms. "I've never been so glad to see anybody in my life," she said, clutching him to her.

"It's all right now. Couldn't you sleep?"

"Not a single wink."

"Neither could I." He tipped up her chin with his index finger. "I need to kiss you." He slipped his tongue into her mouth and sampled every crevice, let his hands roam over her, caressing the flesh that he loved so much to touch, and hugged her. When she trembled uncontrollably, he picked her up, carried her into the thicket and pressed her against the smooth trunk of a witch hazel tree.

She loosened the strings on her jogging pants, dropping them to the ground, and hooked her legs around his hips. Within seconds, he began to storm within her, nearly out of his mind with a passion such as he'd never felt and that threatened to overwhelm him. She started throbbing around him, and he told himself to control it, but when her vagina began squeezing his penis and her moans rose higher and higher, he emptied the essence of himself into her. At that moment, he knew she could have him on any terms she cared to dictate.

He picked up the jogging pants and helped her get into them and held her close to his body. "Are you all right, sweetheart?" he said. "I mean, did you feel it?"

"Did I ever! Oh, Judson. I've never experienced anything like that."

They walked slowly, arm in arm, in the direction of the house. "Neither have I. I don't think it was because I needed relief. I know how to handle that. But it was such an intense emotional need. It was you, and I know of no other way to explain it. I needed *you.*"

"I don't think I'll ever understand it," she said. "I ached for you in the very pit of me."

He expelled a long and heavy breath. "It settled something for me."

"And definitely for me."

He looked up at the house and saw a light in the kitchen window. "Someone's in the kitchen. Do you feel like going in now?"

"Yes. Thanks. I'm all right," she said.

He took her hand, opened the kitchen door and saw no one. "I'll stay here," he said. "Why don't you go on to your room and get comfortable?" He washed and dried his hands, found the coffeepot and a can of coffee, and soon the aroma of perking coffee filled the room. He poured a cup, added some milk. Seeing a television atop a storage bin, he turned it on to distract himself, sat down and began to sip the hot coffee. He'd drunk half a cup and sat lost in his thoughts when Drake walked in.

"Good morning. Say, it's early. Couldn't you sleep?"

"Good morning. The room is perfect. The mattress on that bed was made for me."

"But—"

Judson smiled. "But, heaven was next door."

Drake fingered his chin, poured a cup of coffee, sat down and looked at Judson. "And heaven said no way, not here."

"You got it!" Judson exclaimed, protecting Heather's modesty.

"You're gonna have to do something about that."

"As soon as I get this business about Sparkman settled, I will."

"Let's hope she doesn't lose patience."

"She'd warn me. Heather doesn't know how to be coy or treacherous. I'm not planning to live without her, but I have a compulsion to get this business straightened out before I ask her to marry me."

"Don't ever let her think that marrying her is contingent upon your resolving who your parents are, because she's accepted the matter as it is."

Chapter 11

Heather showered, dressed in jeans, a sweater and boots and walked over to the window in her room that overlooked the bay. She didn't remember ever having been so incautious and so reckless as an hour earlier when she'd made love with Judson in the open where some other early riser could have happened upon them. But at that moment, she'd felt that if she hadn't had him, she would have died. And what an awesome, mind-blowing feeling it was when he'd gotten into her and she'd finally exploded all around him.

She saw no point in thinking and worrying about the control he had over her; she should have worried about that months earlier. If marriage proved to be his terms for keeping him in her life, she'd marry him. She took a deep breath and exhaled it. That was silly, a child's way of thinking. She was not going to fool herself any longer. She wanted him, and she'd negotiate the terms if she had to.

Her gaze caught Drake and Pamela as they walked hand in hand along the pier to Russ's boat. Lovers. All of the Harrington men loved their wives and showed it. And their women exuded not only contentment but happiness. Maybe… She wiped the dampness from beneath her eyes. Could it happen to her with Judson? He'd taught her to need him, and not only for the complete sexual satisfaction that he gave her every time, but for himself. At the sound of music she loved, she wanted to dance with him, and only him. If she enjoyed food, she wanted him to taste it, and if she found anything beautiful, she wanted him to see it. Why hadn't she acknowledged that to herself weeks ago, and when had she begun to want to share everything with him?

"I've been so focused on my career that I almost let something maybe even more important sneak past me," she said to herself, shaking her head as she left the window and started down the stairs where she knew she'd face him…and the others. Her mind told her to skip down the stairs, but she couldn't do it. The last person she'd ever been able to fool was herself.

Heather walked toward the kitchen with a slower gait than was normally her wont, for she hated the thought of engaging in meaningless, friendly patter at a time when she was experiencing something akin to an epiphany. As she reached the dining room, Judson came to meet her with his arms open, and she walked into them.

"Are you okay?" His fingers brushed gentle strokes over her back.

"You know, I like these people so much, but right now, I don't want to be here. I want to be alone with my thoughts. Do you understand that?"

"Yes, I do. But let me tell you something. Kindness is one of the things the people in this family share. Be yourself, and they'll understand. I'm sure they'll all accept it gracefully if you don't want to talk. Come back here with me. I'm helping Velma get breakfast."

"Where's Henry?"

"You have to ask? Henry and Tara are fishing."

In the kitchen, Velma greeted her. "Good morning, Heather. I hope you slept well. Judson's helping me with breakfast. You just sit over there and keep us company."

"Good morning." So Judson hadn't told them that she'd already been out. She took a good breath and relaxed. "Can't I at least set the table?"

"Thanks, but Judson did that. We're probably going to have fish for lunch because Henry and Tara will try to catch every fish in the bay. I packed the crabs on ice to take back with us. Drake said it's too cold to swim up here, so if you want to swim, Russ will take the cruiser down to Cape Charles. For some reason, it's much warmer down there."

"I don't especially want to swim." He looked at Heather. "Do you?"

"No," she said, but it was hardly the truth. "Is Tara good at fishing?"

"Absolutely," Velma said. "The way she trails behind Henry, she couldn't miss."

Judson dipped the bread into the egg batter for the *pain perdu.*

"We're having French toast?" Heather asked, excited, because she loved it.

Judson stopped with the spatula dangling in the air. "My dear woman, this is nothing so simple as French toast. I'll have you understand that I'm making *pain perdu* as it should be made, complete with cinnamon, butter and all the other necessary ingredients."

"Really? Impressive, Mr. Philips," Heather said.

The three of them rocked with laughter. Velma dialed Russ on her cell phone. "Honey, would you please haul Henry and Tara in here? Judson and I are ready with breakfast."

"What about Alexis and Telford?" Judson asked. "Where are they?"

"With Tara out of the way, you can guess," Velma said, and added, "Makes me think I'd better not start a family till the fire dies down a little bit."

Surely the sound she heard wasn't the hand of Russ slapping playfully on Velma's backside. "I'll be back in a minute," Russ said. "Tara's going to be furious with me for bringing her in here now. She's as much of a fishing addict as Henry is. Be right back, baby."

Velma drained two rings of sausage and put that, along with a pound of cooked bacon, on a large patter. "I'll take that to the dining room," Heather said. She met Alexis in the hall, her color high and her eyes sparkling.

No one had to tell Heather that Alexis was still flushed with passion.

"You're just in time for breakfast," she said to Alexis. "Velma and Judson are cooking like we're all a bunch of hard-working ditch diggers."

"Is there anything for me to do?" Alexis asked her.

"No and not for me, either. Russ went out on the pier to get Henry and Tara, and I'm not sure where Drake and Pamela went."

Within the next ten minutes, the brothers, their families and Henry found their way to the dining room along with Heather and Judson. After his usual tease with Tara, Russ said the grace. He tapped the side of his glass, and the rest of the family laughed.

"Those who didn't help with breakfast," Russ said, "can clean the kitchen. By nine-thirty, I want us to be on the boat. I'm thinking of going down to Norfolk where Henry and Tara can fish for Spots. Telford and I can try for some striped bass and bluefish."

"What will you do?" Heather asked Pamela.

"Read, provided Alexis and Velma don't want to play pinochle. Do you play?"

"I do, but it's been a while."

"Good," Pamela said, "they can play with you."

"Suppose she wanted to play with Judson," Henry said. When the group laughed, he said, "Clean up yer minds."

Heather played pinochle, fished and, after Russ's captain dropped anchor near Cape Charles, she finally got a chance to swim that afternoon. But, although the water cooled her body, it did little to reduce the fever for Judson that still raged within her. And that longing for something elusive remained after Russ delivered them to her apartment on Sunday afternoon.

"I'm not going to stay," Judson said. "I have some work to do that's urgent, and if I stay even for a few minutes, I won't want to leave. Please understand. I'll never forget this past weekend and my time with you, sweetheart." He kissed her so quickly that she hardly experienced it. Minutes later, she was alone.

Heather stared at the front door, frustrated as her anger began to furl up. She walked from one end of the dining room to the other and back again, picked up a crystal bowl, raised her arm to throw it and laughed. Just because she'd decided that she wanted Judson didn't mean everything should go her way. "Oh, hell!"

She pulled out a chair in the dining room and phoned Scott.

"Say there, Heather, girl. Where've you been?"

She told him as much of the weekend's events as she thought he needed to hear.

"So where's my buddy?"

"Judson went home to take care of some urgent business. I doubt he knows how I'm feeling. I tried to show him, but he's fixated on Fentriss Sparkman."

"Hold it, Heather. You sound bitter and for no reason. How would you feel if you had to tell your kids you didn't know who their grandparents were? He's worried about it since he was seven years old, and that's an awful burden for a kid. He didn't mind being adopted, and he loved Aunt Bev and Uncle Louis, but he didn't know who he was. Be patient, Heather."

"I know that, but if you have a garden and you don't tend it properly, the flowers wither."

"Don't get dramatic on me. You mean the minute you decide you want him, you think he should kneel at your feet? You're smarter than that, Heather. Judson loves you, and you know it. Instead of standing on the sideline, jump in and help."

"You don't know what you're talking about. I have, and I would if he'd let me." Frustrated, she changed the subject. "When are you going to Lithuania?"

"In a few weeks. This is something I'll love you for forever. I definitely wouldn't have been in line for it for another three years at the least."

"With your personality," she said, "you can't miss rising to the top at State."

"You're a sweetheart. Be sure and give me notice enough to get back here for your wedding."

"You're nuts."

She hung up. "Why do I always feel better after talking with Scott?"

Because he neither pampers you nor lies to you. He tells you the truth and you know that's what you need to hear.

She answered the telephone, certain that she would hear Judson's voice. "Hello."

"Hello, Heather. This is Pamela. How about lunch tomorrow? I meant to ask you during the weekend, but it kept slipping me. Is twelve-thirty good for you?"

"Perfect. Shall we go back to The Grill?"

"That's what I had in mind. See you tomorrow."

"Okay, and thanks."

She jotted the place and time in her pocket *Week at a Glance* and went to the refrigerator to look for the makings of supper. Seeing nothing interesting, she took a quiche lorraine from the freezer and heated it in the microwave oven. With that, a bottle of beer and a mobile phone, she made her way to the living room and sat down to eat and watch the Ravens."

When the phone rang, she could see his caller ID.

"Hi, Judson. I just sat down to supper. Are you okay?"

"More or less. Somehow I got a feeling that you might be distressed about my leaving you."

"That's one way of putting it, but I got it under control...at least for now.

"I'm glad. I'd like to give Scott a party before he goes away. I thought a dinner for about twenty people would do it."

"Twenty people? Judson, that would be at least a hundred dollars a person plus three hundred for the waiters and another couple hundred for the maitre' d. A cocktail party for fifty at a good hotel would be cheaper."

"That's true," he said, "but I don't really like cocktail parties."

"Neither do I. He's leaving in around a month. I'll get the correct date from his secretary. Is this why you called me?"

"No. It's killing me not getting into my car and driving to you right now."

"But if you come here, you definitely won't get your work done," she teased. "We can see each other tomorrow evening maybe. I'm having lunch with Pamela."

There! Henry would be proud of her. "Don't make it easy for him," he'd said, "but don't give him too much rope, either."

"Does that mean you'll have dinner with me tomorrow evening? We can go to that Italian restaurant that we never got to last week."

"Okay. Will you wear a tie?"

"Absolutely, and a handkerchief, too."

After they told each other good night, she finished the quiche and beer, discarded the refuse, extinguished the kitchen light and went to her bedroom, but she couldn't sleep.

The phone aroused her from a tired stupor at a quarter of six the next morning.

She sprang up. "Hello."

"Heather. It's your father. He…he won't wake up."

She jumped out of bed. "Annie! Is this Annie? What is it? What's the matter with him?"

"I think…I think he's left us. Just a minute. The ambulance is here."

She heard her heart pounding, as pain crisscrossed her stomach like scissors gutting her into pieces.

"Hello, ma'am," a male voice said. "I'm the EMS driver. The lady here insists I talk to you. I…I don't think there's much hope. I'm sorry."

Stricken, Heather mumbled, "Thanks. Let me speak with Annie."

"I knew he was gone as soon as I touched him, Heather," Annie said, tears in her voice. "Funny thing is I couldn't sleep last night. He ate a good dinner, and we laughed and talked for the longest time. Every time I said it was time for him to go to bed, he'd think of something else to reminisce about. He got up to go to bed, stumbled slightly and laughed.

"You know what he said? 'Getting old is terrible. Maybe the alternative isn't so bad. If I was twenty years younger and knew what I know now, I'd make you marry me. You've been the true love of my life.' It hasn't hit me yet, but Lord, I know it will."

"I'll be there as soon as I can get there, Annie. I have a few calls to make."

She hung up and telephoned Judson.

"Hi, sweetheart. You're up early again today. Is this getting to be a habit?"

"Oh, Judson. My...my father died. I—"

"What? When?"

She told him.

"Sweetheart, I'm sorry. I'll be there as soon as I can."

"I have to go to Hagerstown."

"I'll take you."

"But you have something important to do today."

"I know, but my senior associate will have to take care of it. Can you make a pot of coffee?"

"Yeah. Don't forget to feed Rick."

"I'll call his sitter. Rick will be one pampered dog when I get back home."

She packed, remembered that she probably wouldn't be back home for at least a week, and repacked. She made coffee, fried some bacon, mixed some pancake batter and set the little table in the kitchen.

The doorbell rang, and she ran to the door. "Hi," she said and collapsed into his embrace.

He stepped inside, dropped a small overnight bag on the floor, kicked the door shut and wrapped his arms around her. For a while, they didn't speak. Then he walked with her to the kitchen. "Let me pour you some coffee," were his first words.

He said grace and they ate in silence.

"You have a lot of things to do today, things with which I've had some experience. I'll stay with you till you have everything in order."

"I don't know how to thank you, Judson."

"Please don't thank me, Heather. You're the most important person in my life and the closest to me. You're everything to me. What else would I do?"

"Oh dear, I had a date with Pamela for lunch."

"You told me last night. I called her a few minutes before I got here. She'll phone you later. How's Annie taking this?"

"She was calm when she called me, but I don't know how long that will last. She said that as he headed for bed last night, he told her that she was the true love of his life. I knew that, and I'm glad he told her. Funny thing was that I couldn't get to sleep last night."

"I think we all have second sights, but they're uncultivated. Remember how happy you were when you left him last week?"

"I do, and right now, I have a wonderful feeling about that. I don't know how long it will last."

He cleaned the kitchen, stored their bags in the trunk of his car and phoned Telford with the news of Heather's father. "She and I are on our way to Hagerstown now."

"We'll be there for her. What is her father's address?" Judson gave it to him. "All right. I'll see you there around one-thirty today."

Judson relayed the conversation to Heather. "You see? They care about you. And about me. Seven months ago, I only had Scott. Now, I have you, Aunt Cissy and the Harringtons. I have a family. And that reminds me. I'd better call Aunt Cissy."

Annie met them at the door. They embraced each other and, as he'd expected, when Heather hugged Annie, she finally cried. An aching emptiness settled inside of him as he watched her struggle with the pain.

"The first thing we have to do is make the funeral arrangements," he said, doing his best to break the mood. "Then, we have to notify his friends and acquaintances. I'll call the minister at Shiloh to schedule the funeral and give the *Frederick News-Post* a notice and report the event to the local radio station. I'll make some fliers on my laptop and print them out in the library."

Annie stared at him in frank appreciation. "Danged

if you're not the most organized person I know, and especially now that Franklin's gone."

His cell rang, and he took the call quickly. He turned to Heather. "That was Aunt Cissy. How many notices do you think we have to mail?"

Within two hours, they had everything organized.

"Child, this ham won't last long," Cissy said a little later after arriving at the Tatum home. She had baked it along with biscuits, corn bread and string beans. "You always need a lot of food at times like this."

Telford and Alexis arrived, bringing three roasted chickens.

"The five of us ought to get these notices done in no time," Alexis said, sitting down to the dining room table and handing out stationery like someone dealing cards. "I'll have to leave, because I'm still nursing, but Drake and Pamela will be here later. Russ and Velma will be here tomorrow."

"Yeah, and we can mail them in the post office when we're on the way home," Telford said.

And so it went. Pamela and Drake arrived with beer, soft drinks and a bottle each of bourbon and aged Scotch whiskey. Relief spread over Judson when Pamela embraced Heather, and the heaviness he'd observed in Heather lifted like fog in the morning sun. He knew then that, of the Harrington women, Pamela would be the one to which Heather would become attached. He looked to Telford as an older brother, but he regarded all of the three with true brotherly affection.

It amazed him that when Russ and Velma arrived

the following morning, Henry accompanied them. "It was easy for me to arrange for the reception after the interment," Velma explained. "You know I plan parties, receptions and such things professionally. Just leave it to me."

Heather found Judson in the kitchen talking with Henry, who was explaining to Judson the personalities and outlook of the Harrington men. "They're behaving like they always do," Henry said. "Whenever one starts something, the other two pitch in and help. I'm thankful that me boys all got themselves women with the same spirit. They're a loving bunch."

"It's very strange," Heather said. "This is a sad and terrible loss for me, but I have this feeling that out of it, I've gained something precious."

"Nothing strange about it," Henry said. "Your friends are showing you that we're yer family."

She leaned down and kissed his weathered cheek. "You're a rare person, Henry. I'm blessed to know you."

"You're all right yourself."

Judson watched the interplay between Henry and Heather. The old man clearly admired and preferred women who possessed intelligence and elegance. One day, he meant to have a conversation with Henry about that.

"Why do you like Heather for me?" he asked when Heather went to answer the phone.

"Oh, that's an easy one," Henry said, seemingly with relish. "Apart from how you feel about each other, she's arrow straight, won't let you down and won't let you walk over her, and she'll stick with you in whatever you do. She's that type, and they ain't easy to find."

"That's a terrific recommendation for a woman."

"She's what you deserve."

Friday afternoon saw the end of the ceremonies and the reception. The Harrington family, including Henry, returned to Eagle Park, and Telford asked his brothers if they could meet for a few minutes to discuss Judson and his paternity. They assembled in the den at Telford's house, and after getting their preferred drinks, Telford leaned back in his favorite chair and opened the topic.

"Judson told me that he's taken steps to try and get his birth certificate. But there's no doubt in my mind that he is Uncle Fentriss's son. So, I don't need that certificate."

"What are you getting at?" Russ asked him.

"It doesn't matter," Drake said. "Add everything else we know and then let him stand beside me, and there's your answer. But if he wants DNA tests, I'll accommodate him."

"So will I," Russ said.

Drake got up and got another drink of bourbon and water. "We split Uncle Fentriss's money between the three of us, and we've already used a lot of it for philanthropic and other purposes. We still have all that property Uncle Fentriss gave us, and we could give him the Beverly apartment building. It's the single most valuable piece of property that Uncle Fentriss left us, but it isn't a quarter of the value of the estate. Am I right, Russ?"

"Yeah," Russ replied. "Income from that building alone would make him a wealthy man, though I sense he's already well-fixed."

"As executor of the will, can you take care of the deed, Russ?" Telford said.

"Absolutely. It may take some weeks to finalize it, though, because town, county and state officials have to sign it, in that order. I suggest we tell him about it when I have the document in my hand."

"All right," Telford said. "Believe me, I feel good about this. When it's a done deed, we'll tell Henry. He'll appreciate it. Let's drink to it."

At that moment, Heather made an important decision. "I know you love this place, Annie, and your memories of my father are tied to it. But you're too young to live another forty years in the past. I don't think you'd be happy in a Baltimore apartment. So, I've decided to sell this house, buy—"

At the stricken expression on Annie's face, she held up her hands, palms out. "I'm going to buy one in Frederick, move the contents of this house and you to a new one, and I'm going to close my Baltimore apartment and live with you in Frederick. What about it?"

Annie sat down, covered her face with her hands and let the tears come. Heather sat beside her and folded the woman into her arms. "You've been my rock since I was ten years old, my mother whenever I needed one and always my friend. What did you think I'd do now that you need me?"

"I…I didn't know what would happen. This is my home. God bless you, Heather." She wiped her eyes with the hem of her blouse. "What about Judson? Surely you're not planning to let him go. Your own husband couldn't have been better to you than he's been this past week. Cissy told him that he's crazy if he doesn't marry you, and I'm telling you the same thing."

A frown marred Heather's smooth face. "Why'd she tell him that?"

"She said she wanted to see him settled and happy before she passes on. He told her not to worry. Your daddy thought a lot of Judson, too."

"I know. So do I. We have to go to Frederick tomorrow to see the lawyer about the will, and while we're there, we can check out a couple of houses."

"May I speak with you for a minute?" Judson's voice came from the doorway.

She looked up and saw Judson standing there. "Of course. Excuse me, Annie."

She walked over to him.

"I need to get back to Baltimore, but I'll leave my car for you and get a limousine," Judson explained. "Also, I've filed a request for my birth certificate along with sworn affidavits from Aunt Cissy and her sister-in-law and a copy of my adoption papers. I'm hoping and praying for the best."

She gazed up at him, seeing the anxiety in his eyes. Whatever concerned her was at that moment of no importance. She wrapped her arms around him and held him close. "I'll be hoping and praying, too, because I know this means everything to you."

A half smile curled his lips. "Well, not everything. You're more precious to me than that or any other document could possibly be." He ignored her inquiring expression. "I also have to prepare for a difficult trial. I'm not basically a trial lawyer, but we can't come to an agreement, so it has to go to trial. While here, I've been working on it with my partners by phone and the Internet, but they want me to argue it in court. Let me know when you'll be home and what you're planning to do with Annie."

"I'll call you at home tonight."

He bent to her lips and, for the first time in a week, she had a need to feel him driving his body inside of hers. He stared down at her. "Soon, sweetheart," he said, reading her mood.

Heather watched Judson get into the limousine, and as it pulled away, she vowed to give their relationship until the end of the year. "If we don't have a contract by then, I'm out of it." She knew it was her fault that they went along willy-nilly because she hadn't encouraged him to believe that she wanted anything more. But now that she understood fully what he meant to her and how rich life with him could be, she was going for it. She went into the living room where Annie sat in solemn silence.

"Come on, Annie," she said, shaking the keys to Judson's car, "we're going house hunting."

She drove through Frederick and its environs, saw three houses that they both liked, and made a note to contact a real estate agent.

* * *

Half an hour after she parked Judson's car in front of her building she answered the bell and opened the door to Judson. "Hi," she said. "I didn't—"

He swallowed her words in his mouth, picked her up and walked inside with her in his arms. "Sweetheart, so much is going on for the next few days," he said when he released her. "I need you badly, and I know you need me. You're my first priority, but that case I'm working on will be the first in five years that I've argued in court, and I admit I'm scared. I'm a corporate lawyer, not a trial lawyer."

She pushed him into a big chair and sat in his lap. Her agenda did not include talk about cases and trials. "You know I'm with you," she said. He eased her up higher in his lap. She locked her hands at the back of his neck and parted her lips over his. His groan excited her, heat snaked up her limbs and arousal gripped her. *He goes after what he wants, and I can, too.* Letting him know what she wanted, she sucked his tongue into her mouth and pulled on it as if she were drawing liquid through a straw from a near-empty bottle.

His arousal was the signal she needed. The ache in her vagina intensified to urgent need, her nipples ached, and she grabbed his right hand and rubbed one furiously. He jerked her sweater overhead, flung off her bra, bent his head to suck her nipple into his mouth and feasted on it, ripping screams from her as he popped the snap on her jeans. He slid his hand down to her clitoris and rubbed it in a double onslaught. She cried out from the pleasure of it and from the harrowing need to have him inside of her.

"Put me someplace and get in me," she said. "I need you. I can't stand this."

He stripped off her clothes and carried her naked to her bed. Seconds later, disrobed, he pulled her to the edge of the bed, locked her legs around his shoulders, and nipped, licked and sucked until she whined for relief. As if hell-bent on staking a claim for all time, he kissed his way up her body at his own good time, stared down into her face and went into her slowly, tantalizing her. She gave as she never had.

When she was on the brink of orgasm, he smiled down at her. "Be still for a minute, baby."

She tried to hold her body still while he drove into her with rapid and powerful strokes. The heat at the bottom of her feet seemed to spread through out her body, and then the pumping and squeezing, the quivering of her legs and thighs, but still it wouldn't come. He put a hand beneath her hips, held her where he wanted her, and with a powerful explosion, relief tore through her body.

"Oh, my Lord, I'm dying. You're killing me. Oh, Lord, I'm… Oh, Judson. I want you to love me." She bucked beneath him and then lay still. Breathless.

"I do love you," he moaned. "You're my life." He poured the essence of himself into her and collapsed in her arms.

"I haven't got enough strength to drink a glass of water," he happily complained. "I'd better stay away from you till I finish this case."

"I'm not sure how much help I'll be able to give you with your case, though I'll try."

He moved from her, fell over on his back and tucked her to his side. "What's going to happen with Annie?"

"Shows you where my head is. I forgot to tell you that I'm going to sell the house in Hagerstown, buy one in Frederick and settle there. Annie's what's left of my family, so my home is her home."

She felt him stiffen.

"I assume you planned to tell me. Actually, I think that's a good idea. I don't like your being farther away from me, though I'm pleased that you'll be near the Harringtons in Eagle Park."

He continued, "Don't forget you're my date at my dinner for Scott. I've decided to ask Velma to handle it. She did a super job on the reception following your father's interment."

He gripped her in a fierce hug, kissed her and said, "Will you be hurt if I leave? Telford isn't going to ask for a DNA test because he's satisfied with the information he has. But I want as much proof as I can get, so I have to request it. I'm going to Frederick tomorrow morning to get an order for it."

She *did* mind, because she hated for him to leave her. Hadn't he noticed that she needed him more? Something had happened to her on that early morning beside a witch hazel tree. She'd developed an ache for something she didn't have. He didn't notice that she'd changed, and she didn't know how to reveal it short of announcing it.

"I mind," she said, "because I'm happiest when I'm with you. But I don't resent your going." He kissed her, dressed and left.

She'd loved him for a long time, months at least, or thought she had. But this was different. She needed him. If he needed her, he wasn't acting like it.

Chapter 12

Judson reached for the handle on the door of his car and paused. Had he detected a slight chill when he kissed Heather goodbye? He shook his head, certain that he must have imagined it. He drove home thinking that Heather was the first person he'd ever let drive his car, and that included Scott. The minute after he walked into his house, he remembered that he hadn't eaten dinner and telephoned his friend.

"Say, man. Anything to eat at your place? I just got in and remembered that I haven't eaten since lunch."

"Sure," Scott said. "I have hot dogs, two frozen pizzas and a Hungry Man frozen roast beef dinner."

"Pizza. I'll be right over with a six pack."

"I'm having a hard time accepting that Heather turned down a second ambassadorship," Judson said to Scott, washing down the pizza with beer. "She was so driven for a post, and she's been working so hard for it. I don't want to question her about it too much, because she might misunderstand."

"Look, Judson, Heather is not stupid, as you well know. Those are graveyard posts, she hates frigid weather and she knows that they know she deserves better. Most of all, I don't think she wants to sign on to be away from you for two full years, and she knows you are not going to Lithuania with her. She loves you, and she's doesn't want to give you up."

"I love her, too, but I'm not sure I'd do that."

"That's the difference between her position in life and yours. You're a man, and you'd expect her to go with you, but if she asked you to leave your practice and spend two years with her at her ambassadorial post, you'd ask her if she'd lost her mind. You and most other guys."

"Yeah, but that's because I can't work overseas. I'm a lawyer, and—"

"You're kidding yourself, buddy. There's an American company in most overseas countries, and they need lawyers."

"Okay. Are you free for dinner next Thursday?"

"Sure."

"Good. Meet me at the Harbor Court Hotel at seven. Also, wear your tux, and don't forget to put on some socks."

"I always wear socks this time of year. What's up?"

"You're invited to dinner. Look, I'd better be going.

That lawsuit's going to trial, and I have to argue the case. Thanks for the pizza."

"Sure thing, buddy. And thanks for the beer."

Judson got into his car, took out his cell phone to call Heather and saw that he'd missed a call. He didn't recognize the number, but he dialed it nonetheless.

"Hello. This is Judson returning your call."

"Thanks. This is Telford. I won't keep you. We're going to have a christening ceremony for Marc, my son, next Sunday at two-thirty in the afternoon. It'll be at Second Presbyterian Church. We'd love for you and Heather to be with us."

"Thank you for asking me to come. I'll ask Heather if she can make it, but I'll be there in any case."

"That's great. We're only inviting relatives and a few very close friends. We'll leave from my house, if that suits you?"

"Fine. I should be at your place around one-thirty. A bit earlier if the weather is bad."

"Thanks. Give my love to Heather."

"I will. Give mine to your family."

Did people give christening gifts? Heather would know. Velma certainly should. As soon as he walked into his house, he dialed Heather's number.

"Hi," she said in a sleepy voice. "Judson?"

"Right. I'm sorry if I awakened you. It's only nine-thirty, or I wouldn't have called."

"I fell asleep in front of the TV. Did you eat any dinner?"

"Yeah. I went by Scott's place and ate a pizza. If I'd

had my head on straight, we could have had something together. Telford called a few minutes ago and invited us to Marc's christening next Sunday. I hope you can come."

"I'd like to."

"Then I'll be at your place at twelve o'clock. And I've invited Scott to dinner on Thursday. He agreed, and he's bringing his girl. I told him to wear a tux, but I didn't tell him there'll be twenty at the dinner."

"Okay. I won't mention that."

"I may increase the number to thirty, because I'd like the Harrington brothers and their wives to attend. It's time I returned some favors."

May as well get it over with, he said to himself. "Sweetheart, are you displeased with me?"

"Am I...why do you ask me that?"

"When I kissed you good-night, your response seemed a little frosty. Twenty minutes earlier, you gave yourself to me so joyously and... What happened during that short interval?"

"It's...I—"

"No matter how it sounds or how you think it will make me feel, give it to me straight."

"I...uh...I guess I lied when I said I didn't resent your leaving me right then. I minded, and I resented it. For the first time in my life, I felt—"

"Say it."

"I feel vulnerable. I mean, I wanted to hold you in my arms, but you wanted to leave me minutes after... after practically taking me to heaven."

"I see. Do you realize that if you'd told me that, I wouldn't have left you? Don't ever mislead me about your feelings, because whatever's wrong will only get worse. If something isn't all right, tell me. That's not all of it, but I get it."

"I'm... Judson, I'm not used to feeling like this."

"I'm sure of that. And neither am I, but knowing that I need you in order to be complete doesn't perturb me. I'm happy about it. We shouldn't be having this conversation over the phone, Heather. *Listen* to me! *I've had no other love. I have only loved you.*"

"It's the same with me, Judson. I've liked other men, but I never before thought I loved a man. It scared me. Kiss me good-night. I'm fine now." They made the sound of a kiss, and he didn't hang up until after she did.

So that was it. She could accept and enjoy loving him, but the realization that she needed him frightened her. As a successful, independent woman who was very capable of running her life as she pleased, Heather had not planned to need a man or anyone else.

The next morning, Heather awakened with the wonderment of how she had changed. After extricating herself from one unfulfilling relationship, she had promised herself that she would forever chart her own course, and love lightly, if at all. Easier vowed than practiced, because she hadn't met Judson Philips.

She got two cups of coffee from the canteen on the first floor of the building in which she worked and, instead of going to her own office, she knocked on Scott's office door. "If it's not important, keep walking," he said.

She opened the door, put a container of coffee on his desk and took a seat. "Have you ever been in love, Scott?"

"Good morning. Thanks for the coffee. Why?"

She stood. "If you're not in a good mood, I'll take my coffee and—"

"For goodness' sake, sit down. I've been in deep like, but I don't know that you'd call it love."

"Trust me, if you'd been in love, you'd know it. It's… is it a good thing to want to be with someone every second of the day and night? For the last week, I just don't want to be away from him, and this thing started before my father died, so that's not the source of it. I want to know what he thinks about everything, and I want him to experience everything that I enjoy. If something exasperates me, I want his comfort. It's crazy as hell, Scott. Maybe I don't like this."

"You don't want to need the guy. Is that it?"

"I don't know. I'm not used to it, and I refuse to become a demanding, clinging woman. I'd hate myself."

"Look, babe, if a man loves you, he wants you to love him and need him. That's important to him. If you don't need him, he'll find a woman who does. Need is the essence of the relationship between lovers and spouses. When it's gone, so goes the relationship. So you watch it."

"I'm almost sorry you got your new job. Who'll I talk to when I get into trouble?"

"You'll talk to Judson. Share with him, and you won't get into trouble, at least not where he's concerned."

She kissed his forehead, went to her office and telephoned Pamela. "Hi, Pam. Judson and I are invited to Marc's christening Sunday. Is there a dress-up reception after the service, or will church clothes suffice?"

"Hi. Any street dress or suit will do it. We're coming back to Telford's after the christening. At the most we'll be about fifteen people. Alexis and Velma's father, my parents, you and Judson, Jack and Melanie Ferguson are the others coming. Russ and Velma are to be the godparents. So, except for Jack and Melanie, it's family."

She digested that for a minute. "But, Pamela, I'm not family."

Pamela's throaty laughter reached her through the wire. "Not yet, but I don't think New Year's will find you single."

At the thought of being married to Judson Philips, shivers raced through her. "How did you feel when you first got married? I mean, before you got used to it?"

"Great. I walked on air from the minute I knew we'd be married, and I'm still high on him. Any sane person can see that you and Judson love each other deeply. Let me tell you that no matter how good it is when you're single, it's better and better when he's yours and you know it. Trust me on this."

"Thanks for sharing. I can see what I missed by not having a sister."

"I don't have one either, but you and I can support each other."

"Thank you, Pamela. That gives me a good feeling." But would she feel good if she surrendered her freedom in exchange for marriage with Judson or any other man? For various reasons, fifty percent of marriages in the United States went sour, leaving one or both spouses devastated. She tried to shake off the thought.

Later, on the way home, she passed a designer dress shop and saw an evening gown that she liked. "Do you have it in red or a pastel color?" she asked the saleswoman. Told that it came only in white, she declined to buy it. She didn't look great in white, and she didn't want to give Judson the impression that she was dropping a hint.

"I can't always wear dusty rose," she said to herself, remembering the royal blue velvet that she'd worn once and headed home. "It would make the perfect dinner dress."

She hadn't expected to enjoy that dinner party, but she did. Velma had placed her at one end of the table opposite Judson, with Scott at her right and Drake on her left. Drake, she discovered, had a droll sense of humor and piercing insight into personalities. He and Scott were perfect matches for each other. Suddenly, it hit her. Some aspects of Drake's personality reminded her of Judson. She made a mental note to ask Scott if he agreed with her.

"Why didn't you tell me that Judson planned this party for me?" Scott asked her. "It's the fanciest thing anybody ever did for me."

"He loves you, Scott, and he hates cocktail parties, so what option did he have?"

"Gotcha. I want the name of the person who planned this shindig for him. It's perfect."

"Drake's sister-in-law is an event planner right down to the lightbulbs," she told him. "I think Judson is about to say something."

She gazed at Judson Philips, who stood resplendent in a black tux and royal blue accessories. He pointed toward Scott. "Our guest of honor is headed for his first ambassadorship, and he and I will be separated for the first time since kindergarten. To his left, and my hostess for the evening, is Dr. Heather Tatum, my date and the woman I love."

Both Scott and Drake looked at her and gave her the thumbs-up sign.

"When a man puts it on the line like that," Drake said, "he means business."

She wanted to stand up and let all of them see the woman Judson Philips said he loved, but she let prudence prevail and remained in her chair. "I'll kiss him for that," she said to herself. After coffee and liqueurs in an anteroom beside the dining room, Judson thanked everyone for coming, said good-night to Scott and walked over to her.

"I'd like to leave now. Does that suit you?"

For an answer she put her arm through his and let the happiness she felt spill out of her in a smile. "I'm with you."

"That's what I like to hear."

He assisted her into his car, went around to the driver's side and got in. She wondered why he didn't turn the ignition, but he sat there and said nothing.

"What is it, Judson?"

"One of the most important trials I've had since I began my practice comes up next week, and I won't be able to see you until it's over."

"But you won't be busy in the evenings," she said and immediately wanted to bite her tongue.

He started the engine, moved away from the curb into the flow of traffic that led away from the Inner Harbor and drove half a dozen blocks. She knew she'd said the wrong thing, but she hadn't thought it would irritate him.

"I didn't mean that the way it sounded," she said.

"I'm glad to hear it. As you know, I do not trust my reputation to anybody."

"And that's why you're one of the best lawyers anywhere. Remember that I'm not a bad lawyer myself. If I can help, I want to, so please let me know."

"Thank you. This is the first time you offered help, and I appreciate it."

What was she supposed to say to that? He did share his concerns with her occasionally, but he'd been so involved with the quest for proof of his parentage that it seemed that goal had overshadowed everything else.

"I'll always be here for you. Always." When he reached over and squeezed her hand, relief spread over her, for that gesture said more than words would have.

"I don't want you to reply to this just now, but I'd like you to give serious thought to a Philips-Tatum law partnership."

When she could catch her breath, she said sincerely, "Okay. I will."

He parked in front of her building, walked with her to her door and stood there looking down at her. "You are serenely beautiful tonight, and I've been a very proud man."

"Not more proud than I was when you told those people that you loved me."

"Yes, I do. I'll be here Sunday at twelve o'clock." At the inquiring expression on her face, he said, "Tomorrow and through Sunday morning, I'll be cramming for my date with the judge on Monday morning."

She opened her arms, and when he walked into them, she sensed that he'd needed communion with her. He held her so close, stroking and caressing her. "I love you, Heather. More that you will ever guess." His kiss seared her lips, and she opened to him. But after savoring it for a second, she stepped away because she knew that, in spite of the late hour, he'd go home and work.

A faint smile played around his lips. "Thanks for the temperance. I'll make up for it."

* * *

After a morning of heavy wind and rain, the sun shone brightly as Judson and Heather arrived at Telford's home in Eagle Park that Sunday afternoon. "I'd been thinking that I'd have to carry you to the house," Judson joked, "in order to protect those pretty shoes on your feet. Fortunately, the sun's shining, and there're no puddles here. I'm beginning to believe that being impractical is part of being a woman."

"You wouldn't expect me to come here in brogans, would you? Anyway, I don't weigh much, so carrying me wouldn't be a big deal."

He took her hand and headed up the walk. "I didn't say it would be." When he stopped walking, she gazed up at him with an inquiring expression on her face. God help him, but she could reduce him to putty with that look. He kissed her lips and reached for the bell at about the time that the door opened.

"Hi. You're just in time for a light snack before we leave," Alexis said. "Come in."

After a light repast of smoked-salmon sandwiches, deviled eggs, tea and Henry's chocolate-chip cookies, they left for Frederick. The ceremony lasted about half an hour, and all the while his thoughts centered on that day long ago when he was christened in the same church in the absence of his parents and in a ceremony of which the record no longer existed. What words had the preacher said, and had his grandmother put the kind of white gown on him that Marc wore? Did anyone play an instrument?

"What is it?" Heather whispered. "Darling, what's the matter?"

"What do you mean?"

She eased her arms around him. "You're... There're tears on your face," she whispered.

"Don't worry. It's all right. I'll tell you later."

At the end of the ceremony, everyone congratulated Marc's parents, and then they returned to the Harringtons' house. Henry walked up the steps with Judson. "I see the ceremony moved you like it did me, Judson. Take matters in yer hands and get some young ones of yer own."

"It was more than that, Henry. They recorded the ceremony for Marc, his children and grandchildren. I've been told that I was christened in that same church before that same altar, but there's no record of it, and I never knew the person who arranged it."

"I know that's tough, son, but as soon as you get yer own family, you'll stop frettin' over the past. You're Sparkman's boy or me name ain't Henry. Far as I'm concerned, that ain't up for argument." Judson put his arm around the shoulders of the frail old man and let the gesture suffice for an expression of gratitude.

He walked into the living room behind Henry and stopped, unable to move another step. Heather sat on the living room floor with her back against the sofa holding Marc in her arms. She gazed down at the child as if seeing a miracle for the first time. He'd never seen her face so soft or her expression so tender. She leaned down, kissed the baby's cheek and, in response, Marc bubbled with a happy grin, waving his hands in delight. Judson wanted to take her and run with her to any place where they would be alone and he could show her how he loved her. He knew that his face betrayed his raw emotions and the powerful effect that this Madonna-like Heather had on him. He turned to walk away and bumped into Drake.

"She's always beautiful," Drake said, "but right now, she's radiant. I imagine that picture set you back a good bit. Let's get a drink. What would you like?"

"Whatever you're serving, brother, so long as it will help restore my balance." He would take to his grave that picture of Heather smiling and serene with Marc in her arms.

"Would you believe that's the first time I ever held a little baby?" Heather asked Judson later that day during their drive back to Baltimore.

"Yes. I can believe that. I wish I'd had a camera. It was the most beautiful, the most touching picture I ever saw. It literally took my breath away. Why were you sitting on the floor?"

"I wanted to hold him to see what it was like, and I figured if I was sitting on the floor, I couldn't drop him. Alexis thought I was off the wall, but I did not want to drop that baby. He was so sweet, and do you know he actually liked me?"

The child's reaction to her filled her with pride. His warm little body in her arms had a life-giving quality, and she had given him back to Alexis with reluctance and regret. "I didn't want to give him up," she said, "and that still surprises me. Judson, it's a little scary. Having children after age thirty-five can be risky."

"Don't worry about that."

She just realized how badly she wanted children. Previously, she'd thought it would be nice to have them, but that it wouldn't bother her too much if she didn't.

"I hope you're right. What are you doing this evening?"

"I was hoping to have dinner with you."

"Unless you have to have a gourmet meal, I can turn out a really nice supper in forty minutes, and then we can eat for a couple of minutes before you dash off to be a lawyer."

"Saying no to you is not something I feel like doing right now. Do you need anything from a deli or grocery store?"

"No. Thanks. I…uh…I have everything I need."

His laughter told her that she hadn't fooled him and that he knew she'd planned all along to have him spend the evening with her in her home. "Oh, all right," she said. *"'When the mountain wouldn't go to Muhammad, Muhammad went to the mountain.'"*

A grin captured his face. "I get it. That's the mark of a good lover and a good lawyer—if it doesn't work one way, try another."

At home, she changed into a peasant skirt and blouse, cooked and, in forty minutes, served a meal of broiled salmon, steamed asparagus and parsleyed potatoes with chocolate pie à la mode for dessert. They cleaned the kitchen and sat with each other on the couch, letting their fingers entwine while listening to CDs of their favorite music.

Suddenly, without thinking, she said, "Why did you cry today? I thought it would kill me to watch those tears roll down you face."

Like a spring overflowing, he began talking about that moment, his voice betraying the pain he felt. Unable to bear it, she climbed on top of him, locked her arms around his neck and rocked on him, loving him until she felt him bulge beneath her. She took him into her body. "What do you need?" she asked him. "Tell me."

"You. Only you and always you." They exploded together, and she relaxed, happy in the knowledge that she'd given him the love that he so badly needed.

He held her close. "I want you to remember this in the next couple of weeks," he said. "When you begin to doubt me, stop and remember this moment. I love you more than I love my life."

Chills plowed through her system. "I will. I have to, because I love you."

He walked into court followed by his senior associate and two law clerks, nodded to the opposing lawyer and took his seat, waiting for the arrival of the judge. The courtroom reminded him of his own search for truth. He still had no response in his birth-certificate search. That didn't make sense unless the information he sent had proved inadequate.

The judge arrived, and he focused on the task at

hand. He turned to walk back to his seat and get a file from his briefcase and glimpsed Heather. She gave him the thumbs-up sign. She was there for him, and he could almost feel his chest expanding.

At a break, he met Heather in the corridor near the trial attorney's office. "Thank you for coming. I know you have plenty of work to do, and I want you to know that your being here means a lot."

"Of course I came. You're doing a great job."

"I love you, woman. Consider yourself kissed."

He went into the office and telephoned the Maryland vital statistics registrar. "When may I expect to receive the copy of my birth certificate?" he asked a clerk.

"But, Mr. Philips, we mailed that to you ten days ago. You didn't receive it?"

"No, I didn't." Every nerve in his body seemed to stand on end.

"I'm sorry, sir. If you come to the office, I'll be glad to give you a copy. We're open Monday through Friday from eight to four. If you call me first, I'll have it ready when you come."

He thanked her, but for a minute, he was hardly aware of his surroundings. He looked at his watch. Four minutes to court time, and he couldn't even tell Heather. After thinking about it and recalling Telford's warning that the birth certificate may not contain the truth, he decided not to mention it until he saw it. And that wouldn't happen until after the trial, because the court recessed at five o'clock, an hour after the vital statistics office closed. Still, his years of waiting seemed near an end.

* * *

Just before noon, three days later and the first on which Heather did not attend a part of the trial, the jury found in favor of his client. He raced out of court and dashed to the registrar's office.

"Here you are, Mr. Philips," the clerk said as she handed him a large manila envelope. He stared down at it, wondering if he'd be sorry that he'd embarked on this effort. "Is...everything all right, sir?" the woman asked him.

"Oh, yes. Yes. I never thought I'd actually have this in my hand. Thank you so much."

He left that office, got into his car and didn't stop driving until he parked in front of the building in which Heather lived and went up to her apartment. Until then, it had not occurred to him that she might not have gotten home, and his heart seemed to hover near the pit of his belly until her voice said, "Who is it?"

"Judson. Open the door, sweetheart."

The door opened, and she gazed up at him with an inquiring expression, for he hadn't previously paid her a surprise visit. He walked past her, turned and shoved the envelope to her.

She looked at the return address. "Oh, my goodness! Do you want me to open it?'

"No, I... Let's sit down a minute." She sat beside him as he opened the envelope with shaky fingers. He stared at the words he had longed nearly all of his life to see. His hands trembled as he read them. Slowly and now composed, he read them again:

Name of baby: Judson.
Sex: boy
Date of birth: December 2, 1976.
Mother's name: Beverly Moten. Age, 23
Father's name: Fentriss Sparkman
Date of birth registration: December 8, 1976

He read it aloud a third time, his voice carrying even to his ears a tone of wonder, then he handed the certificate to Heather. "Did I see it correctly?"

"You definitely did, and I'm so happy for you. I suspect your mother registered the birth herself, and she did it correctly. I hoped that it would come out this way. Do you resent your mother for allowing you to think she was your adoptive mother?"

He shook his head. "I'm over that part of it because I've known since my first meeting with Aunt Cissy. I suppose Mom did what she had to do. For some reason, she didn't want Louis Philips to know she'd had a child as an unmarried mother." He slumped in the chair.

"What's the matter?" she asked him, her voice urgent with concern.

"I'm…washed out, exhausted. I feel as if I've just wrestled a steer. I need to call Telford and Scott, but there's one more thing. I left a DNA sample at Diagnostic Services in Hagerstown. I want a DNA test. For all I know, this certificate was filed by someone other than my mother." He dialed Telford's cell phone number.

"Telford Harrington speaking."

"Hello, Telford. Judson here. You said you were

willing to take a DNA test. Does the offer still stand? I left a sample with Diagnostic Services in Hagerstown."

"We don't need it, but if that's what you want, the three of us will do it tomorrow morning, and I'll ask them to process it right away."

"Thank you."

"Now, we'll really know the truth," he said to Heather after he hung up.

He laughed. "I feel better than I did a few minutes earlier when I doubted what my eyes beheld. If it comes out all right, will you go to Eagle Park with me?"

She wrapped her arms around him. "Of course. Have faith, honey."

"I'm trying, but I'm so close. It's as if my whole life is suspended out there someplace." He waved his hand toward the unknown.

"Come on. Let's get some food. I'll treat you to shrimp and rice Italian style."

He jumped up. "Works for me."

For the next few weeks, he jumped each time the telephone rang. On Friday evening at about five-thirty, he received the news. "Mr. Philips, this Dr. Horace Epps at Diagnostic Services. I have the results of the DNA tests. You're a match with Telford, Russell and Drake Harrington. The tests are ninety-nine percent positive for you with Telford and Russell and show a ninety-nine-point-nine percent probability that you and Drake are from the same blood line. We'll be open Saturday until twelve-thirty."

Thank you, Dr. Epps, I'll be there before noon." He marveled at his calmness, for he had proof more reliable than his birth certificate offered that he was the son of Fentriss Sparkman.

"I'll have the papers ready for you."

He phoned Telford. "I'll pick up the test results before noon tomorrow, and I'd like to leave there and visit with you and your brothers around one. Heather will be with me if that's all right with you and Alexis."

"We'll be delighted. Looking forward to seeing you."

Heather didn't know how to respond when the real estate agent called to say that the house Heather wanted was for sale and could be broom clean for her within ten days. "I'll call you back Monday after I speak with my banker," she told the agent. In truth, she didn't need to check with her bank, but she needed time to speak with Annie and Judson about it. She knew Annie would go along with anything she proposed, but her instincts told her that the weekend could be a crucial point in her life.

She sat down on the edge of the chair, rubbing the back of her neck as she'd so often seen her father do. "Why am I equivocating about this? I should take the house and let the chips fall where they may," she said to herself. *Don't tempt fate,* her niggling conscience prodded.

She got up early Saturday morning, dressed in a red silk dress that had a matching jacket and spike-heel black suede boots. She put a pair of slippers in a small tote, in case they spent time with Telford and Alexis.

"Won't you be cold?" Judson asked when he arrived at nine o'clock. "It's freezing out there."

An hour later, with the incontrovertible evidence of his paternity in a sealed envelope, he drove to Cissy's house. "Well, well. Now this is nice," she said when she opened the door and saw them. "Don't tell me you two got married."

"Not yet, Aunt Cissy," he said. "I wanted you to know that I have my birth certificate, which says that Beverly Moten and Fentriss Sparkman are my parents, and results of DNA tests show a ninety-nine percent certainty that I'm from the same blood line as Drake Harrington and his brothers."

"Hallelujah! I felt from the first that you were my blood kin. Y'all come on in. I'm just about to fix some lunch."

"I'm sorry, Aunt Cissy. We can't stay. I'm on my way to share this with the Harrington brothers. You can't imagine how happy I am. I suppose it will sink in soon, and I'll be delirious. Heather and I will be back soon and spend some time with you."

She'd thought they'd go next to Eagle Park, but he swung in the opposite direction. "We'd better make a quick stop and see Annie." He handed her his cell phone. "Tell her we'll be buy for five minutes."

She dialed the familiar number. "Annie, we're in

Hagerstown on a little business, and then we're going to Eagle Park on some more business. We're on our way to you, but we can only stay a minute."

A few minutes later, it seemed strange walking into that house and not finding her father there. "I hope you came to get a marriage license," Annie said after greeting them.

"Not quite," Judson said. "I came to pick up the evidence that Fentriss Sparkman was my father. My adoptive mother was actually my birth mother."

Annie sat down. "I figured that from all you told me, and when I saw Drake Harrington, I was sure. It must be wonderful to know your father was such a respected man."

"I'm pleased with what I've learned about all this, Annie, and I thank you for caring. We'll be in touch next week."

Heather could see in Judson an anxiousness to show Telford and his brothers the evidence that he was one of them. Judson drove into the circle in front of Harrington House, and before he could park, Telford came out to meet him. She looked up and saw Alexis standing in the front doorway, her face wreathed in smiles.

Telford brought Judson to him in a strong embrace. "No matter what it says, you're one of us. Don't forget this."

Judson blinked rapidly and handed Telford the envelopes containing the birth certificate and the unopened results of the DNA tests.

Telford kissed Heather's cheek, took Judson's arm

and went inside with them. Heather had the strangest feeling when Alexis hugged her, almost as if she hugged her big sister. It was as if something or someone other than her was controlling her life.

"Russ and Drake will be here in a couple of minutes. Should I wait for them before I open this?" Telford asked Judson.

"I regard you as head of the family. It's up to you."

Telford looked at the birth certificate, and his face brightened in a big smile. He glanced at Judson, gave a thumbs-up sign and opened the other envelope. The doorbell rang and Alexis ran to get it. Drake and Russ walked into the room and stopped.

"What does it say?" Russ asked. Telford passed them the two envelopes.

"We had already decided," Russ said, "but you needed the proof, so we gave it to you. Congratulations."

Telford called to Alexis. "Sweetheart, bring everybody in here, please, including Henry." She returned with Pamela and Velma. "Last week, Russ, Drake and I decided that since we knew Judson was our first cousin, we should do the right thing. Uncle Fentriss thought he had no heirs and left what he owned to us, with Russ as executor of his estate. We divided the estate between us, except one apartment house, the largest and most valuable property in the estate. We decided to leave it as it is and to divide between us the receipts and expenses. We're giving that building to Judson, because he deserves it. I'm talking about the Beverly Apartments in downtown Frederick, which Uncle

Fentriss obviously named for Judson's mother. What is the situation, Russ?"

When Judson gasped, Heather eased her arm around his shoulder and whispered. "They love you, darling. It's all right."

Russ stood, walked to the fireplace and leaned against the marble facing. "I have here the transfer of ownership to Judson and the deed supporting it. I had the building appraised. It's fifteen stories high with forty-three apartments, swimming pool and recreation facilities are on the top floor. It sits on prime land. It's structurally as sound as when it was built six years ago and is what he considered his crowning achievement. Its current market value is twenty-five to twenty-seven million dollars and is approximately one-quarter of the value of Uncle Fentriss's estate." He walked over to Judson and handed him the papers.

"We are extremely happy to be able to share this with you, Judson. We were all very well-fixed financially before receiving the inheritance, and we've used some of it to build attractive and affordable housing for poor people, among other things." He put his hand into his pocket. "I forgot. Here's the master key to the Beverly Apartments."

She wondered that Judson would be able to stand. He patted her knee and managed to get to his feet. "I wouldn't be surprised if I had a heart attack," Judson said. "He named that building after my mother. Six years ago. That's a long time to love someone and not know where she is or even if she's alive. He really loved her," he said, seemingly in awe. "I'm not going to try and thank you, because it's not possible. I've never known people like you. From the beginning, you received me as if I were one of you. I… Thank you.

"If anyone in this room ever needs me, you only have to get a message to me. I regard you as my brothers and sisters." His voice broke. "And I love every one of you."

"This calls for a party," Alexis said.

By five o'clock that afternoon, the party was going full sway and, happy though he was, Judson had to get away from it. His father had been a rich man, and though he was wealthy, the largesse of the Harrington brothers made him richer. But he was shaken equally by the love that they and their families showered on Heather and him. He remembered the basement, opened the door to it and went down there.

Almost immediately, he heard the sound of shoe heels on the steps and waited, hoping that it was Heather and not one of the other women. "I guess it's overwhelming," Heather said, when she reached the bottom of the stairs. "Judson, where did you go?"

"Over here." He stood as she approached, opened his arms and brought her to him, restoring some of his sanity. "It's almost too much in one day."

"Do you want to leave?"

"That wouldn't be nice, especially considering how much I appreciate it and how I feel about them. Can you imagine they gave me that building? My name is on the deed as the owner, and they did that before they had proof."

"Now you have three wonderful cousins."

"Yes. Wouldn't you like to be part of this large and loving family?"

He felt her tense, but he was tired of being half a person. He dropped to his knees and looked up at her. "You know that I love you, and you love me. I'm tired of being without you. Will you marry me? I promise to be a good husband to you, loyal and faithful and a loving and caring father to our children." She wasn't looking at him. "In my whole life, I've loved no woman but you. Will you marry me?" he repeated.

"Judson, I—"

He was on his feet in a second. "Do you think the Harrington men and their wives are anomalies, the only happy couples on this planet? Do you believe that all other couples are miserable? Look at me. If you can't trust me to be a faithful, loving and caring husband for the rest of our lives, baby, it's over between us as of this minute."

Horrified that he would leave her, she reached out, detaining him as he headed for the stairs. "What about my career and all that? Everything's set for you, but not for me."

He stared down at her until she felt goose bumps on her arms. "What do you take me to be? Haven't I showed you that I have compassion for you and that I care about your goals and your wishes? Last week

I asked you what you thought of a legal partnership between Philips and Tatum—in alphabetical order. You seemed surprised, and you haven't answered me."

"You mean, you and I practice law together?"

"Yeah. Think about it."

"What will I do about Annie?"

"You sell your house, I'll sell my house, and we'll build our house. Annie can live with us. If she doesn't like that idea, she can have an apartment rent-free in Beverly Apartments, or whatever she wants. Any more excuses?"

"Oh, honey, they're not excuses, just concerns. I don't know what I'd do if you walked out of my life. You asked me to marry you, and by damn, I'm holding you to it."

He stared at her. "What?"

"You heard me."

He picked her up, twirled her around and around, raced up the stairs and into the living room with her in his arms. Spontaneous applause greeted their ears.

"Did you hurt your foot, Miss Heather?" Tara asked her.

Judson put her down, but she had a sense of loss for his having done it. "I got carried away," he said. "She just promised to marry me."

"It's about time," Henry said. "I was about to ask ya about yer intentions."

A round of laughter and applause, hugs and kisses followed. "Stay right where you are," Drake said. "I'll be back in fifteen minutes."

Drake returned with half a dozen bottles of champagne, and the merriment began. "Spend the night," Telford said, "and we'll all go to church tomorrow morning as a family and give thanks that Judson's dream came true. What do you say?"

When Judson looked at Heather, she smiled. "I'd like that."

Alexis took Heather's hand. "Come with me. Your room is waiting for you."

"Where're you going?" Judson called after Heather as the two women headed down the hall.

"She'll see you at dinner," Alexis said, somewhat airily.

After a dinner that featured roasted Cornish hens, they sat in the family room sipping espresso, and she marveled that both she and Judson as well as Alexis, Telford and Henry exuded a peacefulness and contentment that seemed to bind them together.

"Where will you marry?" Alexis asked Heather.

"I'm still in shock, Alexis, so I haven't thought much about that, but probably somewhere near here. We'd like the family to be with us."

"I've had an exciting day," Judson said, getting to his feet, "and I don't want it to end. But I'd better turn in if we're going to church in the morning." He looked at Heather. "I'll walk you to your room."

She hugged Henry, Telford and Alexis and walked down the corridor beside Judson with heavy steps. *Was he really planning to tell her good-night at that door and leave her?*

"Aren't you going to ask me to come in?" he said, standing at the door, his tone wistful.

"I thought you wanted to go to bed."

"You're joking." He walked past her. "Sweetheart, you amaze me. I've been dying to get you alone. Come here to me."

She pushed the door shut, dashed into his arms and let herself feel his strength and the love that flowed from him to her. "Kiss me, baby." The words seemed to seep out of him between pants for breath. "Ah, sweetheart, we'll have a wonderful life together." He locked her to him, hungrily, as if he couldn't get her close enough.

As soon as she parted her lips and pulled his tongue into her mouth, he bulged against her, hard and heavy. She spread her legs and moved onto him, already eager to have him inside of her.

His hands roamed over her body, heating her, possessively claiming her, branding her. The blood raced to her vagina, and that familiar ache took hold of her until, increasingly frantic for relief, she undulated against him. Her unzipped dress fell to the floor. He pulled off her bra, sucked her nipple into his mouth and feasted like a baby while her moans escalated.

"Stop torturing me," she told him, "and put me in that bed."

But he continued to chart his own course. Frantic, she unzipped his pants and stroked him until he groaned uncontrollably, capitulated and took her to bed. Like a wild man, he stormed inside of her while she met him stroke for stroke and twist for twist until she surrendered herself to him in a powerful orgasm and cried out in relief. He collapsed in her arms. Totally spent.

"When are you going to marry me?" he asked, still locked inside of her.

"How about December eighteenth? That way, we can spend Christmas together."

"That will be a perfect time for a warm-weather cruise," he said, hugging her. "Sweetheart, you will never regret this. I'll love you for as long as I breathe."

Her face beamed in a smile. "And I will love you just as long." She reached over and turned out the light.

That December, in Frederick's Shiloh Baptist Church, Pamela Harrington walked down the aisle ahead of Heather, who held Henry's arm as she walked to the altar to marry Judson Philips-Sparkman. Others there to witness their exchange of vows were Cissy, Annie and the Harrington families. As best man, Scott Galloway offered the wedding toast at the reception, the most elegant affair that Velma had ever created. Shortly after the toast, the bride and groom slipped away and headed for their honeymoon in the South Sea Islands.

* * * * *

L♥VE IN THE LIMELIGHT

Fantasy, Fame and Fortune...Hollywood-Style!

Book #1

By *New York Times* and *USA TODAY*
Bestselling Author Brenda Jackson

STAR OF HIS HEART
August 2010

Book #2

By A.C. Arthur

SING YOUR PLEASURE
September 2010

Book #3

By Ann Christopher

SEDUCED ON THE RED CARPET
October 2010

Book #4

By *Essence* Bestselling Author Adrianne Byrd

LOVERS PREMIERE
November 2010

*Set in Hollywood's entertainment industry,
two unstoppable sisters and their two friends
find romance, glamour and dreams-come-true.*

REQUEST YOUR FREE BOOKS!

2 FREE NOVELS
PLUS 2 FREE GIFTS!

KIMANI™
ROMANCE

Love's ultimate destination!

YES! Please send me 2 FREE Kimani™ Romance novels and my 2 FREE gifts (gifts are worth about $10). After receiving them, if I don't wish to receive any more books, I can return the shipping statement marked "cancel." If I don't cancel, I will receive 4 brand-new novels every month and be billed just $4.69 per book in the U.S. or $5.24 per book in Canada. That's a saving of over 20% off the cover price. It's quite a bargain! Shipping and handling is just 50¢ per book.* I understand that accepting the 2 free books and gifts places me under no obligation to buy anything. I can always return a shipment and cancel at any time. Even if I never buy another book from Kimani Press, the two free books and gifts are mine to keep forever.

168/368 XDN E7PZ

Name _____ (PLEASE PRINT)

Address _____ Apt. #

City _____ State/Prov. _____ Zip/Postal Code

Signature (if under 18, a parent or guardian must sign)

Mail to The Reader Service:
IN U.S.A.: P.O. Box 1867, Buffalo, NY 14240-1867
IN CANADA: P.O. Box 609, Fort Erie, Ontario L2A 5X3

Not valid for current subscribers to Kimani Romance books.

**Want to try two free books from another line?
Call 1-800-873-8635 or visit www.morefreebooks.com.**

* Terms and prices subject to change without notice. Prices do not include applicable taxes. N.Y. residents add applicable sales tax. Canadian residents will be charged applicable provincial taxes and GST. Offer not valid in Quebec. This offer is limited to one order per household. All orders subject to approval. Credit or debit balances in a customer's account(s) may be offset by any other outstanding balance owed by or to the customer. Please allow 4 to 6 weeks for delivery. Offer available while quantities last.

Your Privacy: Kimani Press is committed to protecting your privacy. Our Privacy Policy is available online at www.eHarlequin.com or upon request from the Reader Service. From time to time we make our lists of customers available to reputable third parties who may have a product or service of interest to you. If you would prefer we not share your name and address, please check here. ☐

Help us get it right—We strive for accurate, respectful and relevant communications. To clarify or modify your communication preferences, visit us at www.ReaderService.com/consumerschoice.

KROMIO